PAULA WENTZ

Witnesses to Love

DOING CHRISTIANITY
Pastor David Wentz

This book was professionally typeset on Reedsy.
Find out more at reedsy.com

This book is dedicated to my husband, David, for his constant love and encouragement. I have always seen him as the embodiment of this line from his worship song, "Lord, Help Me Enter In:"
'Let people see, looking at me, nothing but You.'

We may shut our eyes,
But we cannot help knowing
That skies are clear,
And grass is growing.

— "The Vision of Sir Launfal"
by James Russell Lowell

Contents

Chapter 1: End of an Internship

Pussytoes were one of Liddie's favorite wildflowers. The bright bluets were a close second. And now, in the late spring sunlight, both were filling the hillsides with their beauty. Tiny blue flowers swayed in the gentle breeze, giving her steps a carpeted path into the woods. There, on the edge, leading into the shady canopy, the pussytoes were just opening their fuzzy little heads. Each one seemed like a tiny nosegay, all gathered together into a bouquet with thin antennas spiraling out from the top.

Liddie waved goodbye to the students she had just been guiding through the fields and bent down, examining the pussytoes more closely. Part of the attraction was, of course, in the name. Who wouldn't love talking about pussytoes? When she was teaching students, Liddie always made sure to use the correct Latin name, *antennaria*, but she also brought in related interesting folklore and herbal uses of plants, as well as their importance to local ecosystems.

In this short internship, she had ample opportunity to share her love of native plants with eager young students. Having just received her college degree in botany, she was excited about the future, but unsure of her next steps. There didn't seem to be a lot of demand for new botanists without field experience. So when the winter internship had opened up in this rural Ozark conservation area, she jumped at the chance. Perhaps it would give her some leads for future jobs, or at the least, some experience to put on her resume. The Ozark wilderness was the perfect place for searching out rare wildflower specimens, and Liddie's notebook now overflowed with her descriptions and sketches of her finds. Most of the sketches were just quick pencil renderings that she intended to complete from her notes.

As the junior person in the camp, much of her job consisted of maintenance, cleaning, and running here and there for the boss. But in the past couple of weeks, they had given her more responsibility for leading the local school groups. The students connected with Liddie's enthusiasm and obvious love for plants. She easily led them into a new understanding of nature's importance when viewed as a whole.

The job had been good at helping Liddie recognize her own joy when she shared plant knowledge with others. She was surprised to discover how much she loved seeing the kids' faces when they looked freshly at nature. But it had also been a fun time hanging out with the other interns. And, there was the unexpected complication of that young law intern.

Initially, she had been turned off by Beckley's confident demeanor. She supposed that one had to be at least somewhat confident to enter law school, but Beckley seemed to have his whole life planned, from following in his Dad's footsteps at Yale to joining the premier environmental law firm in New York. His internship was to gain firsthand knowledge of plant ecosystems so he could work more effectively protecting them.

Liddie and Beckley first discovered a shared interest in climate change when, at dinner one night, they realized no one else was joining their discussion on the impact of hotter summers on the monarch migration. The two of them had been going back and forth for a good half hour. The other interns had long since drifted away for the late evening Carcassonne game. But after that night, the days for Liddie and Beckley routinely ended with conversations about native plants, environmental rights, and the legal implications of water usage.

Although their relationship had never moved beyond this sharing of ideas, Liddie sometimes became aware of Beckley taking more than just a moment to rest his gaze upon her. At such times she would toss her head just a bit, knowing how attractively her long brown hair spun in the air. Then she would quickly glance over to see him watching, quite interestedly, she thought. She admitted that she found him attractive, but she knew their lives were just too different for any kind of relationship to work. There could be no place for her in the high-powered New York law office. Still, she enjoyed dreaming, and she loved the glimpses of his soft, gentle heart that she sometimes heard in their discussions.

Especially the night he was describing the plight of the bumblebee. "The ecological issues are important," he had said.

"Liddie," he added, "the bumblebees, they're so small, so vulnerable. We just need to take care of the little ones."

Her own heart melted.

So it was a bittersweet day as Liddie softly touched the pussytoes at her feet. She was glad for the internship, but it had brought her no closer to an understanding of what her next steps should be. She had no job prospects. And no place to live. She was grateful that her parents had offered that she could come home and stay until she got things figured out. But still, how lame was that? To live with your parents again?

As she was pondering this precarious future, her cell phone rang.

"Hello?"

"Liddie? Liddie, is that you?"

"Yes, Mom! It's always me when you call this number," Liddie answered. "What's up?"

"Sweetie, I just had this marvelous idea! When you head back here from your internship, you will pass not fifty miles from the old family homestead. No one has been there or used the place for at least thirty years. I've just been talking to your aunts and uncles, and we're thinking it might be time to sell. You know, not have the burden of taxes and such."

Liddie recalled vague memories of her parents and their siblings telling childhood stories of their grandparents' farm. But she never knew they still owned the place! How could something like that still exist without her knowing?

"Mom! You mean you still own this family land? And you're selling it now? Before I even know about it? What?"

"But Liddie," her mother replied, "that's just it! We all just kind of forgot about it, what with the busyness of life, and none of us lived nearby, and your uncle handled all the taxes, so I just never thought of it. But now, seeing as you'll be so close..."

"Mom, of course I want to see it!" Liddie interrupted. "Tell me where it is. I've just finished teaching my last class here, so I can leave anytime."

"Well now, Liddie, Uncle Stan's idea was that you could get some new pictures — oh my, the most recent ones we have are from the funeral. No one has been back there since... since... the funeral." Liddie's mom paused here, as if reflecting on a slightly unsettled bit of history. But then she resumed, "And anyway, those pictures don't really show the land. If you can get good pictures, then he can create a listing to sell it."

"Of course I can do that." Liddie hesitated. Her mother was asking for help in selling this land whose existence she had just now discovered. She felt a new emotion, tinged with uncertainty. She remembered the day when she and Beckley hiked to the spring at the Ozark Scenic Riverways. The family land was probably very similar — what if it had a spring? Or, what if...? Her mind started to wander as she recalled the night when she and Beckley stayed up late around the crackling remains of the interns' campfire, gazing at the constellations. Liddie had thought that night perfect, and she wished it would never end. Nature, the Ozarks... and Beckley. Was this land anything at all like the Ozark wilderness where she had just been living? If so, Liddie wasn't so sure it was a good idea to get rid of it.

"But Mom," she said, "what if this land turns out to be something fabulous that you want to hang on to?"

"I don't know, Liddie. Uncle Stan has always been the one handling these things. For right now, let me give you the directions. As I recall, it's quite off the beaten path. Uncle Stan has been paying someone for years to keep the driveway cleared and open, so it should be accessible. I'm sure it has changed, though, given the thirty years since I've seen it. Most places do. Change, that is."

Liddie's mother carefully read her the directions from Stan's email, and they said goodbye. Putting away her phone, her Mom gazed thoughtfully out the window into the misty sky. Just a curious wondering she had — perhaps there was more to this. Perhaps she was being guided with this 'marvelous idea.' She was well aware that Liddie was rudderless, and had been for some time. Perhaps this would lead to her finding that elusive "something more."

With this new goal spurring her on, Liddie made her way back to the lodge. The call from her mom had given her a new interest for the next couple of weeks. Maybe it wasn't a job, maybe it wasn't a long term future, but this intensely interesting adventure had just suddenly been plopped in her lap! And wasn't there something mysterious in the way her mother had referred to "the funeral"? Thirty years ago...

Liddie mused that it must have been one of her great-grandparents, who died before she was even born. Her parents had never talked a lot about family history. Liddie herself was always too involved in her own school and social life to be concerned about what seemed to her like ancient history — although she did know some friends whose families had created massive genealogies that purported to show their lineage all the way back to Adam! She remembered thinking at the time how odd that was, because, didn't we all go back to Adam?

Sadly, she reflected, her family didn't even keep up with living relatives. She recalled meeting Uncle Stan once or twice when she was very young, but she knew nothing of his family, or even if he had a wife and kids. And the other aunts, uncles, cousins — she had no idea who they might be or where they might live. Apparently, none of them lived near this old homestead, or they would have traveled to it. Liddie was somewhat pleased that she was the one called upon to get the pictures. A purpose! She hadn't felt a 'purpose' in her life since beginning college when, along with all the other starry-eyed first-year students, the clear purpose was to study hard, graduate in four years and have the world become your oyster. That hadn't quite happened. So Liddie tempered her expectations with this new purpose. Now, it was enough simply to have it as a pleasant diversion as she headed home.

There was very little packing to do. Liddie basically lived out of her suitcase, washing her jeans and tee shirts every few days. She did have Elizabeth, the stuffed dog who peeked out from under a glittering Christmas tree when she was five years old. Given almost twenty years of hugging, petting, and loving, Elizabeth was not in bad shape. A bit worn, but still recognizable as a St. Bernard, Elizabeth had served as Liddie's confidant, supporter, and friend through many a childhood turmoil. Even at college, the soft toy dog was a comforting presence and reminder that Mom and Dad were still there, still loving her.

Liddie had already filled out her end-of-internship paperwork, so the only remaining obligations were to sweep out her half of the room and say some goodbyes.

Room tidied, backpack in the car, Elizabeth was gently tossed into the passenger seat. The lunch bell rang across the camp, and Liddie's stomach reminded her that it might be a good idea to eat lunch with the staff before leaving. That would give her a chance to see everyone together once again.

Liddie paused to watch for the last time as her fellow workers entered the lodge in laughing little groups. It had been a good internship, and she would miss them all. But none had formed a really lasting relationship with Liddie. More like acquaintances than friends, they had all enjoyed their mutual activities, but she didn't see keeping up correspondence once she left. Except, of course, with Beckley. She wouldn't mind continuing his relationship!

With that thought in mind, she turned and was surprised to see Beckley sitting by the fire pit.

Beckley also had been packing his suitcases, in anticipation of heading back to New York. He had stopped by the fire pit, thinking his misplaced blue sweater might have been left there. But then, sweater found, he slowly sat down on the largest boulder. He couldn't avoid the sick feeling in his stomach any longer.

He knew it wasn't hunger. It had something to do with that girl Liddie. And it had been growing and gnawing at him almost constantly these last few days. He had always been focused on studies and work, moving seamlessly toward his goal of working in a big New York law firm. But out here, his concentration waned. His mind was filled with only one thing: anticipating the next time he would catch a glimpse of this pretty young intern who seemed to toss her hair at him in a most flirtatious way!

"Liddie!" he called, as he saw her walk toward the lodge, "Wait up!"

Her head tilted. Her eyes sparkled. There was no question that Liddie welcomed this encounter.

The two of them strolled into the lodge, laughing about the no longer missing sweater. Neither one noticed what was being served as they filled their plates. They were both acutely aware that this was the end of their time together.

Liddie told Beckley about her mom's phone call. "Liddie, you have no idea what you'll find. You say it's been abandoned for how many years? What about rattlesnakes? Copperheads? You know how many of those we've seen here in the woods. How about squatters? I've read they can be a real problem in the hills! I'm worried about you. What was your Mom thinking, sending you there all alone?"

Liddie was quite touched by his concern for her safety. She had to admit that none of those possibilities had occurred to her. But then, it had just been a few hours since she talked to her mom. Was this really a good idea?

"Okay, you know what?" she finally answered, "I don't need to stay if it gives any appearance of danger. I can just turn the car around at any point and leave! And as far as snakes go, I've got my snake boots. I've learned all the precautions, and I'm sure I'll be fine."

Beckley looked only a bit less concerned, so she added, with that engaging sparkle back in her eyes, "And tell me, have you ever heard of such an exciting adventure?"

Beckley walked Liddie back to her car. Neither one was ready to give voice to the feelings they both had. They each knew there could be something more, and they each yearned for it. But something held them back. Was it fear? Fear of the unknown, of being too vulnerable, of losing control over their lives? Whatever it was, the something more was not to happen, at least not then.

So there they stood, outside the dusty car, in what became a progressively more awkward silence.

"Well then," Beckley finally spoke, "let's keep in touch. You've got my phone number, right?"

It was a totally unsatisfying end to the internship.

Chapter 2: Strangers on the Farm

"These Missouri back roads are leading me deeper and deeper into nowhere land!" Liddie exclaimed.

Worn, stuffed Elizabeth was her only companion, but still, Liddie felt a bit more comfortable talking out loud. She had gone from a superhighway, to a state road, to a smaller state road, and she assumed this new one was the smallest state road ever! No lines marked the edge of the crumbling asphalt. A very vague, faded middle line was all that remained of any maintenance. Still, it was taking her closer to the old family farm.

The surrounding fields were beautiful in a deep, calming way. Not at all like the great National Parks. Her parents had taken her on a grand adventure when she was ten, and they visited the Grand Canyon, Yellowstone, all the major parks. The beautiful vistas were breathtaking. A wide, awe inspiring beauty. But these fields were a different kind of beauty. Rolling hills, tall grasses blowing gently in the breeze, a few scattered majestic old oaks all gave the impression of timelessness. Farmers were still raising cattle on the same hills where their fathers and mothers and many generations before them had done the same. Their children were born, married, and died all on the same plot of land that their ancestors had settled in the early years of America.

Liddie watched cows lazily move toward muddy old farm ponds. When she passed a house, scores of multicolored chickens rushed back from the road, but quickly calmed to resume their pecking, hunting for grubs. She imagined the chicken eggs brought in a lot of breakfast food for those families.

There was more and more distance between the houses as she continued driving. Small dirt roads led off from this main road, presumably to isolated houses even further afield. None of the houses were big. Most had additions added on, providing more room for when children came along. A good number of the houses were trailers. Most had several tractors and other types of farm equipment. To Liddie, who didn't know the difference between a combine and a grader, they were all simply tractors.

She felt a weight falling off her shoulders as she continued driving. Not that she had been weighed down with worries, but perhaps a burden that had been resting on her spirit was being removed. She felt more alive. Liddie hardly took note of the feeling, though, attributing it to simple excitement of this adventure — the same excitement she felt when her mom suggested it.

Glancing ahead, she remembered her mother's directions to be on the lookout for two big red barns. Were they supposed to be on the left or the right? She quickly pulled up the directions on her phone. Yes, right side. There they were. She slowed down to search for the turn. And there it was — another state road. Only this one was gravel. Not even paved!

Wide-eyed, Liddie evaluated the road. In many places gravel had washed out, leaving deep ruts. Fallen trees lay rotting by the sides. Flowering brambles arched over the logs to trail into the road. She was glad it wasn't yet dark, because the overhanging branches made it appear strange and foreboding. She couldn't imagine driving through here at night.

Liddie began creeping down the twists and turns. She navigated several low areas that had been recently washed out by spring rains and were still covered in mud. Apparently there was an abundance of wildlife in the area, because she recognized a number of tracks. Deer, raccoon, turkey, some kind of big cat — most likely a bobcat — and a large footprint that she thought might have belonged to a bear.

At almost exactly a mile, the road ascended up into a small hilltop clearing.

And there, just like her mom's directions indicated, was a deeply rutted side path. At one time it had been cleared for a nice driveway, she was sure, but now it could only be called a pathway. Pine, oak, and hickory woodlands bordered either side. Liddie was grateful that her uncle had arranged for a local farmer to brush hog and clear the driveway. Otherwise, she had no idea how she might have entered.

Just past a rusted gate, Liddie pulled into an overgrown field covering the top of a large hill. Beyond, she could see the patchwork of this field mixing with bits of woodland. Even in its overgrown state, or maybe because of it, the land was beautiful. Liddie stopped her car and got out to inspect it more closely. Native grasses surrounded her — Indian grass, switchgrass, big and little bluestems. She had seen these grasses in native prairies, but never in an old farmstead. Instantly, she was intrigued with the people who had lived here and cultivated this land. Most farm pastures, such as those she passed on the way in, were monocultures of fescue, grown for the sole purpose of feeding cows, and not much good for anything else. But this, this was a veritable treasure trove for wildlife. She watched the grasshoppers jumping from leaf to leaf. Dragonflies of all colors swooped back and forth. Huge bumblebees buzzed among the flowers. She involuntarily jumped back as a harmless hog nose snake startled her.

The creature hid behind a large rock near the gravel. Liddie moved the grass aside with a stick, hoping to see the snake again. Instead, she discovered old, worn writing painted on the rock. Someone must have placed this rock here many years ago, as a welcoming sign! Liddie struggled a bit to decipher it. "THUS FAR" were the only two words on the rock.

"Now, that's really odd." She thought to herself, "Thus far? What can that possibly mean? Thus far… Something unknown, maybe, a reflection upon the past? A far distant past?" She made a mental note to look into possible meanings of this new phrase.

Climbing back in the car, she slowly proceeded down the cleared path. A different field off to her left was bursting forth with early black-eyed Susans, their golden petals waving in the breeze. Tall pines lined the path, causing Liddie to stretch and turn to see through openings to what was lying beyond.

Some of the overhanging branches brushed her car, and she sniffed the lovely pine scent left behind. She was just beginning to wonder where the house was when she rounded a curve, and there it was!

The brush hogger had mown around the house, so weeds weren't encroaching as much as they could have. And the house itself looked solid, with no obvious deterioration, at least to her untrained eye. It was nestled into a little hollow, and Liddie could just see the edges of a large pond on the other side. This was looking more and more interesting, and she couldn't wait to start exploring.

But her mouth dropped open in shock when two people peered around the side of the house!

"Oh, no!" she thought! "Beckley was right! Squatters! Maybe I should turn around right now and get the police!"

As Liddie was putting the car in gear to back up, one of the pair waved at her. Liddie paused, looking at them a bit more thoroughly. They were old. That was her first and most lasting impression. They didn't look dangerous. Rather feeble, she thought. A woman and a man. Fairly nicely dressed, not fancy, but not rags. The man was wearing an old, worn outback style hat. The woman wore a shapeless blue denim dress that came almost to her ankles. She had a solid grasp on a gnarled walking stick. Liddie thought maybe she could talk to them through the car window, if she kept her hand on the control and kept the car running. Maybe she could learn a little something about them.

"Oh my," she thought as she kept watching. "They're holding hands!"

This last observation swayed her more than anything. How many elderly couples still hold hands?

Liddie waved back and shouted, "Hello!"

The old man and woman began slowly walking toward her. Liddie kept her hand on the window control. She wondered if maybe they were some distant relatives that her mom hadn't known about. Surely Uncle Stan would have mentioned it if there was anyone living here.

A great clattering sounded from the other side of the house, and Liddie turned her head. As if the sight of the old man and woman wasn't shock enough, Liddie's mouth dropped open when she saw what was barreling toward her. A giant, fluffy, brown and white St. Bernard! The dog headed straight toward the car, jowls flapping, and eagerly jumped up at Liddie's window. There ensued such a mess of slobbering and licking that Liddie completely forgot her concerns about the couple, who were still slowly making their way up the driveway.

She got out of the car, pushing the dog down so the door could be opened. Then she bent down to pet it, loving her first meeting with a real St. Bernard dog.

The couple had reached the car by that time, and Liddie could tell that they were way too old to be any danger. And their faces were... kindly, she thought.

"Hello there," the man said. "We don't see many visitors out here."

"Well," Liddie answered, "I really didn't expect to see you, either! You see, my family owns this place. They sent me out here to get pictures so they can sell it. Really," and here she mustered up her most authoritative instructor voice, "I don't think you're supposed to be here."

"Oh my!" The old woman turned to the man. "I don't recall any mention of this!"

Liddie thought that an odd remark, but continued.

"So, I'm really sorry, but you'll need to leave."

The old man looked thoughtfully at Liddie. He glanced over at the woman, then paused as if listening, or maybe sorting through his thoughts. Liddie knelt down to rub the dog's belly before he responded.

"I'll tell you what," he said. "We do have permission to be here, but our time is almost done, and we will be gone before you need us gone."

Liddie thought this the oddest answer of all. Who could have given them permission? Maybe one of the relatives arranged something without telling the others? She checked her phone, thinking to call her mom, but there was no signal. She hadn't really expected there to be one, this far into the Ozark wilderness. Things were getting awkward. So she made a snap decision, relying on her gut instinct that the two were harmless, and decided to proceed with the plan.

She answered a quick, "Okay."

Then it was back to responding to the dog, who had continued to nuzzle Liddie. She asked the couple what the dog's name was.

The woman shrugged her shoulders and shook her head. She said, "No one knows! She just randomly shows up here. As far as we can tell, she's a stray, but a really, really loveable one! Look at those eyes!"

Liddie returned to petting the dog and murmuring to it. "Why, who wouldn't want you? You are just the most adorable thing I've ever seen! And you're a girl, are you? Why I know just the name for you — Elizabeth! We'll call you Elizabeth! Yes!" With that, she put both arms around Elizabeth, who joyfully slobbered on them.

As Liddie stood back up, she introduced herself to the couple and explained how she was on her way home after the internship.

"I imagine we gave you quite a start when you drove up," the old man laughed. "I'm David, and this is my wife Paula. As I said, we'll be gone soon, so we'll be no trouble to you. Perhaps I can help you in describing the house and getting your pictures. Here, come around to the other side — the pond is beautiful!"

Indeed, as they walked around the corner, Liddie's breath was taken away. In the dusk, the sun's lengthening rays shone off the rippling water and played hide and seek in the branches of the many different oaks and hickories. There seemed to be an orange glow from the reflecting light. The pond was only about an acre in area, but it maintained that same aura of timelessness that Liddie had felt driving down the road. It seemed to say that this was a special place. A place of mystery. A place of discovery. She couldn't quite put her finger on what physical characteristic made it appear that way. It was more of a deeper, unknown sense.

There was a wandering path around the pond, sometimes close to the edge, sometimes heading back into the bordering woods. A lovely dogwood was still blooming on the far side. Several benches were spaced on the path, waiting for a wanderer to stop and sit a while. On the near edge, an old dock jutted out from the shore, just big enough for two people to sit and fish. Liddie wondered how it could all still be so well maintained, not overgrown at all. Perhaps the couple had been keeping it up.

She saw more pathways leading away from the pond. One had several other spring trees flowering — a pink dogwood, a serviceberry, and some redbuds just about ready to burst into bloom.

Liddie spoke her admiration out loud. "Why, with all these mature flowering trees, this land is like a showplace!"

Paula turned to look at her with approving interest, saying, "You have a good eye! Here, the house is open. Come inside."

The house was a simple one-story, spread out along a small slope not far up from the pond. Liddie was struck by how solid it was, with no signs of decay inside. It still had furniture throughout. Liddie wondered if the old couple had furnished it or if this had been left from the last time her family had been there. She wanted to explore more in-depth, but was fast becoming aware of how tired she was from all the driving and excitement.

It was obvious that the old couple was living in the main part of the house. They led her down a long hallway to an addition with a separate bedroom and bathroom. Seeing the soft bed, Liddie couldn't help herself. She sat down and kicked off her shoes.

"Look, I'm really, really beginning to fade out. It's been such a long day; I'm wondering, is it okay if I just sleep down here at this end?"

"Of course!" answered Paula. "David, go get Liddie's bags. Here, I think there are some sheets in this closet. Let me help you fix the bed. Are you sure you don't want anything to eat first?"

Liddie thanked her, but explained that she was still full from her snacks in the car. She gratefully took the bags from David. Pausing to wonder briefly about the electricity, she remembered her mother had mentioned solar panels and batteries. That was an amazing testimony, if they were still working all these years later!

There would be time tomorrow to ask more questions.

Paula and David murmured good night and headed off to the other end of the house. Liddie went over to check the locks, just to be safe. She opened the door, peering out into the gathering darkness, and met Elizabeth's nose pushing in. Liddie smiled.

"Yes," Liddie said to Elizabeth, locking the door after the dog. "I think the two of us will enjoy each other's company tonight!"

Chapter 3: Immersed

B right yellow rays of morning sunshine streamed through the bedroom window. Liddie stretched, poking Elizabeth with her toes.

"That was the best sleep I've had in months!" she murmured, listening to the sweet song of early spring peepers. She thought the frogs must love the habitat around the pond, with plenty of shallow water for their tadpoles and lots of grassy plants with perfect hiding places. Tall, shady trees provided access to the higher spots where the peepers enjoyed singing. "What a paradise!" she thought.

Just then she heard David calling out, "How's the fishing?"

Another male voice answered him, but she couldn't quite make out the words. She quickly got dressed, lightly brushed her hair, and opened the bedroom door to a garden bursting with early spring color. But she couldn't examine the flowers because her gaze was immediately drawn beyond, to the pond. There she could see an old man fishing from a battered aluminum jon boat. This was not David, but another old man, wearing a well-worn thatched hat. On the dock watching him was a woman, sitting quietly, working with something hidden inside a large pot.

Liddie stepped outside and moved slowly along the pathway to the dock. She caught a glimpse of David around a bend ahead of her. He appeared to be heading to the dock also.

"Good morning!" she called to him. He turned, waved, and waited for her to catch up.

"Why, good morning, young lady! How was your sleep?" he asked.

"One of the most perfect nights I've ever had," she replied. "The bed was so soft! And the frog music was so peaceful!" Then she added, as she saw Elizabeth coming down the path behind her, "And what a joy when that big, fluffy dog nuzzled me awake!"

They both rubbed that big, fluffy dog behind her ears before continuing the walk to the pond.

"I'm glad you're here to meet Osmund," said David. "But I want to let you know, before you get all upset again, thinking we're squatters, that he's with us, and like I told you, we'll all be gone before you need us gone."

Liddie thought the use of 'all' sounded a bit like maybe there were still others in addition to this Osmund. "All?" she questioned.

"Well, yes," David answered. "There are a few more here and there." His arms waved off toward the fields and then the woods. "But," he added very quickly, "they've all been given the same permission to be here. Honest! It's not a problem. Land and buildings have been kept up, and like I say, we'll all be gone before too long!"

Liddie began wondering just how much odder this adventure would become. She would need to find a cell signal and call her mom to check this all out with her.

By this time, Liddie and David were at the dock and the sitting woman turned to look at her curiously. "Sarah," David introduced her, "this is Liddie. She came in last night. Something about needing pictures of the place so her family can list it for sale."

Liddie felt Sarah's questioning gaze move first to her, then to David, then back to Liddie. She was silent, but her head nodded in greeting. She handed the pot to Liddie before motioning toward the other metal chair on the dock. Liddie saw a mess of fresh picked green peas in the pot and understood that she was being asked to help shell them. She dutifully sat down next to Sarah.

"Oh, my!" Liddie ventured, "I haven't had fresh-picked peas since my grandma taught me how to garden when I was young! These look delicious!"

Sarah, still silent, nodded and moved a bowl between them. Liddie picked up a pod, deftly snapped the tip and pulled the string toward her, releasing five big, juicy peas. Pleasing plops sounded as they dropped into the bowl. Enjoying the memories of her grandma, Liddie very quickly found herself entering into the gentle rhythm of a shared chore.

Liddie studied Sarah's face. She could tell that Sarah had been a beautiful woman when she was younger. Now, though, her face was lined with a roughness, perhaps a sorrow, of a life lived in great adversity. Yet her eyes betrayed a deep inner strength, perhaps a strength that came from facing those adversities with a proper mix of determination and humility. Liddie surprised herself when this appraisal came to her mind. She was good at making accurate first impressions of people, but these thoughts were much deeper than usual.

Sarah's dress was a gay red and white plaid. It looked homemade, but very skillfully done. The material was an old fashioned design, slightly reminiscent of the old feed sack material that backwoods people sometimes used for making clothes. Liddie remembered seeing, in fabric stores, material that duplicated the old patterns. She thought the dress was very intriguing and was about to say something about it, but was distracted as the boat came up to the dock.

Osmund had tossed a line to David, who quickly tied a cleat hitch to secure it. Liddie was pleased that she remembered enough of her Girl Scout lore to identify the knot. She watched with great interest as Osmund passed a sloshy bucket to David.

"Whoa! Nice catch!" David exclaimed. "Looks like we'll have a fine catfish supper!"

Liddie set down the pot of peas and stood up to peer at the catfish. A quick smack of a fish tail splashed water straight up into her face. Startled, Liddie stepped backward, missed the dock, and plunged down into the brown pond water!

Quite the commotion ensued. Osmund stared uncomprehendingly at this stranger, then reacted quickly —not to save her, but to save his bucket of fish. He had spent the last hour working hard for them and wasn't about to lose his supper. Sarah busily moved her peas away from the dock edge, protecting them from a spill.

David knew the water was only a foot deep at the dock, so Liddie wasn't in any real danger. He desperately wanted to be somewhere else, but knew this called for a gentlemanly response. He grabbed another rope and tossed it to Liddie, who was trying to push herself upright in the muck. Of course, this was an almost impossible task, with the muck sucking at Liddie's feet and hands whenever she moved. It was all greatly complicated by Elizabeth running down to rescue Liddie. She took a running leap off the dock just in time to smack the stumbling Liddie back down into the water, only this time covered with a soaking wet St. Bernard!

Paula, inside the house, heard the shouting and splashing and came running out. She ran down the path, breathless and frightened that someone had gotten hurt. But instead she saw Osmund and Sarah, each cradling their buckets, standing off to the side. On the dock was her husband, mud splashed all over his soaked clothes. And in the pond, being lavishly licked by that enormous dog, was their new guest!

Paula did the only thing possible. She sat down right in the pathway and started laughing uproariously. The sheer ridiculousness of the situation overcame her desire to help. So she just sat and laughed. She shook and jiggled with laughter. She laughed until tears streamed down her face. And then she laughed some more.

In the meantime, David was still trying to get his rope to Liddie, and after a while succeeded. She grabbed hold and was able to pull herself upright, and then with some difficulty, climbed back onto the dock. The dog, that drenched dog, scrambled over a nearby log and proceeded to shake and spray pond scum over everyone. By this time, Paula had completed her laughing fit and ran to help Liddie. Together they climbed back up to the house, leaving David to corral Elizabeth and make a not totally effective effort at cleaning her up.

Reaching the porch, Liddie looked at Paula. Paula looked at Liddie. Both dissolved into more laughter, each one shaking together in a new, shared bond.

Liddie thoroughly scrubbed and cleaned herself. She discovered a washing machine and got her clothes started. By that time it was mid morning, and she wondered about breakfast or lunch, or actually, any kind of food. Wandering down to the far side of the house she found David and Paula, who had just finished cleaning themselves up.

"I'm wondering," she said, "is there a local grocery store where I can pick up a few things to eat? I'm not sure how long it will take me to check out the land and get my pictures — probably not more than a day or so. I don't need much."

Paula jumped up and, taking her arm, led her to the kitchen. "Look!" she said. "We have anything you might need already here! And it's such a long journey in to town, it would take you all day." She began opening cabinets and pointing to the different boxes and cans.

Liddie was quite impressed with the variety and amount of food they had on hand. Cereals, soups, pastas, oatmeal — quite a well-stocked pantry!

"Why, thank you so much! I'm happy to pay you for whatever I use," she responded.

Paula shook her head and replied, "Nonsense! I won't hear of that."

"As soon as Osmund is done cleaning those catfish," Paula continued, "we can cook them up for supper. Here, come with me and let's go get Bronia — she's the best at frying catfish."

"Hmmm," Liddie thought, "this must be one of those others that David mentioned."

She followed Paula out the door, eager to see what other surprises this place held. Paula indicated that she should choose one of the walking sticks leaning against the wall, and after a brief examination, she chose a nicely twisted staff. It felt quite natural as she followed Paula down the pathway to the far side of the pond.

Soon they could see a small, rustic cabin. The wooden floor was set upon cinder blocks. Liddie could see that the cabin was built into a natural ravine that would collect water during the spring rains, and the blocks kept it high and dry. Although small, the cabin had a pleasing look with a window on each side and a storage area connected in the back. Old metal chairs sat on a porch that extended along the front half. Short steps led up to the porch and entrance.

Paula was already up the steps and calling out for Bronia. A stunningly beautiful woman opened the door. Liddie found herself staring, mentally comparing this woman to the gorgeous actresses she had seen in vintage movies. Katherine Hepburn, Rita Hayworth, Ava Gardner, all rolled into one! And this woman even had the look of that time period. Her clothes were tailored to her trim figure, shoulder pads accentuated the crispness of her blouse, and the pants were neatly creased. Her auburn hair descended in pleasing, naturally curly waves, just loose enough to give a spirited, free-flowing look. Liddie watched Bronia's eyes sparkle as she greeted Paula with a lilting laugh, and Liddie immediately wanted to know more about this person.

Paula was quick to introduce Bronia to Liddie. There was no explanation about who Liddie was or why she was there. Just a warm acceptance. Bronia responded to the introduction by laughing quite heartily as she described standing at her window and watching Liddie fall into the pond earlier.

Upon learning that Osmund had caught a mess of catfish and she was being requested to fry them, Bronia called out a window, "Mac! Mac! Wake up! Catfish time!"

Liddie peered out an adjoining window and could see a figure clambering out of a hammock. A clear view was obscured, though, until he walked around the cabin and appeared in the doorway. Then her eyes widened, her mouth gaped, and it was all she could do to look back and forth, back and forth between the two, Bronia and Mac.

If Bronia was the epitome of a 1940's screen beauty, Mac was totally her male screen idol counterpart. Tall, handsome, with dark curly hair and the most engaging grin. These two were classic heartthrobs.

Once inside the door, Mac strode straight toward Bronia and swept her up in a loving hug. It was only after a warm, lingering kiss that Bronia motioned with her eyes over toward Liddie. Confused, Mac didn't appear to know what she was signaling. Bronia took his arm and turned him face to face with Liddie. A look of surprise registered on his face, but he quickly recovered and extended his hand for a greeting.

"And who is this lovely young visitor?"

Chapter 4: Couples

L iddie reached out her hand to Mac's firm grasp and greeted him with a simple, "I'm Liddie. So pleased to meet you and Bronia!"

Mac nodded matter of factly and refrained from digging deeper. Instead, he exclaimed, "So, a catfish feast, is it? Let me get my stash of special drinks." He then proceeded to rummage in a back room, returning laden with a dozen bottles of Mountain Dew soda. Water glistened off the cool, green glass. Liddie thought it had been some time since she had had a Mountain Dew, and never one bottled in glass — she was only familiar with the plastic ones. She joined the other two women in reaching out to help carry the bottles.

Reaching the main house after the short walk back, Bronia busied herself with examining Osmund's catfish. She pointed out a few places where bones still needed removing, but otherwise thanked him for a good job filleting the fish. Paula was already rummaging around for a coating mix. Sarah found a pot for cooking the peas. David exclaimed over the Mountain Dew and opened a bottle for Liddie, who was slightly embarrassed about how gustily she drank it down.

David pulled an assortment of chairs up close to the kitchen table, and those who weren't cooking sank down into them. He turned to Mac, who had been watching Bronia with a soft, gentle love in his eyes.

"Mac," David asked, "how long before you need to leave?"

"Just over a week," he answered, turning to address David.

The old man shook his head and stared at the floor, his lips pursed tightly, and he answered, "You know, it's going to be hard on her."

Mac sighed deeply. "I wish it didn't have to be so," he began. Then, remembering Liddie, he turned to her and explained, "My Navy unit is shipping out in two weeks. They haven't told us where, exactly, but our mission is vital. I must go. Our country needs me to answer its call."

Liddie could see Bronia looking over at Mac and wondered if part of his intensity was to encourage himself about their impending separation.

Mac continued, "You see, Bronia and I have only been married a month. She swept me off my feet and I haven't been the same since. Of course, every new married couple has adjustments, but I can't imagine living life without her. It's hard, incredibly hard, facing this deployment, knowing that I leave her behind. And yet, I must do the right thing. No matter what the cost, I must serve my country."

Bronia handed her spatula to Paula, who began turning the catfish. She moved behind Mac and gently caressed his shoulders. As he turned to look in her eyes, she said, "Mac, you know I'll always be here. I'll be waiting for you, praying for you, and looking forward to the time when I see you returning safe and whole and I run and jump into your arms once more!"

Mac leapt out of his chair, turning to whisk Bronia into his arms, and the two embraced. As all the others watched with great interest, the two walked out the door and stood together on the porch, still entwined, her head resting on his broad shoulders.

"Wow!" Liddie exclaimed, to no one in particular.

A chatter of new voices came down the hallway. Liddie turned to see two middle-aged women walking into the room. A short, stout woman was carrying a plate of steaming food. The other woman, taller and dark-haired, was gesturing emphatically as she talked quite animatedly to her. The short woman nodded in agreement.

The two continued their lively conversation even as they took notice of the others in the room.

"I tell you, that man is going to be the death of me!" This came from the taller woman. She continued, "I tell him what we need to keep the farm running, I tell him about the fences, I tell him about the crops, I tell him repeatedly! And what does he do? He sits there in that barn, jawing all day long with his buddies! What do they do? I can't imagine what they do! Nothing! No work! Our potatoes are past time for planting. We're going to lose that cow if he doesn't fix the fence. Fallen trees lay rotting instead of being cut for firewood. I am just at my wits' end!"

The shorter woman nodded in agreement, and began in a thick Eastern European accent, "I know what you mean! My Stanley is out with your Henry right now. They're up at that Pond Beyond, fishing and telling tall tales, I'm sure! All they want to do is tell each other those long-winded stories that no one believes. Stanley, he's the most generous person, and I love him. He'll do anything for anyone, and keep them laughing while he does it. But to get him helping around the house, I mention anything, and he is out the door to visit Henry. Of course, he did have that terrible bout of emphysema. And I understand that he can't do as much anymore." She added, thoughtfully, "But I need help, too!"

The two paused at that point. Those in the room nodded in greeting.

"Anna! Adelle!" Paula moved toward them. "Oh, look! You've made pierogi! You are the best cook, Anna. Thank you!"

Anna lay down the plate and turned her attention to Liddie. "I don't recognize you," she said bluntly, with some confusion. Paula once again explained the presence of their visitor.

Bronia spread the fried catfish on a towel-lined plate to drain, and Sarah brought out the peas and set them next to the pierogi. Mac's Mountain Dews were eagerly finished as the group devoured the delicious meal.

Afterwards, Adelle regaled the others as she described her morning. She and Henry apparently lived in a part of the land known as Glen McKay where an old homestead still existed. There was an overgrown garden that Adelle was convinced used to be a showplace, so she had spent the morning scouring the woods looking for bushes and stray flowers to transplant into it. She described some tiny saplings that she had dug and moved.

"They were easy enough to dig," she said, "but my skin just flared up in little red bumps wherever the branches rubbed against me! You can see how much I'm itching right now!"

Indeed, her arms were covered with an angry rash. Liddie peered closely at it and asked Adelle, "Tell me… the little saplings… did they seem to be evergreen — like they would be green all year round, instead of losing their leaves in the wintertime?"

"Why yes," Adelle answered, "they were. Do you know what they are? I hope it's not poison ivy!"

"Well," Liddie said, "if they are what I'm thinking, they will be huge in another 20 years! I always get those same little red bumps when I handle cedar trees. They are beautiful trees, especially when allowed to grow free and unencumbered in a field. But farmers don't like them in their fields because they do tend to produce so many seedlings. I imagine there is a large mother tree somewhere near where you dug these up."

Encouraged by Adelle's interest, Liddie continued, "I would love to come up and see your garden! One of my hobbies is searching the woods and fields for forgotten native plants. And I do need to get those pictures of the land for my mom, so I could do both at the same time!"

The two women made plans to head to Glen McKay after lunch. Cleanup took just a short time and they started out, accompanied by Anna, who said that she was staying in a trailer near Glen McKay.

Adelle led the way down a nearby hill and through a forest of towering, majestic black walnut trees. Liddie guessed the largest ones to be well over a hundred years old. Perhaps a hundred-fifty, she thought. Some of them had a diameter of over three feet. Their bright green leaves had just recently emerged, black walnut being one of the last trees to sprout in the spring. Brushing against some of the leaves, Liddie was greeted with a pungent aroma, which she realized with a start was very similar to the citrusy scent of Mac's Mountain Dew!

On the forest floor, some of last year's walnuts lay surrounded by their broken black husks. She walked carefully so as not to step on them — a memory of twisting her ankle on a stray walnut during the internship was still too fresh. The atmosphere in the woodland was peaceful and serene, the sound much more muted than around the pond with its chorus of frogs and birds. The quietness was only occasionally broken by the cuk-cuk-cuking of what Liddie recognized as a pileated woodpecker.

Liddie made a mental note to start a journal describing the land for her mom. This black walnut forest would be an attractive selling point for a realtor. Its hard wood was in huge demand for the beautiful grain, useful in furniture making and many home projects. Walking through the quiet forest, though, Liddie hoped that whoever bought the land wouldn't cut down the massive trees. Besides, she surmised that the edible walnut crop could be a supplement for homesteaders looking to live on their own.

Adelle led the small group out of the woods into a large field where Liddie could feel the warm sunshine again. They emerged onto a flat plain perhaps a hundred yards wide, but stretching much longer. At its far edge the plain rose rather suddenly into a steep hill that dominated the western side of the clearing. Liddie stopped, sensing something, not knowing quite what, but feeling drawn to the hilltop in the distance. She stood, gazing up at it.

Anna, glancing back at Liddie, called for Adelle to wait up for them. Adelle returned, and the three sat down on a nearby log. Someone, long ago, had apparently formed this log into a rustic bench. There were smaller logs pushed under the two ends, lifting it off the ground, making it a perfect sitting height. The log was situated facing the hilltop that had drawn Liddie's attention.

A bit of silence ensued before Adelle began, "I love the placement of this log. It welcomes a traveler to stop and sit. There is absolutely no reason for it being here, between a woods and a field. It's not like this is a place to wait for a bus, say, or a carriage to come pick you up. It sits here, beside a walking pathway, only for stopping, gazing around and absorbing what is not spoken."

With that, the trio continued to sit, Liddie's brow scrunching up as she began to comprehend the deep truth that Adelle had expressed. Liddie's eyes were drawn upwards, watching the soaring and circling of two bald eagles high in the clear blue sky. Then, lower, the flashing bright blue of Indigo Buntings as they flew from one low tree to another. She was able to pick out the calls from other birds — Eastern Phoebe, Carolina Wren, the many different songs of the cardinal.

The field was mostly open, with native forbs and sedges greening up below the dead brown stems of last year's grasses. Splashes of color from early wildflowers burst out randomly in the field. Tall stems of bright blue spiderworts, purple and white violets with their visiting hungry bumblebees, and, of course, the prolific, cheery yellow dandelions.

Bisecting the lower expanse of the field was a low, washed-out area, presumably, Liddie thought, caused by erosion from spring rains. All along the wash grew native shrubs with the occasional tall sycamore or pine scattered among them. Liddie could identify the white flowers of hawthorns, some dogwoods and redbuds, and what she thought might be false indigo — it wasn't blooming yet so she couldn't be sure. Flowering plum thickets seemed to be activity centers for the myriad birds. The entire wash gave a very pleasing impression of a patchwork hedgerow of varying heights and textures. This would be a fantastic corridor for wildlife, Liddie thought, becoming lost in the beauty.

Time passed. Liddie stood and stretched. Anna was the first to speak. "Perhaps we should keep going" she said. "We could sit here all day. Maybe you can stop again, on your way back to the house?"

Adelle led them on down the path, through a hazelnut thicket where they found clusters of catkins still hanging on the branches. Beyond the hazelnuts, the path wound through a short strip of woodland, coming into another wide field, much like the previous one. Except, off to the south, Liddie caught the delicious scent of blooming crabapples! Delighted to see their pathway head toward the tall, spreading trees, Liddie almost ran to get a closer look. But she stopped short when she suddenly came face to face with a weathered old couple sitting underneath the flowering trees. Liddie's expression of surprise was matched with the shock on their faces.

Behind her, Liddie heard Adelle call out, "James! Mary! It's just us! And a friend!"

Catching up, Adelle and Anna waved to the couple who responded in kind, although still somewhat quizzically eyeing Liddie.

"Liddie, these are Henry's parents — James and Mary," Adelle began. "They are the sweetest people. But," and here she turned to James, who nodded vehemently, "they do like to have their privacy. So let's us just continue on to my garden, shall we?"

Reluctant to leave the enchanting fragrance of the trees, still, Liddie didn't want to be rude, so she waved goodbye to the couple and continued down the path which wound through the middle of this new field. Adelle explained more as they walked.

"James and Mary — they're from the 'old country.' They even still use some of their native language. I think it's Gaelic. For instance, they persist in calling that strip of land Lana na Null. I think it's a Gaelic phrase that means something like Lane of Crabapples. And you can understand why, I mean the crabapples make such a statement there, but still…" And here she trailed off as they entered what apparently was the Glen McKay where Adelle and Henry lived.

The biggest landmark in this field was a rickety house that appeared to be over two hundred years old. Peeling tin hanging from the roof, loose porch steps — all indicated that years of neglect had taken their toll on the dwelling. Liddie's first thought was to wonder how she could describe this building as an asset for her mom, although she was doubtful it would be possible. But there were definite signs that someone had been making repairs on some of the walls, trying to fix it up. The porch itself was neatly swept with several potted plants artfully arranged. Her attention was drawn around to the side of the house as Adelle called her over. "Come! See my garden!"

Suddenly a chorus of loud shouting erupted as Adelle and Anna both started talking at once, occasionally answered by two male voices. Liddie assumed these must be the two missing husbands. She peered around the corner with some trepidation.

Two very pleasant looking men were stretched out on old metal lawn chairs. Despite the torrent of words from Adelle and Anna, they showed no concern, simply nodding in response, but eyeing each other with knowing glances.

Adelle was the most vocal. "Just look at you two!" she chided. "Have you any idea what time it is? Supper was two hours ago! Don't you think for a minute that I'm going to get you anything now!"

The one that Adelle seemed to be most fixated on wore an old set of blue overalls with a broken shoulder strap. Underneath was a baggy, faded, rather worn tee shirt. A straw hat sat somewhat rakishly on his head. He was having difficulty maintaining a straight face and tried to look away from the women. Liddie assumed he must be Adelle's husband, Henry.

The other one, Stanley, was a bit more refined, dressed surprisingly in a clean buttoned shirt and tweed jacket. He seemed grateful that Anna started into him with a gentler tone.

"Stanley," she began, a bit reproachfully, "your cough… You know I worry about you. You just can't keep sitting outside in the cold like this. Have you had any of that elixir today? Anything hot to drink? I'm going to take you right home and mix up a poultice to wrap around your neck. Come on! Get up!" she commanded, grasping his arm and practically pulling him out of the chair. Stanley protested just a bit, shot Henry a sideways glance, and rolled his eyes. Then, noticing Liddie, he nodded his head toward her in acknowledgement, but was only able to call out, "Good day, Miss!" before he was whisked down the pathway.

Adelle seemed not to recognize the awkwardness of the situation but plunged right into showing off her garden. She did pause long enough to briefly introduce Liddie to the man, who was indeed her husband Henry. But then she turned her attention to finding the saplings she had transplanted. Liddie was able to positively identify them as red cedars, and pointed to a large cedar tree in the woods that probably produced the seeds for them. Most of the other plants in the garden hadn't yet sent forth enough of their leaves for Liddie to recognize. However, as she turned to leave, she saw a beautiful peony on the edge of the garden. The large pinkish buds were not quite open, but Liddie could smell the sweet fragrance as she bent close.

"I've never seen such a wonderful specimen," she marveled. "To have this amount of scent from an unopened bud is unheard of! I must come back once it's fully opened!"

Adelle agreed, and then showed Liddie the direction for her walk back to the house. Waving goodbye, Liddie started off down the winding path. Peering around a bend, she caught a glimpse of that enigmatic hilltop she had seen from the bottom of the big field. Realizing she was headed straight to it, her pace quickened.

Chapter 5: Two Phone Calls

Their walk to Glen McKay had been up a gradual incline that ended almost level with the top of the big hill. Glen McKay was behind the hill, to the West. Liddie surmised that she must be close to the edge of the property because she could see fencing through the woods. Her path wound its way through a savannah with widely spaced pines and oaks before giving way to the top of the large field she had first encountered coming out of the black walnut forest. It was just a short walk further before Liddie arrived at the summit. A small metal chair lay on its side inside a clearing. Not far in front of the chair, Liddie could see the remains of an old campfire. Ashes were scattered about with pieces of charred wood. A couple of long sticks that might have been used for poking a fire lay nearby. And a bit further from the remains a jumble of firewood lay as if dropped there in preparation for another campfire.

Liddie straightened up the chair, brushed it off and sat down. A hint of wood smoke still hung over the area, leading her to wonder, was the campfire yesterday? Certainly not longer ago than two days. She didn't much like the idea of unknown people setting fires on this property. Or could it be some of those she had already met? And what was the purpose? The hilltop could be an excellent spot for stargazing, with its large expanse and unencumbered view of the sky. Was it used for cooking? She didn't see any pots or pans or any scraps of food. But then, any number of wild creatures could have come by to eat scraps.

Her speculations did not seem to be finding any solutions, and Liddie was becoming aware of the late afternoon sun on her shoulders. The warmth was oh, so seductive. Her eyes began drooping. Next her head dropped down, chin touching her chest. She melted into peaceful abandonment, allowing rest to overtake her body.

Unsure of how long, exactly, she had rested, Liddie awoke with a start. She shook her head, giving herself a few moments to recall where she was.

What was that? On the clearing edge, opposite from where she had left Adelle and Henry, she thought there was a movement. Tall, slim — surely it was a person. Could this be yet another resident of the land she hadn't met? She made a mental note to ask Paula and David how many people actually were living on her family's land.

The figure walked slowly around the hill's summit. Sometimes he, or she, faded into the slowly gathering dusk. Liddie experienced an odd certainty that there was no danger involved with whoever this was. On the contrary, she could sense a peace, a calmness that emanated from the person. She had felt the same thing when first seeing the hill earlier that afternoon. It aroused something in her, something new. Was it wonder?… no, something akin to wonder, but more a sensation which Liddie could not place, one she did not have in her experience…

The figure disappeared out of Liddie's view. She jumped up, becoming acutely aware of the setting sun. Dark settles quickly in the Missouri hills. Liddie walked hastily, almost running, down the pathway. The dim glow of lights in the house welcomed her back into its warmth and she gratefully plopped down on her bed. Elizabeth, who apparently had been sleeping there all day, nuzzled her, tail wagging, and returned to snoring. Liddie rubbed her ears.

The day had been a whirlwind. From falling into the pond to meeting so many people, Liddie realized she needed to start her journal now in order to keep track of everything. She reached into her backpack, rummaged around and found her sketchbook. It would do.

Almost an hour later, she was satisfied with her recollections. She had even included a few sketches to help describe the land. She placed the journal back in her backpack. Seeing her phone, she pulled it out, checking for messages. No messages, but she accidentally touched Beckley's contact information, and his face popped up with his phone number.

"Oh!" she exclaimed out loud. Then, "Hmmm," as she examined his eyes in the photo and decided they were the most perfect shade of deep blue, with just a tiny touch of green.

"You know," she thought, "maybe I should give Beckley a call. He should know something about the legality of all these people living here." They had all been exceedingly friendly, of course, but she did have a responsibility to her mom and other relatives. "And," she considered, "this would be a good excuse to 'keep in touch' with Beckley!"

Liddie decided to start with a text. That would be slightly less forward than calling on the phone. Surprisingly, there appeared to be cell reception now!

Hey, you! she typed.

Almost immediately came his reply: *Liddie! Great to hear from you!*

A bit of silence followed, as she pondered how to put all of the day's events into a text. She gave up, and decided it really needed a call.

Perhaps she also wanted to hear his voice.

Thanks! Hey, is this a good time for a call? There are a couple of things I want to run by you.

Her answer came in the buzzing of her phone, which she hastily answered.

"Liddie! I've been wondering how you've been getting by. What have you found at your family's farm? Is it desolate? In ruins? What about snakes? Have you been careful?"

Liddie was delighted to hear his concern and couldn't help smiling to herself.

"Why, hello to you, too, Beckley!" she answered with a laugh.

He chuckled somewhat self-consciously.

"Everything has been great," she continued. "The house is in good shape.

It even has the solar power still running! The land is beautiful. And I found a dog!"

She was surprised to realize how pleased she felt when she described Elizabeth to Beckley. Up to that point, she hadn't regarded Elizabeth as her dog. Now, though, as she rubbed the floppy ears, she recognized there was a bond she wanted to keep.

After Beckley effused over Elizabeth, he told Liddie he was scheduled to have his final interview for the law firm the next day.

"You know, Liddie, I'm really glad you texted. Somehow, talking to you makes me feel less worried about it."

That was all the encouragement Liddie needed to plunge into the tale of her day.

"So, Beckley," she wound up after talking nonstop, describing the people living on the farm, "what do you think? As I said, they are all really friendly. I don't think I'm in any danger. And frankly, I am finding that I really like most of them! They're genuine, honest people, even if they do seem a bit mysterious. I mean, how are they all related to each other? It's like a small community, where they do some things together, yet live separately. And they weren't at all concerned when I showed up — just welcomed me in."

Beckley had been listening in silence. Perhaps this was due in part to his law school training — get the whole story first.

"Well," he started slowly, "I think you have good instincts for evaluating situations. I saw some of your actions and responses when you were working with groups at the internship. Yes, you probably are accurate about not being in danger."

Here, Beckley was forcing himself to stay calm and respond logically, because what he really wanted to do was shout, "Get out of there! You have no idea if these are homicidal maniacs! Out! Out! Run!"

But he continued to respond slowly, hoping for inspiration, when it hit him!

"Liddie, have you called your mother about this?"

"Um, no! I guess it's all happened so fast, this is the first time I've stopped. I thought you might have insight from a legal viewpoint, so I called you first."

"Okay, then." He had a direction now. "You need to call your mother! As soon as we hang up. She needs to know about the situation. She or your uncle might be familiar with some of the people, although I would have thought she would have said something if that was the case. I will do some research into laws regarding squatters. We can hope that whatever that first man referred to when he said that they would be gone soon really does happen, and they all leave. However, you need to know your options if they won't leave.

"So, I will call you tomorrow after my interview — it should be late in the day. And, remember, you must call your mother when we hang up!"

Liddie was again touched by his concern. She was glad for the reminder to call her mom and wondered why she hadn't thought of it right away.

"Thanks, Beckley! Yes, I'll do that!" She then encouraged him about his interview the next day. "You're going to do great! I can't wait to hear all about it!"

"Okay, Liddie." He didn't really want to hang up, but knew he needed to let her go so she could call her mother. "I'll talk to you tomorrow, then."

Liddie dialed her mom, first taking just a moment to absorb the warm afterglow she felt from hearing Beckley's voice.

"Liddie! How are you?"

"Mom! I've missed you!"

Hearing her mom's voice always reminded Liddie of how much she enjoyed being with her. Her mom had such a fun outlook on life, and Liddie always felt encouraged and loved when they talked. "I've got so much to tell you!"

Once again, Liddie described the day's events, ending with the same question she had posed to Beckley. "So, Mom, what do you think?"

Liddie's mom was definitely concerned. She, like Beckley, knew that Liddie had a good head on her shoulders, but she was a mother, and she cared about her daughter. She paused before responding.

"Liddie," she started, "you know that your father and I pray for you every day. We ask God to hold you in the palm of his hands, to give you protection, provision, and an awareness of his presence. And that he would give you wisdom and knowledge to know him more fully each day of your life. I trust that he is there with you and that he will guide you. It seems like a grand adventure." She paused again.

Liddie felt the warmth of her mom's love. She knew that her parents had been concerned when Liddie had expressed to them her new doubts concerning God. None of her friends at college shared a belief in God, and Liddie had gravitated to, if not an 'unbelief,' at least a feeling that God wasn't really relevant to her life. She was grateful that her mom and dad were open to discussing it with her in a non-judgmental manner. And, she had to admit to herself, she was glad they still prayed for her.

"Thank you, Mom. I love you."

"I love you, too, Liddie," she answered.

"Now, as as for all these people, I had no idea! There shouldn't be anyone living there. I do remember, when we visited my grandparents, most everyone in the community was good hearted. They mostly kept to themselves, but they certainly weren't dangerous. Of course, that was many years ago. No telling what things might be like now."

"No, Mom, it's funny — I really don't feel like I'm in any danger. And I've already spent the one night here. And, I really think Elizabeth has adopted me and would be some kind of protection."

Her mom recognized the logic of what Liddie said. "I think you're probably right. But I want you to be sure and lock your door! And keep your phone right beside your bed! Are you keeping it charged? And your father and I will be doubling our prayers for you!"

Liddie smiled. She loved her mom.

"And Liddie, I want you to contact the sheriff. Ask him about the characters living there. See if he can come out and visit in person. Do that tomorrow!"

"Yes, Mom. That's a good idea. Now, I've got to get to bed. I'm hearing frogs again. And a whip-poor-will. Did I tell you about the whip-poor-will? I love you so much! Goodnight, Mom!"

Chapter 6: Sarah Confides

The next morning Liddie made sure to call the sheriff right after breakfast. She thought it odd that there was only a recording for leaving a message. "What if there was an emergency?" she thought, becoming a little more aware of the farm's isolation. But, that was also part of the charm — being more isolated meant more opportunities to experience the beauty of nature.

Liddie realized that she had forgotten to get pictures the day before, so she was determined today to get what photos she could for her mom. It made sense to start with the house. She began exploring the other rooms. One appeared to have been a small office, with a large old desk, several bookcases, and plastic bins. She took a few pictures with her phone and turned to close the door, but something pulled her back into the room. She glanced at the bins again. What could be in them? She told herself that she had a responsibility to be as thorough as possible in documenting the premises. Sitting down in the old leather office chair, she gingerly opened the top bin, checking carefully around the edge for insects. Much as she enjoyed nature, Liddie did not want to encounter spiders!

There were no spiders, the bin having a solidly closed and sealed lid. A faint musty smell, as was to be expected, arose from the papers inside. Liddie could see several binders and notebooks. On top of these rested a yellowed map! Liddie's mind began racing with thoughts of buried treasure as she lifted it out. Gently, she lay it on the desk and began to study the depictions.

It was well drawn. Colors had been applied to different areas, but the colors were all muted now. Neatly penciled writing identified different parts.

"Aha!" Liddie shouted, as she laid her finger on what appeared to be a pond. And there was the house, right next to it. "Why, this is a map of the property! How cool is this?"

Paula and David must have heard the shouting because they appeared at the doorway, peering in at her.

"Oh, look at that!" exclaimed Paula. "What an amazing find. And all the names of the places are marked on it." She excitedly pointed to the map.

David said, "It looks like there might be additional interesting records and files in those bins."

Liddie agreed, carefully replacing the lid of the open bin. "I'll leave them for another time." She answered. "It's such a beautiful day out, I think I'll just take this map and explore with it."

Paula gave her an apple and a small bag of nuts to carry along the trails. Liddie gratefully accepted them and placed them in a bag with her filled water bottle and journal. She sat on the porch to examine the map and plan out her route. Yesterday she had visited the cabin with Bronia and Mac. As shown on the map, it was along the trail that circled the pond. If the two of them only had a few days left before he deployed, she thought, she didn't want to bother them, so she decided not to head that way. On the opposite side of the pond was a trail heading up to a place called The Mountain Top, and beyond that, an area to the east labeled The Border. Liddie wondered if perhaps that was the eastern boundary line of the land. Yesterday, she had seen the fencing along the woods near the big hill and assumed that was the western border. Checking the edge of the map, she was able to pinpoint those woods and confirm her thoughts.

Coming east from the woods lay a large field that ended in an area labeled Walnut Hill just below the house. Liddie was sure that must be the beautiful walnut grove they had passed through on their walk yesterday! And the big hill in the field must be the one where she had found the campsite — where the mysterious figure wandered. Sliding her finger to the center of that field, she stopped at the penciled words, "Carn Ingli."

"Carn Ingli?" She questioned out loud. "I've never heard of that. Is it even English? I wonder what it means." She continued musing, repeating the name to herself.

Liddie was feeling comfortable with her understanding of the lay of the land. This map would be a most fantastic resource to show her mom. She looked again at Walnut Hill and saw that it led into an area labeled The Wetland.

"That would be interesting to explore," she thought, guessing that many of the frogs she heard at night might live there.

Liddie was most intrigued by all these names, thinking there must have been reasons behind them all. She wondered if this map was drawn by some of her ancestors or if it had been created by someone who lived here after her family left. She would need to ask her mom.

It occurred to her that James and Mary had referred to their crabapple trees as Lana na Null, and the area was labeled as such on the map. So what was the connection there — had they found the map, or maybe there was some sort of sign near the trees? She noted this in her journal and returned to examining the map.

Between Walnut Hill and the house was a section called The Pilgrim Path. Liddie, looking up from the map toward the walnut trees, recognized the beautiful flowering smaller trees she had seen and commented on when she first arrived. The flowers on the redbuds had now opened and were varying shades of red and pink. Surely, that must be The Pilgrim Path.

She decided to start her exploration there. She wasn't too familiar with Pilgrims, but she knew the word had something to do with exploring, wandering, traveling. And ever since arriving at this place she had felt like she was wandering through a type of grand adventure. The Pilgrim Path, then, was an appropriate place to start.

The twisted walking stick Liddie had used yesterday was leaning near the door. She picked it up as she headed off toward The Pilgrim Path. Her pathway took her along the pond edge where two huge bullfrogs leapt out of the swampy weeds and plopped into the water with loud splashes and croaking. The sudden noise startled Liddie, and she paused to watch them resurface in the pond.

Continuing on to The Pilgrim Path, she found a metal bench situated at a turn. After examining it, she sat, using the opportunity to take a few pictures of the house and pond, as well as the blooming trees on the pathway. She could only look twenty feet or so down the path before it curved out of sight.

"That's interesting," she thought. "Yesterday, most of the pathways were also curved with lots of bends and twists. I've always heard that the shortest distance between two points is a straight line. So, what is going on with all these curves?" She pondered a bit and then rose to continue her walk.

The dogwood petals were beginning to flutter down off the branches, carpeting the pathway with pinks and whites. Liddie thought she could identify a large old mimosa tree. Several huge crabapples gave forth the same enchanting scent of the ones at Lana na Null. She found at least three different species of crabapples, basing her identification on their flowers and leaf shapes, again leading her to consider what a wonderful place for birds and other wildlife this must be. At the base of the trees clumps of wildflowers and grass-like sedges were beginning to grow.

"Whoa!" Liddie exclaimed! "What was that?" She had caught just a bit of a horrid scent wafting in from beyond the path, on the side away from the house. Not overpowering, but enough to disturb the peacefulness of her walk. Peering through the branches, she could make out an extremely small pond, covered with green algae. Identifying it as a drainage pond, she retreated back to the pathway and continued on her way. She was struck by how quickly the bad smell faded and was replaced with the crabapple scent.

Checking her map, she could see that a left turn ahead would take her down Walnut Hill. Instead, she chose a path labeled The Coneflower Field. Two minutes pleasant walking brought her to another wooden bench where she stopped for water, sat down, and gazed at the surroundings.

From this bench, aptly labeled The Overlook on the map, she could see the entire wide valley of the large field, almost straight across to the top of

Carn Ingli. To her right, the path continued through a sparse woodland — more of a savannah.

After a brief rest and more pictures, Liddie stood and began walking into the savannah. There, she was startled to discover two weathered concrete statues. One, a bit lower on the hill, was of an Indian chief gazing into the distance. The second appeared to be Jesus, outstretched arms reaching over the valley.

"I wonder what the story is here," she mused. She turned, looking back over the valley again. As she did so, a slight movement caught her eye. Across the valley, near the top of Carn Ingli, she thought she could see one solitary figure.

"Why, that's where the campfire was," she thought. "Is this the same person I saw there yesterday?"

The figure moved out of sight before she could focus her camera on it. Instead, she took photos of the concrete statues and walked on. Shortly, the path took her to a rustic lean-to beside a pond, this one smaller than the pond near the house. Checking her map, she identified it as The Pond Beyond. Behind the lean-to was a well-maintained garden plot. A woman bent over, working in the garden. Liddie recognized the red and white dress and the woman who had asked for her help in shucking the peas.

She called out, "Sarah! How are you? So this is where you grow those delicious peas!"

Sarah looked up, startled. After a moment, she regained her composure, sat down on a nearby log and responded, as she patted the log, "Liddie, is it? Here, come sit a spell."

Liddie smiled and sat beside the old woman. There was a brief silence, not awkward but more of a settling down of thoughts, a waiting for inspiration of where the conversation should begin. Liddie knew, and somehow sensed that the old woman also knew, that sometimes sitting in silence was the best way to visit.

They watched the fish jumping in the pond. A tall blue heron swooped in, looking every bit like a prehistoric pterodactyl. It began its peculiar stiff-legged stalking around the perimeter of the pond, hunting fish or frogs, or maybe even a small snake.

Eventually, Sarah began. "I know you're new to these parts, Liddie." She paused for several moments.

"Yesterday, when we met, I felt a connection with you. I wanted to talk more…. But it's hard for me. I've always felt like we're just supposed to deal with life and move on. For the most part, that's how I've lived. And yet, I think there's value in being able to talk about things. For some reason, when I saw you yesterday, these old memories came flooding back in. Memories of difficult times — times that I would rather forget. But now, seeing you again, I wonder, am I being reminded of them for a purpose? It's odd."

Sarah shook her head with a small, wry smile. "I suppose it's really odd for you, Liddie! Sitting here with an old woman rambling on about who knows what!"

Liddie smiled compassionately as she looked at Sarah. She murmured, "Not at all…"

Liddie remained silent, respecting Sarah's vulnerability. She wasn't quite sure where this conversation would lead, but she also felt a kind of connection with Sarah. Their eyes met, and Liddie nodded affirmatively.

Sarah continued.

"You see, I'm not proud of the life I've lived. I don't know what happened, exactly. My father, he was a preacher. A traveling preacher. Wherever we moved, and it was quite often, moving from place to place, he made it his responsibility to tell people about God, and how much he loves them. So, you see, he wasn't the kind of preacher that had a church, or anything like that. And he certainly didn't get paid for it. He was mostly someone who just kind of lived what he knew was right. And he tried to lead people into knowing God the way God wanted to know them.

"He had the most beautiful hair. Long, shiny black locks. I would watch him tell people all about God's goodness, his hair flowing off his shoulders, and I would think how much he looked like Jesus. I wanted to be just like him. Just like Jesus."

Sarah paused, remembering. The tiny hint of a smile appeared, then faded almost as quickly as it came. She shook her head.

"I just don't know how I ended up the way I did…

"I tried, once I was on my own. I did try to do what was right. Hardships came, and I stumbled through them as best I could. But then I just couldn't do it anymore. I had nothing left."

Liddie was drawn into Sarah's pain as she listened. Her eyes teared up, and she reached to take Sarah's hand.

"Liddie," Sarah turned to look straight into her eyes. "It was bad. Really, really bad. I can't tell you all the specifics now, maybe I won't ever be able to tell you.

"But, you know… one day, when I was much older, after years of this despair, I met someone. He talked about hope. I don't even remember exactly how he said it. Whatever the words were, what he said connected with the tiny bits of faith still lying in my soul. It was like I saw this glimmer of hope, a remembrance of what I had seen in my father. He — my father — was long gone by then, of course, but there was something about this encounter that reminded me of him. Almost like he was there, too…

"Anyway, after that day, life didn't so much get easier. There were still terrible trials. But, I felt like I could handle it now. I remembered the beauty of what I had been taught as a child. I was able to find occasional joys. A few times, I even felt something very close to peace.

"The time I lost — maybe it was because of my own bad choices, I don't know. Maybe it wasn't my fault at all… I regret the time that was lost. What I'm trying to say, I guess, is that out of it, in spite of it, because of it — however it's to be described — I found grace."

Sarah repeated, "Grace." She nodded thoughtfully.

"I began living in a knowledge of grace. And that grace moved me on — through a deliverance from my past and into a knowledge of God's blessings. The same kind of knowledge I had as a child, listening to my father and watching the sun shine on his long black hair."

The two sat in silence. Liddie recalled her first impression of Sarah, that she seemed to have encountered great adversity. She didn't know why Sarah had shared this intensely personal story with her. But she trusted the sense of connection they had found. There was a reason, she was sure. Sarah's story had touched her deeply. She felt almost envious of Sarah's knowledge of God.

"Sarah, you remind me of my mother." Liddie began. "Her faith is so deep, just like yours. Thank you for telling me your story. I will remember what you said."

After a short pause, Liddie continued, "Me, I don't know… I yearn for knowing the things you know. I'm not there, but I do think I want to be there."

Their time together ended with a quiet hug in the serenity of The Pond Beyond.

Liddie returned to the house following The Pawpaw Path, which was aptly named for a large grove of pawpaws. The odd purplish flowers were still blooming, making it a treat to walk among the trees. The tall trunks and lush leaves gave the area a tropical feel. Liddie stopped in the grove to give Beckley a call.

Chapter 7: Beckley Drops Everything

"Liddie!"

The excitement in Beckley's voice gave Liddie pleasant tingles. She smiled, listening to him.

"So how are you doing? What did your mother say?"

"Well, Beckley," she started, "she agreed with you. She also suggested I call the sheriff to check in with him. I did that this morning, but haven't heard back yet. I had to leave a message on the number. But I've been fine! I really feel very safe. The people living here — whoever they are — are very friendly, very welcoming. And I'm enjoying learning more about them. One of the women just spent a long morning telling me all about herself and her past struggles. I have no idea why! But we had this kind of connection, and it seemed so right!"

"Huh!" Beckley wasn't quite sure how to respond. "So, that's interesting."

"Yes," Liddie jumped back in. "I think I've met all of them, well, except that one mysterious person at the campfire place. I told you about him last night. I think I saw him again, this morning on my walk.

"Oh! Let me tell you about the map I found! It appears to be of this property, and it details all the little pathways. The one I took this morning was labeled The Pilgrim Path, and it took me down a beautiful walk through spring-blooming trees. I just love seeing the different plants here. I'm not sure if it's a natural remnant of prairie, or if it was planted intentionally.

"Anyway, Beckley, I think I'm going to stay here a few more days. I feel so refreshed, so happy here. Maybe it's because I don't have any schoolwork, or students to take on field trips. Whatever, I feel like this is a time for me to just enjoy!"

"I'm really glad that you feel that way, Liddie. Certainly, it's good to take a break!" He was aware that she didn't really have a job waiting for her anyway, but Beckley didn't think it would be appropriate to bring that up. Instead, he described his meeting with the law firm.

"They are very, very focused on making a difference in the world," he said. "That's one of the things I really liked. They all seem very knowledgeable about the environment. I recognized some of the cases they referenced as ones that I had studied. It's a good fit, Liddie! I think I'll enjoy working there."

"Oh, that's wonderful!" She was truly happy for him, even though his experience was miles and miles away from what she was going through.

"They said I can take my time finding a place to live and begin the job when I'm comfortable."

Beckley stopped short as a new thought entered his mind.

"Wait a minute!" He paused ever so briefly to consider what he was going to say, and then plunged right in. "Since I don't have to start right away, why don't I take a week or so to fly out there and see what you've discovered firsthand?"

He was so very pleased with himself!

Liddie's eyes widened. For a moment, she was speechless. "Whoa," she thought, "this was unexpected!" But there was no denying her excitement at the prospect! Beckley — here? Beckley — meeting these people! Beckley — here! Beckley — meeting Elizabeth! Beckley — HERE!

She tried to control her voice, but was unsuccessful. "Beckley! That would be wonderful! I would LOVE to show you this place. And of course, it would be really helpful to get your input. You can tell me all about your research on squatters in person! And I know Mom would like to have someone else here. Yes! I think that would be a great idea!"

By the time they hung up, plans had been made. Beckley would fly into St. Louis the following evening, spend the night at a hotel, rent a car the next morning, and drive down.

Liddie was ecstatic!

Beckley was ecstatic!

Liddie's mom was ecstatic when Liddie called to tell her about it. But she was even more ecstatic to hear how her daughter talked about this Beckley person. There was definitely something promising going on here!

Returning to the house, Liddie considered doing a bit of cleaning before taking more pictures. She rummaged through some storage areas, but was unable to find the supplies she wanted. David, napping in an old recliner, was awakened by her search. He stretched, groaned, and called out, "Is that you, Paula?"

"Oh, I'm so sorry!" Liddie exclaimed. "I didn't realize you were here!" She moved into the room and sat down.

"I can't seem to find dusting cloths or window cleaning spray." She continued, "These big picture windows are so lovely. I want to get photos showing the sun shining through them. But I want to clean them up first — I suppose all the supplies are long gone."

David's brow knitted up while he thought. "No, I don't recall seeing any. But that doesn't mean they aren't here. I imagine Paula has used something or other to clean. You know what? I bet Frankie carries supplies up at his store. You might enjoy a trip out there. It's only a couple of miles up the road. And you can pick up some more eggs while you're there. His chickens lay the best eggs around!"

Liddie loved the idea of exploring further afield from the land. After a quick walk with Elizabeth, she checked the cabinet for any other food needs and started off. Driving slowly up the gravel driveway, she noticed a small group of deer in the top field. They raised their heads and watched her, seemingly unafraid. By the time she moved past, they were back grazing the clover.

She was struck again by how primitive the gravel road was. Liddie wasn't sure if anyone lived further down the way. She decided that if so, they must drive something pretty big to navigate this rutted lane on a regular basis. She was glad when she reached the pavement and turned toward the small settlement of Hartshorn.

Following David's directions, she saw several small buildings ahead. Peeling paint dropped off their sides onto the dusty gravel. Rusted metal rooftops may have held color at one time, but no tint was visible now. It was hard to guess the age of the structures, but Liddie thought they must be over a hundred years old.

The largest of the buildings featured two antique-looking gas pumps in front of a sagging screen door. Two women of indeterminate age idly perused tables of what looked like flea-market items.

A number of wandering chickens scattered as Liddie pulled up next to the building. She climbed out of the car. Closing the door, Liddie was amazed at how much dirt and dust had covered the vehicle just from the short gravel drive. This appearance, however, was no different from any of the four pickup trucks parked around the store. They all matched with their dusty brown coating.

Liddie gave a cheerful, "Hello!" to the women. They smiled and nodded, but did not seem to encourage more conversation, so Liddie turned to the door. Above it was a handwritten sign proclaiming, "Hartshorn Grocery."

Inside, the dim light required a few moments of adjustment for Liddie's eyes. Several worn chairs almost blocked the entrance. They supported a young Amish man and two grey-bearded specimens who looked like farmers, one leaning so far back in his chair that Liddie wondered how he didn't fall over. She heard a snatch of speech.

"Grass is growin.'"

"Yup. Prob'ly be able to stop hauling' hay to them cows in another week."

Conversation abruptly ceased as Liddie walked in. The men eyed her with great interest.

Liddie was beginning to feel uncomfortably under a microscope. Believing the best defense to be a good offense, she repeated her cheery, "Hello!"

The men seemed a bit more responsive than their female counterparts.

The one leaning back let his chair fall forward with a thud. He was first to speak. "And hello to you, Missy!"

"You visitin', or just passin' through?" another asked.

A husky voice came from the right side of the room. "Give her some space! She's prob'ly gonna actually pay for something here — not like you deadbeats!"

Liddie turned and saw a large, clean-shaven man wearing faded bib overalls and sitting behind a counter. On the counter was an ancient cash register and several jars of local honey with hand-written labels. Behind, leaning against the wall, was a shotgun. Liddie noted that it was within easy reach of the man, who she assumed must be Frankie.

"Just visiting, I guess," Liddie stammered. "I'm taking pictures of my family's old farm down the road. They're thinking of selling."

The men all perked up with interest at this news. Liddie described the land, where it was, and explained how she needed to get supplies to clean up the house for pictures. Frankie set about locating the window spray and other materials. Liddie remembered to ask for a dozen eggs.

"I wonder," Liddie began again, "there seem to be some squatters living on the land. Is that common for this area?"

One of the men frowned and shook his head. "I ain't seen anyone around that I don't already know. And I expect I know most everyone in these parts." The others silently nodded in agreement.

Frankie was adding up the cost of Liddie's items in a dog-eared notebook. He looked up and studied her face.

"You know, I remember my Grandpa Frankie, the one I was named for, talking about an old couple who used to live down on that land. I suppose maybe they were relatives of yours? But that was so long ago. There ain't been anyone there for years and years. Leastwise, not that I know of. You want a baloney sandwich with that?"

Surprised at the offer, Liddie took a moment to respond.

"No, thanks, they're waiting lunch for me."

"Then that'll be $12.47, with your discount."

Liddie started to ask, "My discount?" but decided it was a joke. She paid and thanked Frankie for the supplies.

This whole experience was just getting odder and odder.

The afternoon sun was quite low in the sky as she pulled into the long driveway. Its long rays cast a lovely orange glow onto the pond and trees. Liddie paused to admire the scene. Doing so, she caught a slight whiff of wood smoke. She turned around, nose in the air, trying to identify where it was coming from. It wasn't the house, of that she was sure. Could it be coming from that campfire area? She walked up Coneflower Hill to get a better look. Far down the pathway, she saw figures walking toward Carn Ingli.

"Ah!" Liddie exclaimed to herself. "Whatever is going on there, it looks like it's continuing tonight. I'm going to head up and see for myself!"

As quickly as she could, she brought in the supplies, changed into her snake boots, and grabbed an apple and nuts. Elizabeth, sleeping on the bed, barely looked up. Liddie turned back, gave her head a quick rub, and pulled on a sweatshirt. Then she was off, stopping only to pick up the twisted walking stick.

Dusk fell swiftly as she walked, and Liddie found herself wishing she had searched for a flashlight before rushing out. The rising moon did cast enough of a glow that she could discern the pathway and by now she had a general idea of the lay of the land, so she was able to find her way.

The scent of wood smoke became heavier as she headed up Carn Ingli. Coming within sight of the blazing campfire, Liddie could see a number of figures, some seated, some standing, gathered around the fire. She recognized their faces in the flickering light. One, two, three… she began counting. Yes, all ten were here. Even the reclusive James and Mary.

Liddie stopped just outside the circle of light. Impolite as it might be, she wanted to observe unseen.

Chapter 8: Land Rush

Several folding chairs were set up around the fire pit. Most of the people were sitting in them. Some were resting on logs. Bronia and Mac sat on the ground, leaning on a large oak tree. There seemed to be a lot of conversation going on.

"Stanley, how's your cough?"

"Still bad. Sometimes I think it's getting better, but then I cough all night…"

"Look at Mac and Bronia!"

"Yeah, I'd be holding her tight, too, if I was leaving."

"Anna, did you make this kielbasa? I just cooked one over the fire, and it is the best!"

"You get your potatoes in, James?"

"Yep."

"Grass is growing!"

"You sent that young girl up to Frankie's? David, what if she can't find her way back?"

"Any more Mountain Dew?"

The conversation slowed somewhat, and Liddie watched as Henry stood up and moved toward the fire. His walk had a bounciness to it, conveying an inner excitement. Reaching the fire, he turned and scanned the rest of the group, lifting his arms as if to emphasize what he was about to say.

Liddie had gotten a little more comfortable watching and must have leaned out from the tree line a bit too much. Henry saw her, dropped his arms and his jaw, and stood in silence. Everyone else, of course, turned to see what he was looking at. Liddie, not sure what kind of reception she would get, being uninvited to what was obviously some kind of party, was gratified to hear the chorus of welcomes. Adelle jumped up, ran to take Liddie's hand, and led her to the log where she had been sitting. Bronia handed her the last Mountain Dew.

"As I was saying," Henry began, "well, actually I wasn't saying. I was beginning to say." He looked into the distance as if to center his thoughts. Then, with a burst of excited recollection, he began.

"I'm going to tell you all the story," and here he paused dramatically, "of my ride for the Oklahoma strip!

"I had not yet turned thirty years old. Times were as bad as they had ever been. No, no… times were worse. We were working harder on the farm, but we just seemed to be getting further and further behind. My parents — it was so hard to see them struggle with the weather, the hard rocky ground, trying to grow food. Dad worked every year to grow his potatoes, but every year, he just kept pulling out more rocks. Their one cow had died, and Mama was trying to sell eggs so they could buy another one.

"I was the the youngest — no, actually my brother Albert was two years younger, but he had already been married for three years so it felt like I was the youngest. I hadn't met Adelle at the time, so I didn't have any of the responsibilities they all had for their families. There was a whole passel of us. Seven brothers and sisters, all living mostly within a day's ride of my parents.

"My sister Mary Ann had gotten married some twenty years prior to this. She was the oldest of us kids. She and her husband Jacob, they had two kids. Another had died young. The kids were getting to be an age where they could help in the field work. But Jacob, he had just a small house in town, with no land. You can see how they would want land where he and Mary Ann could work with the kids and build a future.

"So Jacob came to me and started working on me, pushing the idea of free land. He kept after me, looking for me in the fields, in town, it was like he was hunting me down, and he wouldn't give up! He wanted me to go down with him to the strip opening. There had been several other openings already, but this one was called the Cherokee Outlet Opening. He told me, 'It's going to be a great adventure! You'll see things you've never, ever seen in your life!' And of course, after a bit, I began to believe him. I had never been further from the farm than Bethany, our county seat, which was a fairly small town. I had no idea what was out in the world. The more I thought about it, the more excited I became.

"Once Jacob had me on board, there were four or five others from our town who found out we were going and wanted to join in. So we gathered what supplies we could find. Jacob's horse, Ol' Betsy, could pull the wagon. A few old mules could carry people and baggage. And one of the fellows did have a nice riding horse.

"Our route would take us from the top corner of Harrison County, down through Kansas City, on to Wichita, and finally the Cherokee Strip. Four hundred miles. Some of the roads were expected to be fairly passable, but we knew the trail would sometimes be rough. It would probably take two weeks of pretty solid riding to get down to Oklahoma.

"We took our leave of the womenfolk and started off, whooping and hollering until the town could no longer be seen."

Henry stopped for a drink of water. Liddie glanced over at Adelle. She and all of the others had been sitting entranced with the story. Liddie also found herself drawn into the tale. Henry's natural storytelling ability added to the enjoyment. Liddie was, however, confused about Henry putting himself into a story that Liddie was fairly certain happened over a hundred and fifty years ago! Her knowledge of history wasn't super great, but she thought the Oklahoma land rushes were around 1900.

"Well," she thought, "maybe this is like some kind of storytelling practice, like maybe they are practicing their speech skills? I suppose he just found the story and thought it sounded interesting, and is pretending that he's in it? Whatever, it is a good story."

Henry tossed another log on the fire and began his story again.

"Kansas City! What a place! Being from such a small town, you can imagine how we were just flabbergasted at Kansas City. We didn't get to go deep into the city, mainly because the mules and horses were spooked by all the streetcars. But we could see the huge brick mansions, everyone dressed in fancy clothes, and someone said there was one building that was twenty-nine stories high! Land sakes, it was a mess of noise. People here, there, doing all kinds of stuff that I ain't never laid eyes on.

"Maybe it would have been nice to explore the city some, but we had just over a week left to get down to Oklahoma. Besides, that big old town and me — we didn't have anything in common! So, another hard ride down the trail and we pulled into Wichita — I heard a lot of people calling it Cowtown. There was one huge herd of cows driving through that we just narrowly escaped. Mooing and calling. I heard tell they came down the Chisholm trail. Nothing like that ever happened back in Eagleville where we lived. I mean, we had our one milk cow, but she was more of a pet, and she stayed in her little pen. And now, of course, she was dead... These cows off the trail, now, they tried to wander all over town, and like as not would have been more than happy to stampede and slam you into a wall somewhere.

"Anyway, I was happy to get out of there, just as much as I was to get out of Kansas City. About that time, I think we all were wondering if maybe we should just turn around and head home. This adventure had already been more than we expected. But, 'No,' Jacob says, 'we got to keep going. Imagine what we can do with more land, better land than those rocky Missouri hills.'

"Jacob's enthusiasm kept us going on. The last day, we camped just a couple of hours from the line, got up early and headed in as fast as we could. The line would be released right at noon and you had to be there or totally miss out on the run. We passed others on the trail, some still getting up, others working as hard as we were to get there.

"Just after 10:00, we pulled in to see massive crowds. I learned later that it was over 100,000 people there, looking to grab their bit of land, just like us. One of the other guys figured out where we needed to register and took care of that. The rest of us elbowed our way in and around, trying to get closer to the front. The whole scene was amazingly chaotic.

"People on foot, people on bicycles, people on horseback, people in carriages and buggies, and the most amazing thing, there was a train packed full of people. I suppose maybe there was a track leading further into the strip, and they would get a bit of a head start that way.

"Almost noon! Our friend with the registrations found us, we shook hands all around, wished each other good luck, and waited for the gunshot that would signal the beginning. Jacob and I crouched in his buggy. His mare sensed the excitement, muscles tensed and ready to leap into action. The other guys were two each on a mule. You may think a mule just plods along, but these animals were some of the best runners in Harrison County. And our riders were a far sight better off than the men on foot. I can't comprehend how those guys thought they could compete. I felt sorry for them, having come all this way and having so much competition.

"The shot rang out! More shots followed, all down the line. Mass confusion! Immediately, collisions between man and horse, buggy and buggy, fights breaking out, screams, gunshots, broken wheels, panicked animals, and the sad, desperate faces of men realizing that the sweat and determination of these last few weeks had amounted to nothing. They were left in the dust of those with faster horses or more skilled riders.

"Jacob and I, we hollered for ole Betsy to git going. He cracked the whip, and she took off faster than I had ever seen. Off to the side, I could see one of the mules heading into a clearing. The other mule, I don't know where it was. Jacob steered Ole Betsy straight ahead to an area no one else seemed to be heading towards, and I thought we had it! There was an unclaimed parcel! Got there and I leaped out, ready to pound my stake into the ground. Then, poking his head around an old cottonwood tree, some old codger said, "Sonny, you best get off my land!" To reinforce it, he pointed not just one, but two shotguns at me.

"Backing up, I was able to see that this codger had apparently staked the claim thoroughly — could it have been the night before? How could that be? It was only later that I heard the story of the Sooners. But for right now, all we could do was get back in the buggy.

"Ahead of us, we only saw dust, kicked up by those who had now left us far behind. Jacob and I looked at each other, shook our heads, turned and headed back. It was easy to find the one mule still on the line. It had got a sore leg and never even started. Maybe another animal had kicked it in the excitement. A few hours later, the other mule returned but with only one rider. Apparently they had gotten a stake — not a great one, but at least it was a start.

"We still had the buggy and supplies, but none of us was thrilled with the outcome of this adventure. At this point the chances of getting a decent piece of land were slim to none. We left the one friend to homestead his parcel, and we started back up the old Chisholm trail the way we came. The one lame mule kept slowing us down. So I volunteered to drive the buggy, taking it slow for the mule to heal some. Jacob and the others — they boarded the train in Wichita.

"It took me weeks, maybe a month, wandering back to Eagleville. The mule healed up fine with the slower pace. But, I got caught in one of those cattle drives, and the cows stampeded. They kicked up so much dirt and dust that Ole Betsy, she was blinded by it all, and the buggy was nearly destroyed."

Henry stopped, looking down at his feet with a frown.

"You know," he began again. "Sometimes I wonder about that trip. I gotta say, it was one of the highlights of my life. I mean, up to then, all I knew was how hard life was. My parents, they had to scrape by every day of their lives. The crazy thing was, they always believed that God was guiding them. Like even when there was nothing for dinner, still they believed in a purpose, and they thanked God for it.

"But, all I could see growing up was that I didn't want my life to be that poor. I did not want to be poor. On this trip, though, I saw those thousands and thousands of other men, some much older than myself, who, when they didn't stake a claim, didn't even have my poor life to go home to. For the first time, I saw masses of people who were worse off than I was.

"Maybe I wasn't really seeing life the way I should. Maybe my parents knew something after all. Maybe I needed to start looking for something more. I was clearly missing something."

Henry bent down and placed another log on the fire. He poked around in it with a long stick. No one else spoke. Henry walked slowly back to the log. Adelle and Liddie moved closer together, giving him room to sit.

Chapter 9: Seeing Stars

Liddie watched as Adelle patted Henry's arm. Despite Adelle's sharp tongue when chastising Henry yesterday, Liddie could see the genuine love they held for each other.

"Look!" Mary called out, pointing overhead to a streaking falling star.

Liddie glanced up quickly, catching the last of the disappearing tail. She continued gazing at the incredible night sky, full of twinkling points of light.

Her thoughts went back to the night Beckley showed her the Andromeda and Perseus constellations. It was shortly before the internship ended, not quite a month ago. A beautiful evening, begun by joining a charades game with the other interns. For this night, the rule was that each charade had to be related to something in the camp. There were the obvious items like tree, bird, campfire, but then it moved into more esoteric entries — how do you portray the child camper who professed to know everything in the world, and refused to listen to anything the interns tried to teach? Actually, Beckley had done a remarkable job with that one by simply clamping his hands melodramatically over his ears, causing several interns to yell out, "Brandon!" followed by much shared laughter. Later, after most of the other interns had retired to bed, Liddie and Beckley continued to sit together, staring into the dying embers of the campfire. They had become comfortable in each other's presence. At the beginning of the internship it would have seemed awkward to be alone together, but they were now at a point of friendship where they didn't need to talk all the time. They could enjoy a bit of quiet, almost solitude, together.

"Look there, Liddie, you see those four stars?" Beckley pointed up to the sky's northern edge.

Liddie's brow scrunched up as she tried to pick them out. To her untrained eye, the sky was simply a mass of sparkles, some brighter than others, but mostly just a hodgepodge. Astronomy was not one of the subjects she took in college, but she admired those people who could pick out specific stars. Her own knowledge was limited to, "Oh, there's the moon!"

Beckley directed her. "Here, get that tall tree in your sights. Now, go straight up from it and call that 12:00. Okay, move your eyes over to 2:00. You see that bright star? Keep coming to your right from it. You see the second bright star? Good."

Liddie didn't know if the warm tingles she was feeling were from learning something new or from the touch of Beckley's hands on her shoulders as he guided her. Now, thinking back on the night, Liddie was pretty sure she knew the answer to that question.

Beckley continued, "We come on around to these other two stars and they form a square! You see that?"

"Yes, yes!" Liddie exclaimed. "I see it!"

Pleased with his teaching abilities, Beckley pressed on.

"Now, that is the cup of the Big Dipper. And as we continue over this way, to the left, you see three more stars that make up the handle. So, you can see why it's called the Big Dipper, right? But even more exciting, let me show you how to find the North Star, using the Big Dipper!"

"Oh," said Liddie. "Would that tell us where the North Pole is?"

"Yes, exactly!" Beckley answered. "So you go back to those first two bright stars, on the end of the cup. Pretend there's a line between them and go up above the cup, maybe five times more in distance, to another bright star. There! That's the North Star!"

Liddie could tell that Beckley was super excited about finding this star. She enjoyed seeing his excitement. There was something endearing about it.

"Now," he continued, "if ever you're lost, out in the woods, or even on the ocean, you can find the North Star and know which direction to head!

"Let me tell you about some of the other constellations — depending on the seasons, different ones appear in different areas of the sky.

"Andromeda is my favorite, but we won't be seeing it here until the fall. The constellation next to it, Pegasus — we can't see it now, either — Pegasus also has four stars forming a box, kind of like the Big Dipper, that is the body of a winged horse. You remember the story, I'm sure. The one about Perseus and his winged horse Pegasus?"

Liddie, though, had gotten completely lost. She was trying to place the name Pegasus, but was distracted with trying to imagine its body as a box. She vaguely remembered Greek myths from elementary school, vaguely remembered the idea of constellations, but honestly, Beckley's arms were way too close to focus on those things!

"Hmmm. Kind of..." she answered.

Beckley seemed to recognize that perhaps the flood of excitement he was feeling about being able to share some of his love of the stars was a bit overwhelming for Liddie. He needed to scale it back some.

"Oh, I'm sorry for getting so detailed back there..." he said. "Astronomy was one of my first merit badges in Boy Scouts, and I love looking at the constellations. They're old friends now."

"What?" Liddie exclaimed, quite incredulously. "You were in Boy Scouts? I was in Girl Scouts!"

The two spent several animated moments trading stories of favorite skills and badges. Both began looking at the other with, if not yet questioning where the relationship might go, at least a great deal of interest in their newfound connection.

After a lull, Liddie got back to the stars. "I have to admit," she said, "I don't remember too much about the Greek myths — that is what these constellations are? Based on the Greek myths?"

That was all the encouragement Beckley needed.

"Why, yes! I'm sure you remember more than you think! Pegasus was a winged horse given to Perseus, along with a few other items, to help him fight the evil Medusa. You remember her — the one with snakes in her hair, and if anyone looked directly at her, they were turned immediately into stone. Well, through a series of trials, Perseus conquered Medusa. Cut off her head, actually. And then carried her head around, turning other enemies into stone by bringing it out to show them."

"Oh my goodness!" Liddie exclaimed, totally shocked. "You mean, like in his back pocket, just carrying this dripping head full of snakes around. And if he got annoyed at someone, he just whipped it out and said, 'Ha, Got you!' How utterly gross!"

Beckley smiled. "Well, from what I recall, he was quite the honorable character, and didn't go around randomly flashing the dead Medusa's head at strangers. He used it wisely.

"In between Perseus and Pegasus is the constellation Andromeda, and she figures into the story, also. Because after Perseus had conquered Medusa, he was heading home — I believe he was flying over Africa on Pegasus, the horse. Perseus spots the beautiful Andromeda chained to a rock in the ocean. The background here is a long, convoluted story about how beautiful she is, and others who are jealous developing a plot to feed her to an ocean dragon. But Perseus kills the dragon, rescues Andromeda, and takes her home. They marry and live happily ever after, having, I believe, seven sons and a daughter."

It may have been the late night, or it may have been something entirely different, but Liddie closed her eyes and could just see herself being swooped up by the dashing Perseus — alias Beckley — and riding off into the far reaches of the sky on their fabulous winged steed. And secretly pleased she was, as she watched the horrid head of Medusa fall out of Beckley's pocket and disappear into the ocean below.

Liddie was aroused from her reverie to see James walk in front of her. He nodded to Henry and stepped around the others, moving to the front of the campfire.

"Thank you, Mary, for drawing our attention to the stars," he said. "They're beautiful. Endless. They go on forever and ever." James paused. He was a man of few words. Knowing this, the others put great value on the words he did speak.

"There was a time when the stars saved my life. My life, and that of Mary, too." Mary, still standing from watching the shooting star, walked up to join James. She sat down beside the fire, poking at the logs.

"We were so happy when Mary became pregnant with our first child — John. We named him John after my father. It seemed that life was beginning to hold some promise for us. My father had worked hard as a tenant farmer, building up the land to where it produced some of the best crops in Portadown. When Mary and I got married, we began working the land along with him. The best harvest, of course, was the potatoes, and we looked forward to it all year long. But this one year, 1845, I noticed something strange about the plants. Along about June, I found one plant that developed some small black spots on the stems. Then it spread to other plants. Soon the stems wilted, leaving nothing but mush. I began digging, trying to harvest the potatoes that might have already grown, but they were all brown. Some had even turned mushy. The whole crop was lost that year.

"The next year, before John turned a year old, both my parents died. It was just Mary and myself left. We cleaned the fields. John followed us around, picking up rocks, just like us. We hoped and we prayed. We asked God to bless the crops and we watched plants sprout after a wet spring.

"Our neighbor down the lane was first to find the blight on his plants that year. There was no way to protect ours — I guess it was spread by wind, or maybe plant debris. I don't know. What we did know was that we were going to lose our entire crop again.

"Mary and I, we fell to our knees in prayer. We had always done what was right in God's eyes. At least as far as we could know. But we could see no way out. Maybe we could plant other crops, but the season for planting potatoes was done.

"We knelt there in the field most of the day. What started as total despair eventually eased into numbness. Then it was that Mary said to me, "James, God has our plans in His hands. He will show us the way, and it will be well. God has not brought us this far to leave us.""

"As I looked at her, with just a kernel of desperate hope, I knew she spoke truth."

Silhouetted against the campfire, James and Mary turned toward each other, their eyes gazing knowingly, reaching a depth that few would ever reach. Liddie stared, her mouth dropping open in awe. Liddie didn't know where these stories came from, but she thought the delivery was so authentic, so real, that she felt like she was living in them herself.

The group sat in silence. Out of the corner of her eye, Liddie caught a slow movement across the campfire. Just into the edge of the woods — was it that same person? She turned to look more closely. The others also were watching. Oddly enough, none of them seemed surprised to see the figure. The silent hush continued.

Liddie couldn't quite explain what she was feeling. Was it still the sense of awe over the story? Or did it have something to do with how the others were watching the figure? There was a definite sense of otherworldliness, like something surreal was going on.

The figure disappeared, moving into the woods.

James turned his gaze from Mary. He looked back out at the group and returned to the story.

"We continued to kneel. But our prayers turned into worship. For we knew, once again, that God had our times in His hands. We worshipped and thanked God for his deliverance.

"It was not long before we heard the clip-clopping of our neighbor's horses. They were packing up and leaving for America. We had heard of others leaving. Mary and I both knew this was God's answer. We stood up in the field. Mary cradled John in her arms. We walked into the house and packed one small bag, mostly with what food we had left, and we rode with our neighbor to the port of Liverpool.

"I won't go into that long voyage tonight. It is something I would rather forget. The terrible conditions, the mass of humanity pressed into so little space. Of course, the saddest of all was when our little John fell sick and died, and we had to bury him in the middle of the ocean. We all suffered so much, but we all suffered together.

"I started this story by talking about the stars, how they saved our lives. Soon after we started, the ship's compass got broken somehow, so the captain had to navigate our course by watching the stars. Each night, he would check whether we were still on course by locating the North Star. It was always in the north, and if we ever found it not on the right side of our boat, we knew we were off course.

"Three weeks into the voyage, we hit a terrible storm. Rain and wind pummeled the ship for three days and nights. Waves tossed us, almost upending us. And the most difficult, at night, no stars were visible for charting our course. Finally, on the third night, the captain's mate called out, 'Stars! I see stars!'

"Quickly, all those on board were straining to find the North Star through the remaining fog."

Here, James stopped his story and turned, pointing up at the night sky. He pointed straight at the Big Dipper. "See, look there — the Big Dipper. It's easy to find once you know it. Take those two stars at the far side of its cup. Follow their line up above the cup's opening, and they point to the North Star!"

"Just like Beckley taught me," Liddie thought.

James returned to the story.

"It was the captain who first found the North Star that night. It was straight ahead of us, actually almost on the left side! We could have been heading north for days. Surely we would have perished if we continued into the arctic with limited supplies. The captain immediately called for the crew to adjust the sails and turn the ship, which they did. And eventually, we did reach New York City, but with no extra food or water."

Mary started to stand, and James reached down to help her.

"James," she said, "remember how we made that monument to mark God's faithfulness? Once we finished our travels and ended up on our own little homestead, you found that huge rock in the field. No amount of digging could dislodge it. You said that it would be our Ebenezer Stone — our stone of help. And forever after, it reminded us of how God brought us through, from that potato famine, through that horrific voyage, the travels across the new land, and finally setting us up in that tiny hamlet of Eagleville."

James nodded and softly agreed, "Thus far, he has brought us."

Liddie recalled how Henry had described his parents having 'something more.' Were James and Mary really Henry's parents, as Adelle had described them the day before? They didn't seem that much different in age, and none of them could have really lived through the stories they described. They happened over a hundred years ago!

A totally new thought occurred to her — this one rather disquieting. And for the first time, she felt a bit uncomfortable in the group. Were all of these people quite right in the head? Did they really believe that they had experienced these stories? Liddie supposed that her first thought about them just telling stories for the fun of it could be true. They could be just really polished storytellers. But Henry, and now James and Mary — they were just so good, so authentic. Did they really believe they were telling true stories about themselves? And if so, just how crazy were they?

Liddie turned to ask Adelle about the stories. Adelle, however, jumped up from her spot on the log and threw her arms wide.

"Okay, everyone! I'm going to end with a different kind of story!" She exclaimed. "Some of you probably won't enjoy it," and here she sent a stern look toward Osmund, "but I think it's a good story, nonetheless."

Chapter 10: Ambush

"So, let me set the stage!" Adelle began as she walked up to the campfire. "We lived way in the backwoods. There wasn't even a road that came near our house. They called it a trail. Shain Trail. But what fun for me, as a young girl. I loved running through the woods, finding berries, catching frogs, exploring the hills with my sisters and brothers. Sometimes we would come across these massive blackberry thickets, just brimming with huge, ripe, juicy berries. We would pick and stuff them so fast into our mouths, over and over, that it might be an hour before we stopped to rest! Such a wonderful, heady feeling, sitting at the base of an old oak tree, feeling a bit dizzy from the sudden realization that you are just stuffed to the gills with blackberries!"

The ripple of laughter through the group included a number of those answering, "Oh, yes!" and "I remember!" and "MmmMmmMmm!"

Adelle nodded and joined in with the "MmmMmmMmm!" chorus. Only she drew it out, ending with a loud, satisfying grunt.

"We learned when the berries would ripen — gooseberries, which were so thorny it didn't much make sense to go after them, wild plums we made into the most delicious jam, and wild strawberries that could be found hiding under their leaves, surrounded by pretty purple violets. And of course, black walnuts were everywhere. We had to use rocks to crack them open.

Hazelnuts were easier, but still involved a lot of work.

"Those were the parts I loved. Exploring and discovering the bounty of nature. It was all there for the taking. You just had to be on the lookout for poison ivy, chiggers and ticks. I must have scratched myself raw each summer from the itching!

"And snakes — there was always a shotgun near the door, and we learned to use it young. Most snakes we welcomed because they kept the mice and such in check. But let one of us see a copperhead or rattlesnake, and it was a mad rush for the shotgun. We knew too many neighbors who suffered from those venomous bites.

"We all had chores that kept us busy, caring for the chickens, cows, and horses. And we kids did go to the local one-room school when they had a teacher. But mostly we were left on our own. Until the year I turned 14.

"That was the year Mama left. Looking back, I might be able to piece it all together, but mostly, I think whatever happened, Mama and Papa just did not live up to what they should have been doing. I don't know why. Maybe something in the way they had been raised locked them into bad responses, and they could never figure out how to get above it. I don't know.

"That's the background to my story. The background was set by two flawed people — my parents — and how they fell short from being the people God wanted them to be.

"So, my mother left. We did get to see her sometimes — she lived up in Iowa and would visit when she could. But when she was gone, we had a completely new dynamic in the family with my dad. My three older sisters, they were all married and living in different towns. Still at home with me were my four younger siblings. Peter and Ben, being boys, were expected to do all the physical farm work with my father. Melissa and Blanche were young — Blanche was only four years old. They helped where they could, but mainly in the house.

"So I was the oldest at home, and everything else fell on me. Cooking, cleaning, sewing, everything that goes into running a household. I had, of course, learned much of that from Mama, so I knew how to do it. But I was just fourteen years old. I didn't really want to have all that responsibility.

Yet, most of us learn that you do what you have to do. Life is that simple. So we all did what we had to do!

"Until, that is, when I met a very special someone just after my nineteenth birthday!"

Adelle gave a sideways glance toward Henry, smiling and tilting her head. Henry, obviously pleased, but embarrassed, dug around in the dirt with his feet. "I had gone into Eagleville to buy some things we couldn't grow on the farm — sugar, flour, and such. Going into town was always an adventure, not just because the trail was such a scary ride, but because it was a chance to see new things and people. And there was plenty of gossip to catch up on. That's what I was doing this particular time. Leaning on the counter at the dry goods, I was listening to Flora, the clerk, talk about the latest goings on.

"The store door creaked open with a new customer. Flora turned and gushed in a very familiar way, 'Why Henry, it's so good to see you…' I turned around and saw that it was one of those McKays from north of town. Henry was the only unmarried one, but he was going on forty years old and not so great a prospect anymore for most of the women. Rumor had it that he enjoyed a good time on the town. There was that time he went down to the Oklahoma strip looking for land, which showed initiative, but then there were all those questions about what happened on his return trip, so a lot of people had their doubts about him. He never really gave the impression of wanting to settle down with a family, either. But, he wasn't bad looking… and, I don't know… maybe I saw something more in him."

Liddie thought this a startlingly candid description, and she turned to watch Henry's reaction. He apparently was enjoying the story as much as everyone else, nodding and laughing along.

"I had seen Henry sometimes at the evening church meetings. As a matter of fact, I was planning to stay in town for the service that evening. Usually I went to the White Chapel Church, where my grandfather preached. But the new preacher at the Methodist Church in town had quite a fervency about him and was drawing in more and more of us. So I did try and go when the service was the same time as my town visits.

"Flora's sultry voice as she greeted Henry interested me. Was there something going on here? Perhaps there was more town gossip that she hadn't told me! I watched the two of them. She was definitely interested — reaching out and patting his arm, batting those long eyelashes at him, murmuring very quietly up close. Henry, though, seemed uncomfortable. He avoided looking straight at her, moved behind a display of canned goods and stood there, shuffling his feet. She followed him, again trying to touch his arm and whispering to him. Henry shook his head at her, continuing to stare at his feet.

"The clerk appeared to get the message and tossed her head as she flounced back to the counter. The fire in her eyes was unmistakable! She clearly thought the two of them had something going on, but it seemed Henry didn't feel it. I reached across the counter and held her hand.

"'I'm so sorry Flora,' I said.

"'Yeah,' she answered, 'I didn't really want him anyway!'

"Flora packaged up my flour and sugar and offered to carry it out for me. Both of us were shocked when Henry jumped into action, came rushing across the store, and said, 'Here, Flora! I'll get that for her.'

"Flora and I stared at each other wide eyed! I shrugged my shoulders at her, trying to say that I had no idea what was going on. And I really didn't! As I said, I had only seen Henry a couple of times in passing at the service. But apparently, he thought that was enough!

"So Henry carried out my packages and set them in the buggy. He didn't let me get away with just a polite 'thank you.' Instead, he placed himself right in front of my buggy step. Shuffling his feet again, he was obviously having a tough time saying what he wanted to say. Finally, it came out.

"'Adelle, I think you're just about the prettiest girl around. And whenever I see you in the service, I just can't keep my eyes off you, and I've been going to the services way more than I normally would, just so I can see you, and I've been waiting and waiting 'til I can screw up enough courage to talk to you! And when I saw you in that store, I knew I had to do something right now!'

"Henry had to stop for a breath after that long rush of explanation. But that was good, because the pause gave me time to adjust to this new, very intriguing situation. Before I could respond, he started talking again!

"'So, Adelle, please, I really want to see you. Can I please take you to the service tonight? Maybe sit with you there? Please?'

"What could I say? I told him, 'Of course,' and the look on his face was almost comically full of relief!

"'Oh, thank you, thank you!' he responded, but then he added, 'Oh, I forgot my dried beans I was supposed to pick up! Wait for me, Adelle!'

"Henry rushed back into the store. I could hear the conversation through the screen as he told Flora how many pounds of beans he needed. She packed them up and somewhat stiffly asked Henry if he needed help taking them out to his wagon.

"'No, no, Flora! he answered with a big grin. 'And it looks like the beans aren't the only thing I'll be taking out tonight!'"

Adelle laughed along with the others as she told this story, shaking her head at the memory of Henry being so completely clueless when it came to saying such a thing to Flora. She got a drink of water and asked the group if it was getting too late to finish. Everyone wanted to hear the rest of the story, so after a bit of leg stretching, they settled back down and Adelle began again.

"That evening at service, we did sit together, and the preacher had another outstanding sermon. People were becoming more aware of their need for God, and it was good to have a regular time to spend with the church.

"After that, Henry and I would regularly get together and talk each week before the service, after the service, and sometimes even during the service! This went on a couple of months, and Henry knew he was interested enough in me to maybe want to end his single status. So he came down south of Eagleville to formally meet my father.

"Now, my father was a mean old man. Everyone around knew that he was mean. Mean to the animals, mean to people, mean, mean, mean, through and through! Who knows why? The fact is, he was mean! The last thing my father wanted was to have some man come around courting his daughter. He knew I was the one that kept the house together, and he didn't want that to change. But I had cooked and cleaned for him and four young ones for over five years by this time. And, you know, I was just plain tired of it. I thought it would be heavenly if someone like Henry would rescue me from it.

"That first visit, my father was caught off guard. He had heard rumors that I was seeing someone in Eagleville, but he refused to believe it. So, when Henry showed up at the front door, and my little sister, Blanche, answered it, my father looked up from his chair with a frown.

'Who are you?' he demanded.

"'Uh, I'm Henry McKay. From up north of town… Sir.'

"'What in blazes do you want?' This was an angrier question.

"'Uh, uh…' It was as if my sweet Henry was totally struck dumb. All he could do was stare in horror at my dad!

"My father narrowed his eyes. He jumped up out of his chair and reached for the fireplace poker.

"'You get out of my house!' he bellowed.

"Henry turned and ran! I tell you, I wasn't at all sure that I'd ever see him again. I turned to my father, and much to both of our surprise, I started into lecturing him about how terrible my life had been!

"'Papa!' I yelled. 'Look what you've done! That was my friend Henry. I've been seeing him for nigh onto two months now, and we have hidden it from you just because you act this way! I am so sick and tired of being the maid and caretaker of this house, and I'm not going to do it anymore! I don't care if you want me to stay! I'm leaving! And I'm going with Henry!'

"Of course, it was night time, and I couldn't just up and leave right then. But I had put the idea in his head. And, quite frankly, he looked like he didn't know what to think. He sat back down and was still sitting there long after the rest of us had gone to bed.

"The next trip into town, Henry and I arranged for him to come to the house when we thought my father would be out in the fields. Three days later, Henry showed up, riding his old mare. Sure enough, my father was gone to the fields with the boys. I told Peter to give us some signal when they were headed back and getting close to the house.

"It was a good visit — Henry had fun with Blanche and Melissa. I made a delicious apple pan dowdy that we all shared. Henry and I were even more convinced that we wanted to marry.

"Well, Peter and Ben showed up, unannounced. There had been no signal. And there was no sign of my father. It turned out that as they got close to the house, my father spotted Henry's old mare and he told the boys to go on home. He said he had something to take care of.

"Henry jumped up, quickly got his things together, and ran out the door, hopping on his old mare and taking off down the trail. I busied myself with dinner.

"It must have been half an hour, maybe forty-five minutes later that my father came in. He grabbed a towel and washed up, muttering to himself, 'I did what I had to do. I did what I had to do.'

"He glared at all of us, daring us to question him.

"Of course, none of us said a word. But I'll tell you, I didn't sleep that night, imagining all the horrible possibilities in 'I did what I had to do.'

"Next morning, I prepared the buggy to go into Eagleville for supplies. I was surprised to not find Henry at our usual meeting place. Then I saw a group of townsfolk with Henry's brother, Big Jim in the midst of them. He was talking excitedly.

"'That's right,' he said. 'His horse came home all alone around midnight. No one knew where he was! So we were getting up a search party to head out this morning when we heard a sound on the stoop. We opened the door and there he was, crawling on his hands and knees up the step. He saw us and he dropped right there in front of the door! Head all bloody, blood all over his clothes, half dead if you ask me!'

"Well, of course, I knew he was talking about my Henry! So I pushed my way through to Big Jim. He saw me and instantly suggested that we ride up together so I could see Henry for myself. Big Jim tried to fill me in on the way, but he knew very few additional facts. He'd been sent into town for bandages before Henry was up to talking about what happened.

"Reaching their house, I jumped out of the buggy, handing the reins to Big Jim. Henry's mother, Mary, opened the door and showed me into the parlor where Henry was laid on a couch. At first I thought he was dead, lying there so still and pale. But I softly called his name, and oh my! What a relief to see his eyes flutter open. We all worked together to finish cleaning his head wound and bandage it up. Actually, everyone else worked to clean it. I mainly held his hand and gazed into his eyes.

"Head bandaged, Henry was able to sit up and weakly sip some of Mary's chicken soup. Then he told us the story.

"He had started off down Shain Trail, heading home. Since dusk was falling, he had the mare go slowly in the shadows beneath the overhanging tree limbs, picking her way around fallen branches. Just as he passed under a big old red oak he heard a loud whoop and yelling.

"'P'shaw! Take that, you varmint! That'll teach you to be coming 'round my daughter!'

"Henry looked up quickly enough to see my father leaning down from the oak branch, swinging what looked like an enormous log straight at his head. He wasn't quick enough to avoid the crushing impact.

"Poor Henry must have lain there for hours, drifting in and out of consciousness before being awakened by the early sun rays. It was only by God's help that he slowly stumbled and crawled his way back home."

Adelle stopped and was silent. All of the others, with the exception of Liddie, turned and stared at Osmund. Shocked, stunned, trying to comprehend the enormity of the story, they continued to stare.

Liddie, too, was shocked by the tale. But, as she became aware of the others staring at Osmund, she started putting two and two together.

"Wait a minute…" she thought, "Osmund? Osmund and Sarah? Sarah, who spent so long telling me about the hardship in her life? What's going on here? Is Adelle's father Osmund? Was Osmund the really mean, mean, mean man? And, my goodness! Did Osmund really try to kill Henry?"

Liddie's head was spinning. These stories were becoming way too interconnected. And way too real. Either they were all different chapters taken from a book, or there was something really, really weird going on here.

Adelle spoke again.

"Henry survived. It was many weeks before he was back to normal, though. Neither one of us said a word to my father about what happened. I mean, we didn't want to cause any further problems. Instead, we made secret plans.

"That's how it came about that one very early morning on a cold January day, I slipped outside before anyone else was awake. I carried my bag down Shain Trail and waited for Henry. Soon I heard the plop-plopping of the horse's hooves. Jumping inside the buggy, leaning against Henry beneath the heavy blankets as he drove, I knew this was the right decision. It was a long, cold ride into Bethany, where the county judge would marry us, but it gave us plenty of time to talk.

"We shared our dreams on that ride. Dreams for children, dreams of a new future. We remembered how our love began, sitting together in the back of the church service, holding hands. And we talked about pushing forward into the unknown, confident that it would be a good future. We had nothing but dreams. But we knew that God inspired our dreams.

"Yes, it has been good."

Chapter 11: Jehoshaphat

The group sat silently after Adelle's story. It had gotten very late. James separated the charred wood from the spent fire and poured water on it. Sparks flew briefly, followed by a lazy smoke swirl drifting up to meet the twinkling stars. He kicked dirt onto the remaining ashes and walked off with Mary. The others silently left, leaving Liddie to sit, still processing the stories.

David and Paula turned back.

"I don't want to disturb your reverie," David quietly said, "but we could walk back together if you're ready."

"Thank you," Liddie replied. "I appreciate that."

The three walked in the peaceful stillness of the night. Occasionally a whip-poor-will called. High in the trees owls hooted, one to another. Coyotes' mournful howls echoed from a distance.

Liddie was grateful to have Paula and David's company, especially when the coyotes started up. She found the Big Dipper in the sky, returning her thoughts back again to that campfire with Beckley when he first told her about the stars. She wanted to share this evening with him. She wanted to ask him what he thought about these people. She wanted him to tell her that they weren't crazy. She wanted him to come up with some explanation as to what was going on.

Mostly, though, she wanted to tell him that she was falling in love with these people who had welcomed her in. Not, of course, the romantic kind of love. But the kind where you truly care for one another, as a family. Listening to the stories, knowing there was something deeper going on — whatever it was! —Liddie felt like her heart had joined with theirs. Even more, she felt that they loved her, and not just loved her, but loved her unconditionally.

She had been here at this land for three days now. From the beginning, her purpose was to get pictures so the property could be sold. She knew that the people here needed to leave, and she had been upfront about that with them. But none of them ever expressed anger at her, or acted in any threatening way. Instead, she strangely felt almost like they were wooing her. Almost like they knew her innermost being and loved her. It was a very confusing feeling.

A few minutes later the three arrived at the house. Elizabeth barked from within, happy to know Liddie was back.

"Oh, you poor thing!" Liddie exclaimed. "Left alone, and no dinner. I must take better care of you!"

Elizabeth scurried out the door and ran in circles around Liddie. Each time Liddie tried to head back in for the dog food, Elizabeth came barreling into her. Finally yielding, Liddie chased after her, ran from her, and in general, had a lovely romp — girl and dog in a beautiful poetry of joy.

Next morning, Liddie was shocked to discover she had slept through till noon. Shocked, but not displeased. She enjoyed the luxury of no deadlines, waking to see what the day holds without any plans.

After a quick breakfast, she called her mom. It was always so good to hear her voice.

"Liddie! How are you, sweetie?"

"Mom! I love you! I can't wait to tell you all about yesterday! Do you have some time now?"

They both knew Liddie's question was just a formality. Her mom always stopped whatever she was doing to talk to Liddie.

"I'm just making a cup of tea," she answered. "It's one of those teas you made for me last year. You called it Rosehip Bliss. I think you put in chamomile and lemon balm, too. It smells so intoxicating! Let me sit down while I sip it. Oooohhh, yes! Perhaps there is a hint of turmeric in it, too?

"Now, tell me everything! Have you talked to that Beckley boy?"

Liddie was pleased that her mom was using the teas. She had started foraging for herbs last year after learning of their medicinal properties in one of her classes. The shelves in her bedroom at home now held dozens of jars, full of dried herbs. Liddie loved organizing them — calendula, elderflowers, goldenrod, heal-all, echinacea, basil, the list went on and on. Her dad called them weeds, and hadn't quite come on board with the whole idea. He didn't drink tea, anyway. More of a black coffee drinker. Perhaps he was turned off from the herbs that time Liddie insisted he chew a feverfew leaf for his headache. His eyes popped, his nose scrunched, and a violent spitting ensued. She was sure it took care of his headache, though, even though she didn't have the courage to ask him.

"Yes, Mom! Just a bit of turmeric, because it tends to have such a strong flavor. And, actually, no, I haven't talked to Beckley since yesterday. I wanted to call you first!"

"Well, then, tell me all about it!"

"So, let me see… I think the last thing we talked about was how Beckley will be coming out here — he should get here tomorrow, maybe around noon. One of the men here found an old hammock so Beckley can sleep out in the oak grove. You know, he was an Eagle Boy Scout! So I'm sure he will enjoy it — the oak grove is right on the pond and should be a lovely place for him. The weather has been warm during the days, but we'll give him blankets for nighttime. I'm peering out the window right now and watching two men hanging the hammock. Not sure they're agreeing on which trees to use… they keep pointing to other trees and moving from place to place.

"Okay," Liddie continued, "yesterday afternoon, I went to a local place called Frankie's."

"What?" her mom interrupted. "Frankie's? Really? Is he still there? Well, not him, of course, because he was an old man the last time I was on the farm. But the store — it's still there? Oh, my, the stories I've heard from my parents about going to Frankie's!"

"It seems to be pretty much unchanged from the last hundred years, I would guess," said Liddie, describing the worn building and cluttered aisles of the store. "There were some very nice people there, although they all seem to kind of keep to themselves. I got cleaning supplies so I could do a bit of tidying up before taking pictures of the house."

"Don't worry too much about cleaning, Liddie. I think panoramic pictures would be all we need. But, you do what you think best!"

Liddie's mother stopped and called out to her husband, who had begun shouting in the background. "What's that? What? No, I'm not going to tell her what you think! You get on the phone and tell her yourself!"

After a few clanking sounds while the phone was passed around Liddie heard her father's concerned voice.

"Hello, honey! How are you doing?"

"Dad! I'm doing great! This is such an awesome place! Has Mom told you all about it?"

"Yes… and I want to tell you, 'Be careful!' When your mom told me there were people there, I wanted to get in the car right away and drive up there. Of course, it's a two-day drive, but I'm worried about you! Your mom seems to think you're okay, and she says you have some protector dog now, although I never heard of a St. Bernard that was any good as a watchdog! And what about this guy — Beasley? Who's going to protect you from HIM?"

Liddie had never heard her father talk so fast and so much at one time. She laughed involuntarily.

"Dad! I'm okay! These are all really nice people. And most of them are really old. I could certainly outrun any of them…well, maybe not Bronia or Mac… And as for Beckley… his name is BECKLEY, Dad. He was a perfect gentleman at the internship, and I fully expect him to continue being so when he gets here. And there are certainly plenty of chaperones around."

Liddie's father was silent. She recognized the love he was expressing in his concern, so she added, "I love you so much, Dad. Thank you for caring. I promise I'll be careful!"

"Okay, honey. I love you. Keep in touch."

Liddie's mom got back on the phone and asked Liddie if there was anything new that happened the day before.

"Yes, Mom! It was really interesting. Remember I told you about the people who were living here? I didn't know if they were distant relatives, or squatters, or what. Well, last night, I discovered that they have evening campfires up on a hillside. I followed them up there, and they made me feel so welcome, it was just the nicest time! They take turns telling these fascinating stories, all about different time periods. I can't figure out if they are all doing some kind of self-improvement study, where they practice this public speaking, or if they're preparing to be wandering bards, or even if they are just a little off, because they tell the stories like they're talking about themselves... like these things really happened to them!"

"What kind of stories?" Her mom interjected.

"Well, there were three last night. The first one was about heading to the Oklahoma land rush to stake a claim on some land. Then, there was another story about the potato famine and a voyage over from Ireland. And the last one, that was the strangest of all. A kind of love story, set in the late 1880s, I guess. This one had one of the characters trying to kill the man who was courting his daughter!"

"Liddie..." her mom interrupted, "this sounds very odd. Interesting, of course, but odd. Tell me more about that last story."

Liddie's mother set down her cup of tea and stared out the window, her brow wrinkled as if trying to recall tales long lost in her memory.

"Okay," Liddie said. "Well, Adelle — she's one of the people here — very nice, very outgoing — she started out talking about how her mom left the family when she was a young teen, and she had to cook and clean and take care of the house. Then she meets this guy Henry in town and they start to see each other, but her dad — his name is Osmund — he's this really mean man. And he tries to kill Henry by ambushing him and hitting him over the head with a big stick! Henry very nearly dies, but he recovers, and he and Adelle elope.

"The thing is, Mom, Adelle told the story as if it was really her in it. And

Henry really is one of the other people here — they're married. And Osmund, he's here, too! And it's just really weird, like I said — I guess it makes the most sense that they have found some book with all these stories and just enjoy putting themselves into the situations. But they are really good at it — I mean each one has just been riveting to listen to."

Liddie's mom continued to gaze out the window silently.

"Mom? Are you still there?"

"Yes, Liddie, of course!" she stammered. "I was just listening, absorbing. It sounds like a really neat group of people. And you do say that you don't sense any danger? In that case, I think you're having a fascinating adventure. Who would have thought stopping to get some pictures would lead to all this? Will they be having more campfires, do you know?"

Liddie answered, "I hope so. And I hope they have at least one more when Beckley gets here. I'd really like him to experience it. This afternoon, though, I think I want to explore some more in the house and maybe even take a nap! You know we didn't get back until two in the morning last night?"

After their goodbyes, Liddie's mother continued to sit by the window. She strongly felt that God was involved here somehow. She was familiar enough with the ways of God to know that she didn't need to understand exactly what was going on. In cases like this, she understood the importance of not trying to speculate on what God is doing, and certainly not trying to manipulate it. Pray, yes, for God to work his purposes. But other than praying, simply to watch, in expectation of seeing God's hand at work.

Liddie wandered down to the kitchen and spread the old hand-drawn map of the property on the table. Paula came in from planting spinach seeds and sat down next to her. Together, they pored over the different area names.

"Oh, look here!" said Liddie. "This spot, off the Overlook Hill, where I walked yesterday — it's not labeled on the map. But I found two statues there. One was Jesus with his arms outstretched at the top of the hill. Then, a bit lower, there was an Indian chief looking out over the same hill. I wish the map indicated something about why they are there."

Paula jumped up excitedly. "Liddie, when we came here, I kept discovering so many neat places, like where those two statues are. David and I, after walking around and getting a feel for the place, well, ideas just popped in about the different areas. So we created our own theories. Let me tell you what I see in those two statues!"

Liddie sat back, pleased to hear another story.

"Okay," Paula began. "Let me start by saying that things aren't always what they seem to be on the surface. You can look at something, or someone, and choose to see just the plain physical facts. Or you can look below the surface and see much, much more. Sometimes it's just to see more beauty in the world. Sometimes, it's to learn about truth.

"Take this particular statue of the Indian. He's tall. His long headdress hangs down his back, on top of the flowing robes. That's what we see on the surface. Now, under the surface, we see that he carries great authority. He is unmoved by the forces that come at him from all sides. He conveys great strength, not only physical, but strength in knowing who he is and what his job is.

"Now, what do I see when I stand on that Overlook Hill? I see a valley that stretches over to that other hill — it's called Carn Ingli, right?"

Liddie nodded, outlining it on the map with her finger.

"And then we have the Indian chief halfway up the Overlook Hill. He's looking over the valley. That's also what we see on the surface. But underneath… underneath… the great story emerges!

"The Indian chief represents someone else. Have you ever heard the story of Jehoshaphat? No? Hmmm. Then I'll need to tell you the whole story!

"Long, long ago, there lived a man named Jehoshaphat. There are lots of stories about what he did throughout his life, but I want to tell you about just one story — where he faced a certain battle that took place in a valley, very much like the valley between the Overlook Hill and Carn Ingli.

"Jehoshaphat was a great king. Perhaps that's why the Indian chief reminds me of him; they were both persons in authority who commanded armies. But the day came when three other nations, with vast armies, came together to attack Jehoshaphat's land. He was totally outnumbered, and it looked like they would all be killed. So what this king did was call all his people to fast.

He told them to seek God for help.

"And that's what the people did — they prayed and waited for God's answer. But you know, they didn't just sit there waiting. Jehoshaphat stood up before them and spoke to God! He reminded God of how God is all-powerful and how God had brought them through many troubles. He reminded God of how he gave them this land, but now they were facing a great enemy who threatened to destroy them. Jehoshaphat saw no way that they could prevail without God's help.

"Then, something really, really neat happens! The Bible — for this is a story from the Bible — says the Spirit of the Lord came down upon one of the men in the crowd, and this man began talking for God. He told Jehoshaphat, 'Do not be afraid or discouraged because of this vast army. For the battle is not yours, but God's.'

"Just think about that, Liddie! First off, God's Spirit spoke through this ordinary man. How astonishing is that? But, more importantly, what did he say? 'Do not be afraid or discouraged. For the battle is not yours, but God's.' This common citizen told King Jehoshaphat that God would fight the battle for him!"

Paula stopped here and shook her head in amazement. She saw David coming in the door and called out to him, "David, where is the story of Jehoshaphat?" And in a quiet aside to Liddie, she whispered, with a smile, "He's my Bible Answer Man!"

"Chronicles." David responded. "I think it's Second Chronicles... is it chapter 20?" He sat down to listen to the rest of the story.

"So this man starts telling Jehoshaphat exactly how God will fight the battle."

"Jahaziel." David interjected. "The man's name was Jahaziel. He was a helper, like a custodian, in the temple."

Paula turned toward him with another smile. "You know so much! I had just told Liddie how you're my Bible Answer Man!" Then she got back to the story.

"So Jahaziel told Jehoshaphat to march down to meet the armies, take up his position, and stand firm. Then, they all, from King Jehoshaphat on down to all the men, women, and even children, they bowed down and worshipped God in thanksgiving.

"Next morning, they did as they were told, and took up their positions. Then, God told Jehoshaphat to do a most remarkable thing. Jehoshaphat instructed his musicians to march in front of his armies, playing their instruments and singing praises to God, worshiping God for his holiness. So the musicians sang loudly, 'Give thanks to the Lord, for his love endures forever.'

"And do you know what happened? When they got to the overlook they saw that the three armies that were coming against them had turned upon each other in the night and completely slaughtered one another. By the time Jehoshaphat arrived there was not a single soldier left to fight. King Jehoshaphat listened to God, and God fought his battle."

The three sat in silence. Finally, Liddie began.

"So, I think I see it now… The Indian chief — Jehoshaphat — is anticipating a massive battle in the valley, but he doesn't need to command his armies to fight. He holds them back, so that God can fight the battle. Oh! And now I see Jesus standing at the top, holding out his arms, representing God fighting the battle for him! Wow! I can almost see the armies down there in the valley! What an incredible story."

"My favorite part is sending the musicians in front of the armies," said David. "The worship of God is what enabled the victory to happen. Another interesting part of the story is that Jehoshaphat dedicated a monument to God after the battle and called that place 'The Valley of Blessing'.

"I love that," replied Liddie. "The Valley of Blessing — what a beautiful name. And," here she turned to Paula, "I love that you could see so much in the statues. Why, it's almost like you could go sit there and be reminded of how God can fight battles for you.

"I like that."

Chapter 12: Two Special Teachers

After a snack, Liddie found Elizabeth and the two went on a walk around the pond. A great bald eagle swooped down, caught a large bass in its claws and rose majestically above the pines. Liddie had only seen a few bald eagles in the wilds, and each time it was a thrilling sight. She stood, watching until the eagle faded into the distance.

Elizabeth followed some random scent up a pathway into the woods. Liddie was happy to follow her and explore a new area. There was a clearing at the top of a wooded hill. One large oak stood in the middle, hollowed out, but still alive. Liddie peered inside, but not too closely, wondering a little nervously if any animals lived there.

Another of the numerous benches was set on one edge of the clearing. She sat, sipping from her water bottle. From the clearing, she could look across the pond to the house. Bronia and Mac were paddling in the boat. From their animated actions, they seemed to be having a lovely time. Liddie enjoyed gazing at the scene, sensing the peacefulness. But she was also aware of Mac's impending deployment and how hard that would be on the newlyweds.

Elizabeth, done exploring the clearing, started back down to the pond. Today, Liddie was content to let Elizabeth lead the way. It was kind of nice not needing to make choices of her own. Heading down she noticed, off to the side, a clump of wild blueberries, filled with tiny white blossoms. She stopped, got down on her hands and knees to examine them, and felt a new appreciation for nature's bounty. She could imagine the tiny blueberries ripening in a few months. Liddie had only eaten them from the store, but she hoped someday to grow her own.

They rounded the path on the pond and she waved to Bronia and Mac, listening to their sweet laughter. Elizabeth bounded on down the Pilgrim Path and led Liddie back to the Overlook Hill with its statues. There Liddie lay down in the soft green grass, feeling the warm rays of the late afternoon sun.

"What an indescribably beautiful day!" she exclaimed..

She continued lying in the warmth, simply being. Elizabeth lay down beside her, and the two nodded off to a symphony of meadow music. Fluttering dragonflies, chirping crickets, singing birds, all combined with rustling grasses and leaves blowing gently in the breeze. It was a most refreshing nap.

A sudden loud cawing of crows startled Liddie. She stretched and shook herself awake, not sure of how long she had been napping. She stood, brushing off the stray grass leaves, and moved a few steps to the Overlook Hill bench. She was grateful that she had a bag of nuts in her pocket. It made for a rejuvenating snack as she gazed over the valley and recalled Paula's story.

The whole idea of God fighting your battles was intriguing. Actually, to Liddie, the whole idea of God was intriguing. Her parents had taken her to church and Sunday school when she was a child. Liddie remembered enjoying the Bible stories, the fun games, and especially the snacks. She understood the reality of God in, maybe, a historical sense. But she had never really taken it any further than that. And, as she learned after going away to college, none of her friends ever talked about God. So she just sort of drifted away from any connection with him or religion.

"But here," she thought, "all of these people mention God in their stories. Is this some sort of commune, then?"

She had heard stories of people gathering together into communes, kind of like the Amish, and living apart so they could share their experiences of God. She also knew of bad communes from the news, where evil leaders oppressed trusting followers.

"So, is that what's going on here?" Liddie pursued the thought. "I don't think anyone here is evil. On the contrary, they all seem very loving and kind. And there doesn't even seem to be a leader. They all just kind of live here, together."

Liddie sat, staring at Jehoshaphat's statue.

"And what about this battle story? I mean, that sounded almost like a fairy tale, or one of those Greek myths — that God would actually fight a battle for them."

She knew of some neighbors who had relatives in the army, and she understood that some of them had actually been in battles. Her parents always put out flags in support of them. But she had a suspicion that there might be more to the story. Paula's reference to 'looking beneath the surface' came back to her. Was there more than just a physical battle here?

Liddie had always been easygoing, finding it easier to adapt to life's twists and turns, rather than pushing for a particular agenda. So the idea of fighting battles as part of life took a lot of thought.

"You know," she again started musing, "what about that time I went out with that group of girls last year — it started out as dinner, but then they wanted to go party at a bar, and I was really uncomfortable, but I didn't know how to say anything… And I remember thinking that I didn't want to be there, that it wasn't going to end well. I suppose that was a kind of battle. One that I wasn't very good at fighting. I remember wishing for some excuse so I could leave. Then that guy — the one from my ecology class — called and asked if we could get together and study. I remember being so relieved when he came and picked me up. I suppose…. I suppose… if God really is ready to fight our battles, that could have been God looking out for me. I mean, Mom and Dad do pray for me."

Liddie's thoughts were interrupted by laughing voices. She turned and saw Paula and David with Bronia and Mac coming through the Coneflower

Field.

"Liddie!" Paula called out. "We didn't know where you had gotten off to! Are you coming with us to the campfire tonight? Here, I brought you a sandwich."

"Why, thank you!" Liddie replied, giving her a quick hug. "How sweet of you! I would love to come hear more stories."

Dusk had fallen while she was contemplating battles. So Liddie welcomed the company and started off down the pathway with them.

James and Henry were already laying the campfire when the group arrived. Anna and Stanley sat on a log watching. As Mac passed out more Mountain Dews, Liddie noticed that Stanley's cough was worse. She sat down next to Anna and asked about it.

"I don't know," said Anna. "He developed this bad cough from those chemicals at work. And it just keeps getting worse. I've tried different medicines, but I'm really concerned."

Liddie noticed a tall spiked plant growing next to them. Excitedly, she went over and plucked three or four huge fuzzy leaves.

"Anna! I don't know if this can cure what he has, but I know it can help ease his symptoms!" she exclaimed. "This is a native plant that was used in many old folk remedies for coughs and lung issues. Here, let me show you how to prepare the leaves and use them. I tried it last summer when my mom had a bad cold, and it took the cough right away!"

Anna and Liddie huddled over the leaves while Stanley watched with interest. The rest of the group arrived and Liddie heard more random talk as they greeted each other.

"Wasn't that sunset beautiful?"

"Did you hear that Frankie got kicked by a mule?"

"No! I hope he's all right!"

"You got any kale growing in your garden?"

"Nope. Rabbits got it. But grass is growing."

"How about that bald eagle."
   "I think it nests in the big pine."

"Chilly tonight."
   "Just look at that moon!"
   "Whoa, was that an owl or a coyote?"

"Grass is growing."

Liddie enjoyed the warm, comfortable feeling, being a part of this group. She sat back and sipped her Mountain Dew. In the green bottle she could just barely see a faint reflection of the evening's sunset.

Mac squeezed Bronia's hand and stood up. Liddie marveled again at how the two looked like movie stars, so breathtakingly handsome. She watched as Mac strode to the campfire, wondering if he would talk about himself and Bronia.

   "I will only be here a few more nights," he started. "It has been such a wonderful time — this interlude with Bronia before I ship out — I've been thinking back to how it was that I got here. Of course, there was our chance meeting at the circus, when I asked for her phone number and she thought I would never call because I didn't write it down. I memorized it as she spoke. I did call, and we did go out dancing, and it was a whirlwind leading to our marriage just a month later.

   "But let's go back — I memorized her number. I still have it memorized — Hammond 8915. It was easy for me to remember it, because memorizing is one of the skills I was taught as a young lad.

   "Do they still teach memorization in schools? I suppose we'll find out..." Mac turned and smiled at the blushing Bronia.

   "The thing is, looking back, I realize how that simple skill helped me become the luckiest man alive when I did call Bronia. So, I want to tell you the story of two very special teachers, and how they helped a dirt poor boy from backwoods Missouri become that luckiest man alive.

"Our family had nothing, and we were barely scraping by. I was the youngest of seven. All the older ones were girls, and they loved to help Mama care for me. It was a happy childhood, roaming the farm — a lot like Adelle described her early years yesterday.

"Until I began school, I never really was aware of how poor we were. It was just the way life was. But once I started school, I noticed how my clothes were different from the other students. Oh, there were some like me, but for the most part, they dressed better. Their clothes didn't have patches; I wore old hand-me-downs from relatives, sewn up to fit me. They had shoes without holes; I wore whatever leftovers we could find. My manners weren't as good, and my speech wasn't as good as the other children. Now, understand — I'm grateful to my parents for persevering, for working hard and providing for us. I'm just saying that once I got to school, I was aware that there was another strata of life where people lived with a little more money to provide extras.

"We had good teachers who encouraged us all through school. But once I reached high school, I don't know why, but they seemed to see something more in me. And I began to notice them pushing me a little more. It made me think — maybe there was some hope for me to move to that other strata. Maybe I could better myself.

"One of these teachers — Miss Womel — taught English. She enjoyed having us memorize different passages, and then spent quite a bit of time getting us to argue different aspects of the passages. One of these… well, listen as I recite it for you. It's from 'The Vision of Sir Launfal' by James Russell Lowell."

Mac paused, reaching back in his mind to the still-memorized passage. He cleared his throat and began, his deep voice ringing over the group.

And what is so rare as a day in June?
  Then, if ever, come perfect days;
  Then Heaven tries the earth if it be in tune,

And over it softly her warm ear lays:
Whether we look, or whether we listen,
We hear life murmur, or see it glisten;
Every clod feels a stir of might,
An instinct within it that reaches and towers,
And, groping blindly above it for light,
Climbs to a soul in grass and flowers;
The flush of life may well be seen
Thrilling back over hills and valleys;
The cowslip startles in meadows green,
The buttercup catches the sun in its chalice,
And there's never a leaf nor a blade too mean
To be some happy creature's palace;
The little bird sits at his door in the sun,
Atilt like a blossom among the leaves,
And lets his illumined being o'errun
With the deluge of Summer it receives;
His mate feels the eggs beneath her wings,
And the heart in her dumb breast flutters and sings;
He sings to the wide world, and she to her nest —
In the nice ear of Nature, which song is the best?

Mac stood silent for a moment. Then he repeated the last line.

"'In the nice ear of Nature, which song is the best?'

"That was her question to me — Miss Womel's question. She asked me directly, 'Which song was the best?' I knew right away which song was best! Why, the little bird that sits on the bough and sings to the whole world! That was obvious! That bird was singing to all of Nature, to all the people who might listen, and to God up in Heaven. He's singing to everything in creation. How could there be anything better than that? The other bird was just singing quietly to those eggs in the nest. There was no comparison!

"Well, Miss Womel let me talk. Then she let other students talk. Then she talked. I began to listen. Something began to change in me. I began to wish

I hadn't spoken quite so emphatically. By the end of that class, I had totally changed my mind. The male bird singing to creation was important and beautiful and part of God's plan. But, the female bird sitting on the eggs, nurturing the future, was equally important and beautiful and part of God's plan.

"The problem was in the question itself. It should never have been asked. The songs are equally complementary, both parts of a whole. Neither one is better than the other.

"Miss Womel inspired me to look deeper, to look for something more in our readings, in school, in all of life. This, in addition to the memorization skills she taught, helped me believe that I could move into a better life."

Mac paused to sip from his Mountain Dew. Then, he continued.

"I want to mention one other teacher. You know, once you start listing the good things in your life, those things that have shaped you, people for whom you're grateful, sometimes the list goes on and on. For me, it just takes shifting my mind to that view of gratefulness, and then the memories of people and situations start flooding in. I could list people all night long.

"But I only want to talk about this one — Miss Crystal Reed. Actually, her name was Miss Crystal Holbrook — she married a Mr. Reed later on.

"I mentioned that my family was extremely poor. And until high school, I did not see anything that would lift me out of that existence. Until Miss Holbrook came to teach at the small Eagleville High School.

"Miss Holbrook took a special interest in me. She encouraged me, even to the point of driving me up to apply for the State University when I graduated. She motivated me to believe that I could do more. But more than that, she taught me how to see beauty in life. How to see the beauty in nature. How to see beauty in people.

"She taught typing, which I took but did quite poorly at. She taught Business Practice, which I also took. It was in that course that I first learned about the free enterprise system and the importance of getting practical experience in different lines of work.

"Miss Holbrook also taught music, and even though I didn't think I had any musical talent, she put me in a boys' quartet. Well, we did our best, and she kept working with us. For a school competition, she had us learn a song popular at the time. It was based on the poem, 'Little Boy Blue,' by Eugene Field. A sad song, it told the story of a small child who passed away. We did not win the competition. But the other boys and I enjoyed learning and singing the music.

"A few days later, after the competition, one of the Eagleville families experienced the tragedy of their own son dying suddenly. The whole community was devastated. On the day of the funeral, the father asked Miss Holbrook if our boys' quartet could sing that song at the funeral. She hustled us together, found us dress clothes, reviewed the song with us, and got us down to the church in time for the funeral. Looking back, I don't know how she put it all together so quickly.

"We four boys sang our best. Toward the end of the song, I looked out at the father. He was leaning forward, his head thrust almost over the pew in front of him. Peering at us, he studied us intently. It was as if he was trying to get as close to us as possible, to capture every word and sound. Great tears were rolling down his cheeks.

"I looked around the crowded church. Every person there was crying. I felt tears coming to my own eyes, and fought to control my emotions so I could continue singing."

Liddie looked around as Mac paused. She was surprised to see that Henry and Adelle were crying.

"We did finish the song. We were grateful to support the family in the way we did. But over the years, I've thought back to that time, and the impact it had upon me. I still think of it as remarkable that four green kids could be led through such a strong emotional contribution, by a high school teacher, in a circumspect little town. The remembrance and reflection has helped me understand what humanity is all about.

"And it has helped me understand more about how God works in our lives. We four boys were simply doing an extra activity at school. Miss Holbrook was simply teaching.

"Yet, when this tragedy happened, God said, 'Who can I use to ease their pain?'

"And he saw us. He said, 'I can use them.'

"He saw Miss Holbrook. He said, 'She can be my hands.'

"And God reached down into the little country church, touching the pain of that family.

"At the same time, he touched the hearts and minds of those four young boys. He revealed to them a great truth — how the love of God transcends all and dwells in the depths of humanity with them."

Chapter 13: You Do What You Need to Do

Liddie became aware that Stanley was struggling to stand. Anna jumped up to help him. Stanley shook his head, indicating that he wanted to walk to the fire pit. He started off with a somewhat wobbly gait. Anna followed him, providing support when he swayed. Liddie watched, curious to see how Stanley would do, talking through his emphysema.

She didn't have to wait long, because the effort sent Stanley into a long protracted coughing fit.

"You. Talk." Stanley croaked as he pointed at Anna.

"Me? I'm not the one who came up here!" Anna replied in a somewhat irritated manner.

"You." *Cough.* "Talk." Stanley repeated. As if to emphasize his command, Stanley lowered himself onto a nearby log and watched Anna expectantly.

Anna's hands flew to her hips and she stood there, giving every indication that this pose was a familiar one she used often on Stanley. She turned and faced the others, shook her head and then turned back to Stanley. She uttered a long stream of a language unknown to Liddie. But there was no mistaking her intent! Liddie and Adelle looked at each other with raised eyebrows, waiting to see what would happen. Stanley, however, held his ground and smiled resolutely at his wife.

"Humph!" Anna nearly snorted at him. But she did slowly turn back to the group.

"I suppose what Stanley was going to say," she began, "was something about his family back in Poland."

"Ah!" Liddie thought, "so that must have been Polish she used on him! There's quite a spark there!"

Anna continued. "I didn't know Stanley then. He grew up in the Limanowa area. And I grew up in Krakow, north of there. He immigrated to America earlier than I did. Your father," and here Anna turned to Stanley, "he was a cobbler, wasn't he? Didn't he have a store where he made shoes?"

Stanley nodded. Just then Henry called out loudly.

"Look! My shoes — Stanley repaired the soles and patched the holes. They're good as new! See!" Henry pulled off an old leather shoe and held it up high. Everyone else nodded approvingly.

"So," Anna continued. "That's where you learned the trade — from your father. But didn't you tell me that you gave the shop and business to your brother? You thought there would be more opportunity in America?"

Stanley quietly answered, "That's right. America offered a better life. But the work in Chicago was different. After years of working in the Pullman upholstery shop, the asbestos just ate away my lungs."

Another coughing fit interrupted Stanley. After a sip of water, he continued. "But Anna, I want you to talk about yourself!"

Anna looked at him, confused. "Why?"

"Just do it." Again Stanley smiled at his wife.

"Well, Stanley, if it's important to you, I'll give it a try. But I'm not happy about it!" Anna continued to look at him, still a bit befuddled. Then she turned and spoke to the group.

"As I said, I grew up in Krakow. At that time, girls were only educated through the fourth grade. When I reached ten, I had to make a decision. Did I want to work on the farm or in the coal mines, or did I want to do housework and take care of children? I definitely did not want to work on the farm or in the mines, although many children did. The pay was better. So I started working for neighbors, caring for the kids, cooking, cleaning, and generally taking care of housework.

"After a few years, I began hearing about America. I did something very unusual for me. I told the immigration people that I was older than I was! I guess I lied…"

Anna was obviously uncomfortable with this admission. Her brow wrinkled as she stared at the ground. Liddie thought it was very sweet that Anna regretted a past indiscretion that many people wouldn't think twice about.

"I wasn't that much younger than the required age of eighteen. Just two years younger," Anna continued. "But I felt ready for a new life. It wasn't until I was on the boat and began seeing other immigrants that I realized how unusual it was — a young girl traveling on her own, heading into the unknown.

"Once in America I made my way to Chicago, where there was a large Polish community. We all helped each other out. I was welcomed in to a family, and they paid me to do exactly what I had been doing in Poland! Yes — cooking. Cleaning. Child care. But still, it was all good.

"This family introduced me to Stanley, and they pushed us — very insistently — to marry. Perhaps they were concerned about me being a young single girl in a strange country. Anyway, we did marry. I loved Stanley for being so fun-loving and so generous with everyone. He brightened my life. He showed me how to make the most of what you have. See, we didn't have much of anything. But his attitude has always been — make the most of it. Be thankful for what you have, and be generous with it. Act like you have plenty!

"We laughed a lot in those years. But then, when the asbestos in the shop made Stanley so sick, life became very, very hard. Stanley couldn't work anymore. I was the only one responsible for providing for us. Stanley stayed home and helped with what he could do — maybe cooking or a bit of shopping.

"I was grateful to get a job cleaning offices at the Field Building in downtown Chicago. We lived out toward the edge of the city. For my job, I would catch the streetcar at the corner of our road and ride it all the way to State Street downtown. For me, that was a scary challenge — much like heading off across the ocean to a new land, I suppose.

"I still hadn't learned English very well. In our little community, it was easy just to speak Polish to neighbors and rely on our children to translate anything else for us. But, I couldn't take my children with me on the streetcar to work! So I got one of them to write 'State Street' on a piece of paper. I kept that in my pocket and each time I boarded the streetcar, I showed it to the driver, and he let me know when we got there. Eventually, I was able to recognize the stop because of the huge clock on the building.

"So this became my daily routine — boarding the streetcar at four in the afternoon, cleaning offices for eight hours, and then getting home at two the next morning..

"I tried learning English from a little dictionary book I always carried in my pocket. It had Polish words translated into English, and then it had English words translated into Polish. What a helpful book!"

Anna smiled. "I remember being so excited to find *morela* translated into English! I took that dictionary right into a local market, pointed to the translation and held out my money! Sure enough, the grocer gave me dried apricots! I ran home with my apricots and made kolaches! We hadn't been able to make them since leaving Poland! I put a checkmark beside the word so I could easily find it again!

"It was a hard schedule. My knees hurt constantly from scrubbing floors. But you know, there were good parts. This building — the Field Building — was so beautiful. It was something like thirteen levels high. A skyscraper! And in the middle, you could look all the way up to the top, just like looking at heaven. There were beautiful designs in the ceiling — blues and golds, and they would shine in the most glorious fashion! They told me it was done by a famous artist. I forget the name, but I do remember how much joy it brought me to enter the building and gaze up at the beauty before starting work.

"There were also amazingly fast elevators and moving stairs. It took me a while to get used to them, and I used the old-fashioned stairs that stood still for weeks before becoming comfortable with them.

"One other memory was Christmas time when the huge store windows that lined State Street were filled with the most magical displays! It was always busy on State Street, but even more when crowds and crowds of people came into the city to see those displays.

"One year, before Stanley became too ill, he brought our five children into the city. I met them below the big clock, and we must have walked up and down the street four times, soaking in the sights in the windows. Stanley kept pointing out different parts for the children. The snowmen, the reindeer, the train, an enormous dollhouse with figures, and the huge Christmas trees! He even bought us a box of Frango mints. They didn't last long...

"But, yes, most of life was hard. Sometimes neighbors would ask me, 'Anna, how can you do all that? How can you handle Stanley being sick, when you are so exhausted all the time from your job?' I really didn't understand their question. To me, it was simple. You do what you need to do. You just do what you need to do."

Stanley reached up for Anna's hand. He didn't try to stand. He took another sip of water and focused on speaking as loudly as he could.

"Anna, you say it was so simple. So many other people don't see it that way. They give up, they drink, they run away. You didn't. You continued to love me even through my sickness, and you did the right thing all along the way.

"Anna, thank you.

"A Bible verse I learned many years ago I think must have been written with you in mind. To me, it describes you, and how God poured his love through you.

We rejoice in our sufferings,
knowing that suffering produces endurance,
and endurance produces character,
and character produces hope,
and hope does not put us to shame,
because God's love has been poured into our hearts

through the Holy Spirit who has been given to us.

"You, Anna, have the most beautiful character I have ever known. *Jak cie Kocham.*"

Anna continued holding his hand, and whispered in return, "*Kocham cie.*"

Henry called out, after a bit of silence, "Hey, has anyone seen Osmund?"

"He walked here with me," Sarah replied. "But he got up the same time Stanley did. I assumed he was just stretching his legs. You all know how that old leg injury gets him if he sits too long."

She stood up and scanned the edge of the woods. Henry and James also stood and walked out into the darkness a ways, letting their eyes adjust.

"There! There he is!" Henry saw him first.

Osmund was slowly walking in front of the woods. His head hung, as if deep in thought. Occasionally he would raise his head and gaze at the stars. The rest of the group was now standing and watching him with interest.

Someone emerged from the woods. Liddie recognized, even from the distance, that it was the mysterious figure she had seen earlier. The new figure walked toward Osmund, who had stopped moving. Osmund's shoulders drooped. His head hung, almost, it seemed, in shame.

The figure moved closer, arms extended, hands open.

Osmund crumpled and fell into the open arms, just as the figure reached him. Liddie could see Osmund's shoulders shaking, as if sobbing. The figure held him, the two of them a stark silhouette against the moonlight.

Behind her, Liddie heard a beautiful tenor voice, singing into the night stillness. She turned to see Mac, his arm wrapped around Bronia's shoulder, singing one of his long ago memorized songs.

Softly and tenderly Jesus is calling,
  Calling for you and for me;
  See, on the portals He's waiting and watching,
  Watching for you and for me.

Come home, come home,
  You who are weary, come home;
  Earnestly, tenderly, Jesus is calling,
  Calling, O sinner, come home! ...

Oh, for the wonderful love He has promised,
  Promised for you and for me!
  Though we have sinned, He has mercy and pardon,
  Pardon for you and for me.

Come home, come home,
  You who are weary, come home;
  Earnestly, tenderly, Jesus is calling,
  Calling O sinner, come home!

The group drifted home, singing the chorus together as they left. Osmund, however, remained in the healing embrace of Jesus.

Chapter 14: Kolaches and Chocolates

"What is this?!" Liddie exclaimed. She had just taken a bite of a cookie. "This is the most delicious thing I've ever tasted!!" Paula and David looked over and smiled.

"Ha!" Paula said. "I knew you would love them! Remember Anna talking about kolaches last night at the campfire? She showed up early this morning with a plate full of them. She must have worked late after we all left!"

Liddie examined the cookie more closely. Flaky, lightly browned dough was folded over an orange apricot filling. The whole cookie had been dipped in what Liddie guessed was powdered sugar.

"Oh, my goodness!" she continued, "I'm going to have to learn how to make these! Maybe I can teach my mom!"

Liddie picked up more kolaches and sat down at the table. Just then, Bronia came in the door. Seeing the plate full of kolaches, she got herself a cup of coffee and sat down to enjoy the delicious treats.

Liddie finished her plate and moved to get more. There was something addictive about them.

"Say," she said, remembering Anna's story from the night before. "Does anyone know what Anna and Stanley said to each other after they finished talking? I'm guessing it was Polish, but they didn't translate." Liddie looked up at Paula.

Paula turned quizzically to Bronia. "Bronia?" She asked.

Bronia laughed enchantingly. "Of course," she answered. "Stanley said, 'How I love you.' And Anna replied, 'I love you' back to him."

They all smiled knowingly and reached for more kolaches.

Bronia continued, "You saw some of Anna's spunk last night. She once told me about a time she was walking to the neighborhood market. On the way there, some young thug jumped out, grabbed her purse and took off down an alley! By then she wasn't a young woman — certainly not in shape to outrun a young man. But that didn't stop her. She started running after him, yelling all the way, 'Stop! You stole my purse!' The guy turns and looks at this mad woman, cape flying off her shoulders, waving at him and screaming. Shopkeepers are poking their heads out of their stores. Shoppers all around drop their packages and take chase. Well, he flat-out throws the purse back toward Anna, takes off down a side alley, and disappears!"

"You know," she added, "it makes perfect sense to imagine her starting out alone on that journey to America when she was just sixteen. She wouldn't let anything stop her!"

The cookies were all gone. The coffee pot was empty. But everyone felt full and comfortable. They moved to the softer chairs and sat contentedly in peace.

"So!" Paula started. "I've heard that you have a friend coming in today. Tell us about him."

Liddie blushed. "It's not what you think!" she quickly responded. Then, "Well, maybe… I… I… I don't really know!

"His name is Beckley. I met him at the camp where I was a counselor, just before coming here. He is a lawyer. He'll be joining a firm in New York that works on environmental law. So we have a lot in common. I love plants. He wants to work with plants, only… with legalities and all."

"Hmmm." Paula began. "So… why is he coming here? I mean, as near as I can tell, none of that would explain why he is coming here. The only thing here that might interest him is you!"

"Paula!" David jumped in. "We mustn't pry! If Liddie wants to tell us anything, I'm sure she will."

Paula turned to David, "Now, look here. I've seen this girl laying in our pond, covered in mud! I've seen her shucking peas, and wandering the fields and woods. I've seen her adopt a huge lost pup. I've seen her listen to all our stories at the campfire, seemingly enjoying them. I've even seen her helping Anna with medicinal herbs! And, I've seen her jumping up to clean the kitchen after devouring those delicious kolache! This girl is now family!

"So," she continued, "if this boy Beckley is coming out here with anything on his mind, I want to know about it!"

Liddie bent over, shaking in laughter at Paula's outburst.

David shook his head in a "what can I do" kind of way. Stepping to the front door, he opened it for Adelle, who had just appeared.

"What's going on?" she asked, noting Liddie's laughter and Bronia's smile.

"All right, all right!" Liddie burst out, still laughing. "Yes! I'm interested in Beckley!"

Adelle's eyes lit up. Her face brightened into a big smile. "Looks like I got here just in time!"

"All right!" Liddie repeated. "Beckley and I only met each other about a month ago. So, it's way too early to know anything…"

She was interrupted by laughter coming from Adelle and Bronia. Adelle asked, "Bronia, just how long did you and Mac know each other before getting married? A couple of months, did you say? Was it that long?"

"That's about right," Bronia said. "And you, Adelle, you and Henry — a month or two?"

"Yes, but oh my! Definitely too early for Liddie to know anything!"

The two women chuckled and snickered together on the couch.

"Okay! Okay!" Liddie gave up in exasperation. "Yes! I like him! I like him a lot!"

"Ah," Bronia's eyes twinkled. "What do you like about him? Tell us!"

Liddie smiled shyly. "I like that he looks into my eyes. When we're talking, he focuses on my eyes and he's totally there, present to me. He makes me feel important. And he makes me laugh! And he knows so much! It's like he's one of those renaissance people who knows something about everything!

And he's comfortable talking about it. But he doesn't make fun of me for not knowing all the things he knows. And I like that he cares about plants, and the environment, just like I care about them.

"And… and… I really love that he has rosy cheeks!"

This last admission was met with a knowing chorus of "Ah, yes!" and "Ohhhh!" and "Mmmm-hmmm!"

"And," Liddie continued, "I love that he wanted to come out here to check on me. He was concerned that I would be safe. And he was kind of goofy in that he didn't really know how to express it, I guess, because he's a man… No offense, David — I mean I love men. It's just that they relate differently, I think… than women, I think."

"No, no offense taken!" said David, laughing. "I've been married long enough to become well acquainted with those differences! When is Beckley expected to arrive?"

"Oh, my!" exclaimed Liddie. "He should be here in about an hour. I need to walk Elizabeth and then tidy up a bit."

David headed out to check on the hammock where Beckley would sleep. Paula and Bronia busied themselves finding pillows and blankets. And Adelle joined them, but mainly so they could talk more about Beckley.

Once Liddie felt suitably prepared, she walked up the long driveway to meet Beckley at the old gate. Given the sudden interest of the women, she was more comfortable greeting him without them watching.

She was glad to be out in the sunshine soaking in the peace and quietude of nature. There seemed to be more grasshoppers and dragonflies than when she first drove in — was it only four days ago? Five days? She was losing track of time. But she was more and more certain that she loved being here. She recalled how Paula had called her 'family,' and how that seemed so right. So good.

Liddie found that odd rock — the one painted with 'Thus Far' — and sat down on it to wait. Not five minutes had passed before she heard crunching gravel in the distance. That must be him! She jumped up as the sound came closer. Sure enough, as she peered out into the road, she spotted a grey car rounding the bend! Liddie felt just like she thought Elizabeth must feel when she wagged her tail in excitement. She tried hard not to wiggle.

"So," she thought, "the way I'm feeling, this is probably an indication that I really do like Beckley. A lot! I wonder what he's thinking and feeling? I mean, they were right — he must be coming out here just to see me! Why else would he be here?"

Liddie abruptly stopped musing and started waving excitedly as Beckley turned into the driveway. Beckley's face showed everything she was hoping to see — eagerness, anticipation, excitement — and she was sure that her face reflected the same to him. Beckley parked the car, turned off the engine and flung the door open. He leapt out, ran the two steps to Liddie and grabbed her up into his arms!

It only took a moment for them both to realize with a shock what they had done! A hug? A BIG hug! What was this?

They both awkwardly stepped back and looked at each other with the same look of 'Oh, my goodness! Where did that come from?' Liddie, however, had mixed into her reaction, 'Wow! I really liked that!'

Beckley immediately started stammering. "Oh, I'm so sorry, Liddie. I… I… I… don't know what came over me… I was just so excited… I mean, it was such a long trip out here… and, um… I was worried about you, um… I just don't know what came over me."

He trailed off, ending with a very quiet but very gentlemanly, "Please forgive me."

Liddie, of course, was quite amused at his reaction. Not at all upset. In fact, she had difficulty not laughing at his confusion. And she loved his perfectly polite manner — it was quite chivalrous. That characteristic was part of what had drawn her to him. But she was also quite pleased to know that underneath that chivalry, there was apparently some passion directed at her!

"Beckley, it's all right! I'm not upset! I'm super happy to see you, too!"

Beckley's countenance brightened as he appeared visibly relieved.

Liddie continued, "I have so much to tell you. And show you. I can't wait for you to meet all these people. Beckley, do you know what they called me this morning? Family."

She paused for that thought to sink in.

"I have so many questions. And of course, I really haven't done much of anything in getting all the photos and descriptions for Mom, so there's all that. But I'm loving being here. You know, Beckley, it's almost like being in an amusement park — not with all the rides and everything, but kind of like it's somewhere different than where you really live, and you go there to have fun or do something different.

"Does that make any kind of sense?"

Beckley listened and watched Liddie as her thoughts tumbled out. Some of what she was saying he could understand and identify with. There was a lot he didn't get, but here was a question he could respond to.

"Yes, yes, of course that makes sense. I can't wait to hear more!"

But Beckley's main thoughts as he listened were, "I had no idea I felt this way about Liddie! She is so beautiful. I am so glad I came. Why, I want to sweep her in my arms again!"

Liddie, however, was already getting into the passenger side of the car.

"I left some of the women at the house looking for blankets for your hammock. They were asking about you this morning — they're very excited to meet you. It's right down this driveway."

Adelle, Paula, and Bronia were lined up in front of the house as Beckley drove the car around the last bend. They all squinted into the sun, trying to get the best view of Liddie's young man.

"I'll come around and get your door for you." Beckley said to Liddie, as he opened his door and stepped out.

Adelle looked at Paula. They each nodded at the other. Bronia raised her eyebrows and said, approvingly, "Oh, yes!" They had not been prepared for Beckley's striking image.

Tall, not thin, but physically well built, he moved with an air of authority. Curly, dark brown hair was cut just at the top of his collar. His clothes were casual, but clean and good quality. His blue eyes reflected knowledge, but also the inquisitiveness of a mind seeking more. And the squareness of his jaw revealed the solid determination of a man who knew what he wanted to do, and would do it!

This was what the three women saw. They could not know that just a few minutes before, Beckley had not projected any of that as he was reduced to a twitterpated young man beginning to realize that a young woman very likely held his destiny in her hands.

The three watched as Beckley opened Liddie's door. She stepped out and turned to them with a shy smile. In unison, they nodded approvingly at her with broad smiles.

"Adelle, Bronia, Paula, this is Beckley," Liddie began. "And Beckley, this is Adelle. Bronia. Paula."

Beckley firmly, but not too tightly, grasped each of their hands as Liddie introduced them.

"I'm so glad to meet you, Ma'am," he graciously greeted each of them. Then, he spoke to all of them. "This is a beautiful place here. Liddie has told me so much, and I look forward to learning more. But first," and here he reached inside the car, "I brought you all some candies. I was told these chocolates are the best in all of New York! I hope you enjoy them."

The box Beckley handed them was huge. Wrapped in gold foil and red ribbon, if the outside gave any indication of the quality inside, they knew they were in for a treat! They thanked Beckley profusely. As he turned to get his bag from the car, Bronia whispered to Liddie.

"You didn't tell us what a hunk he is. He's gorgeous!"

Liddie blushed and said, "Well, yeah, I guess I forgot…"

"And what a perfect gentleman!" Paula added.

After a suitable time visiting, and eating lots of chocolates, Liddie suggested that she and Beckley walk to the Overlook Bench. But first, she took him to meet Elizabeth. It was as if they had known each other their whole lives. Beckley called Elizabeth and she came running, ears and jowls flapping. A few happy barks, a few repetitions of "Oh, what a good girl," and lots of rubbing and slobbering, and it was clear that the two were solid friends. Liddie was surprised at how happy that made her.

She was not surprised, though, at how happy she was looking at Beckley.

Chapter 15: Swooning

Liddie took Beckley along the Pilgrim Path, across Coneflower Field, and finally to the Overlook Hill. She pointed out the Black Walnut Grove on the way. Beckley was entranced with the beauty surrounding them, from the pond to the riotous flowers, and finally, as they reached the Overlook Hill bench, the expansive view over the valley with Carn Ingli in the distance.

Oak trees were filling out their leafy green canopy, so it was difficult to see through the woods. But Liddie pointed out the path to the Pond Beyond, where Sarah was probably working in her garden. They sat on the bench, enjoying a moment of silence, the two of them feeling the comfortable warmth — was it from the sun's rays, or was it from the nearness of each other?

Liddie looked directly into Beckley's eyes. "I'm glad you're here," she said.

Beckley's eyes held something more than the simple friendship they used to enjoy. Perhaps it was his newly recognized desire to know Liddie on a different level. Perhaps it was the rush of experiences since he had arrived, that impulsive hug at the gate, meeting the women, seeing the beauty of the land. Regardless, what Liddie saw was an aching in his soul — a seeking of something he could not identify.

Beckley quickly answered, "I'm so glad to be here with you, Liddie." But then, overcome with unfamiliar emotions, he turned from her gaze. The two sat in silence.

Liddie began to fill the silence by talking rapidly, explaining Paula's hypothesis of the story behind the two statues — Jesus and Jehoshaphat. Beckley, having been raised attending a small country church, was familiar with the story and thought it very appropriate for the setting. He looked more intently over the valley.

"The Valley of Blessing is a good name," he mused. "It reminds me, and the story reminds me, that we shouldn't take things for granted. That there is a purpose in many events, and like you described your experience at school with the group at the bar, sometimes we don't realize how God fights our battles.

"It's interesting, Liddie. It sounds like the people here talk openly about God. Paula's description was all about a Bible story where God worked in many lives. And you, in telling me about it, you brought up how God might have worked in your life.

"To be honest, I haven't really thought about God since my last Sunday School class in grade school. I have no doubt that all I learned was real and true, but I guess maybe I got distracted by how capable I believed I was on my own. That was about the time we started having more difficult work in school, and I found that I was good at academic subjects. It all came easily to me. So, the stories from Sunday school didn't seem relevant, and they faded away.

"Plus, that was also the time that my parents moved us into the city, and we never did find another church that quite connected with us.

"I guess, what I'm saying, is just… just that it's interesting — this talk about God."

"I know what you mean, Beckley," Liddie replied, brow furrowed. "I actually wondered a day or two ago if this was some sort of cult or religious commune! But, I don't think so. They are all so genuine, and my gut tells me they are all good people.

"But there definitely is the weirdness of it all!" she said with a laugh. "Tell me, what was your impression of the three women you met?"

Beckley spoke slowly. "Well… I've got to say, I liked them. Like you just said, they came across as good people. I saw them eyeing you with secret signals, I assume about meeting me, but that was all in good fun, I'm sure. And when you talked back and forth with them while we ate the chocolates, well, it seemed like the kind of talk that good friends share.

"I'm looking forward to meeting the other characters you've described. And this campfire you mentioned. Do they have them every night? Will I get to go to one? Will I be welcome at one?"

"Oh, yes! I'm sure!" Liddie answered. "And that will be the perfect time for you to meet the others. Well, if not before. I never know exactly where they are during the day. Sometimes I run into someone out walking, or I see them fishing in the pond. This is a big place, and they seem to live in far corners. I think Mom said that it's almost eighty acres. That's a lot of land!"

Liddie stopped talking, and there was an awkward pause. She remembered reading somewhere that every seven minutes, conversations develop these awkward pauses. She cast around for a new topic, then continued.

"How about I tell you some of the stories from last night?"

"Yes!" answered Beckley. "I'd love to hear them."

"Okay, well… let's see. Anna, who seems to be from Poland — she talks with a heavy accent — and Stanley, her husband, talked about life in Chicago. Apparently he worked a job where he was affected by asbestos, and he got very sick. Oh, but Beckley, I was able to find a plant and show Anna how to use it for his cough! I'll need to ask them how it worked tonight.

"I'm not sure what the message of their story was. Most of the stories seem to carry some kind of message, maybe not an obvious one, but something that does kind of stay with you and makes you feel good about life and hope and such.

"Mmmmm, perhaps the message with Anna was simply to keep persevering. Yes! Stanley said something about persevering and character and hope."

"So the persevering had to do with Stanley getting sick?" Beckley asked.

Liddie answered, "Yes, I think so. But more with Anna's response to it.

She had to support the family, and she was an immigrant who didn't know English, and it was all very difficult, but she said, at the end of her story, that you just do what you need to do. So, I guess that's what perseverance is — just doing what you need to do.

"Oh, and Beckley, Anna brought over the most delicious cookies early this morning — apricot something. She had talked about the cookies in her story. I intend to get the recipe so I can help Mom make them."

Beckley interrupted, "So is there any order to who tells stories? I mean, do they have some sort of publication that you can follow along and know who will be talking?"

"No," said Liddie. "I don't think so. It appears to be totally random, like one person just decides it's their turn. Anyway, before Anna, who was it who talked? …Oh, yes! Mac! Mac is the husband of Bronia — you met her this morning. You know, they've only been married a couple of weeks? It's very sad — he needs to be leaving in just a few days with his Navy unit.

"Mac talked about a number of different things — his youth, teachers, and a poem! The poem was lovely. He recited it from memory! I can't remember all of it, but there was a part that had two birds, and one was singing to the world, and the other singing to her nest of eggs. And Mac talked about needing to tell his teacher which one was best. Isn't that odd?"

Beckley smiled and answered, "Yes, I suppose it was odd."

Then he stood up, broadly gestured across the field and turned back to Liddie, looking happily at her as he began.

And what is so rare as a day in June?
  Then, if ever, come perfect days;
  Then Heaven tries the earth if it be in tune,
  And over it softly her warm ear lays.

Liddie's mouth dropped open. Overwhelmed with Beckley having the same poem memorized, overwhelmed with his classically good oratory as he delivered it, she felt as if she would swoon! Liddie had never swooned before, and her only knowledge of the word was from a romance novel she read long ago. But, 'I'm swooning' was the phrase that came to her mind as she stared in wonderment at Beckley.

Beckley, sensing a positive response in Liddie, continued reciting the passage, ending with

He sings to the wide world, and she to her nest —
  In the nice ear of Nature, which song is the best?

Finishing the passage, Beckley sat down next to Liddie.

"Beckley! How in the world?" She began, struggling to speak because she was still in the midst of her swoon.

Beckley laughed. "That was one of the passages we had to study in high school English class. Didn't your school cover it?"

Liddie was a bit embarrassed that she just barely got through high school English, so she just remained silent.

Beckley continued, "Whenever I came across a poem that I really liked, I memorized it. It was just another one of those things that came easy to me, like I was saying earlier about school.

"You know, Liddie, today is the first day of summer. What a great time to remember that poem! Do you know what I love about it — why I memorized the poem?"

Liddie, still very much overwhelmed, shook her head.

"The entire poem is an ecstatic description of nature, and how beautiful the world is. I mean, it's almost like a love song from heaven to the earth, with the two of them in tune with each other — like all the different parts of nature singing and playing together to make this beautiful music that reaches a pinnacle with the birds singing.

"Honestly, I suppose this poem, and others like it, helped me realize how much I love nature — the cowslips, the buttercups, the little birds. And I wanted to protect it — nature, that is. That is why I went into environmental law. It seemed the best way to make a difference."

Beckley was somewhat confused by Liddie's silence, not being aware of her inner swooning. So, after a moment, he continued.

"You know, this is actually part of a larger poem about one of the knights of King Arthur's roundtable. And it's interesting, given what we were saying about the people here always talking about God. The knight — Sir Launfal — is planning a quest in search of the Holy Grail. But he has a dream, or maybe it's a vision, and there's all kinds of symbolism in what he does and who he meets in the dream. It basically ends up with him awakening and deciding that going on his quest would be futile. That the more important thing, the message of the Holy Grail, was to aspire to love."

"That's really interesting," Liddie responded, "the part about King Arthur and the search for the Holy Grail. I remember reading those stories as a kid. They were presented as myths, but I always hoped they were real — such great adventure stories."

"Me, too," Beckley answered. "I always liked the inspiration of striving to do better. Of course, there were lots of people failing in different ways throughout the stories. But the general theme is striving to do better."

The two sat quietly, content now, in the silence. They had reconnected to the point where their relationship had been back at the internship. Liddie recalled the long times of just sitting silently together back then. She was glad they were getting back to it. She looked up at Beckley and was surprised to see him leaning back with eyes closed.

"Oh, my!" she thought. "He's fallen asleep! Is he bored? What should I do? Maybe he's just worn out from his trip — I guess it was a long drive from St. Louis."

Beckley opened his eyes, looked at Liddie and smiled.

Her angst disappeared instantly.

"I was just thinking, Liddie," he began. "There's another part of that same poem that I love. Here, let me see if I can recite it correctly." He paused a moment longer, then began.

We may shut our eyes,
  But we cannot help knowing
  That skies are clear

And grass is growing.

Liddie looked at him in astonishment and burst out laughing!

Beckley was totally caught off guard by this response. Here was a very deep and thoughtful passage that meant a lot to him, but her response was to laugh! Maybe he didn't really know this girl after all. What kind of reaction was this?

He stammered, "I… I don't understand…"

It didn't take Liddie long to realize how her laughter came across. The stricken look on Beckley's face was a huge giveaway. She immediately stopped laughing, and touched his arm.

"Oh, I'm so sorry, Beckley! I wasn't laughing at you. Or the passage! No, no, no! It's a beautiful passage! And I want to listen to it again. But… it's just that phrase, 'grass is growing.'"

Here Liddie began laughing again and shaking her head.

Beckley, though, was only half listening to her explanation. His focus was turned more toward the touch of her hand on his arm. He stared down at her hand, resting there. The simple touch had stirred unknown feelings inside of him. Feelings that he liked. A lot.

His gaze moved from her hand up to her face and he thought how beautiful she was, trying not to laugh, but having very little success. She slowly gained control of herself. As she began talking, much to Beckley's dismay, she removed her hand and pointed across the valley at Carn Ingli.

"The campfires! Beckley, at the campfires, that's one of those things they say! At each one, before they really get started with their stories, they make small talk about the weather and such, and always someone — and I think it's a different someone each time — says, 'Grass is growing.' Every time!"

She repeated, "'Grass is growing.' I mean, how strange is that? What's the point of saying the grass is growing? Of course it's growing. What's it supposed to do?"

"Well, Liddie, I don't know why these guys would say it. Have you ever asked anyone about it?"

After Liddie shook her head no, Beckley continued, "No? Then I think I would start there. Get it straight from the horse's mouth!"

Beckley laughed loudly, cracking himself up with his own wit. Liddie looked over at him, a bit confused. So Beckley explained the idiom and how he made it a joke by connecting it to the grass growing. She joined him with a chuckle, thinking it wasn't really that funny, but not wanting to say so.

"Anyway," Beckley said, "the point of the verse I recited about the grass growing is the sense of peace in knowing that all is well with the world. As we close our eyes, it's not that we fall asleep and don't notice anything, it's that we become more aware that, yes! The sky is clear. The grass is growing. Everything is doing what it's supposed to be doing. And it is good."

Liddie nodded. She closed her eyes, breathed deeply, and felt very, very close to Beckley.

"Yes," she thought. "It is good."

She opened her eyes with a start, hearing squirrels chasing each other on the boughs above them. Checking her phone, she saw that it was nearing dinner time.

"Beckley, do you realize we have been sitting here talking for four hours? My goodness! I had no idea!"

Beckley agreed, "I thought it had been just a short time, too. Catching up with you has reminded me of how much fun it was back at the internship. I loved those nights talking together, looking up at the stars."

Liddie smiled with him at the memory. Then her practical nature broke through.

"Look! I stuck some hard-boiled eggs in my pack before we left. And some apples and nuts. Why don't we have a picnic right here, for dinner? Then we can wander up to the campfire and see if the others are gathering."

Beckley was quite impressed with Liddie's planning ahead. What he couldn't know was that Liddie, like so many other women, did not go anywhere without having three times as much food as might be needed. She always had a bag of nuts stuck in a pocket. Other snacks were carried in her pack, "just in case". And more often than not, those snacks came in handy when she or someone she was with needed to eat.

Beckley took off his jacket and spread it on the grass near the bench. The two of them sat, watching the sunset. Sitting there, in each other's company, they both thought this food was some of the most delicious they had ever eaten.

Liddie pointed out the path down the Overlook Hill and across to Carn Ingli, and the two started off. Halfway down the hill, she stumbled on a rock. Beckley instinctively reached for her hand to steady her. She looked up at him with more than gratitude.

"Thank you, Beckley. I guess I didn't see that rock in the pathway."

"Of course," Beckley answered. "I wouldn't want you falling into the blackberry brambles. I remember how viciously they scratch from the last time I went blackberry picking!"

"Oh," Liddie said, "I love picking and eating them fresh!"

She noticed that Beckley was still holding her hand, even though the rock was quite a ways behind them now. His hand felt warm, solid and strong. She was most taken with the strong feeling. She thought she could enjoy holding his hand for a very long time.

Beckley looked down at her. He wasn't about to let go of that hand! He smiled warmly at Liddie. And her smile back gave him all the encouragement he needed. He straightened up, chest puffed out, full of anticipation and excitement for the future.

"My goodness!" thought Liddie, looking up at him with amusement. "He's strutting like a rooster!"

Chapter 16: The Circus

"Ah, so you're Liddie's young man!" Henry greeted Beckley. "Adelle has been telling me all about you!"

The two couples had found each other on the trail leading to the campfire. Adelle pulled Liddie up ahead, walking a bit faster, leaving Henry to walk beside Beckley. The two men could see Adelle questioning Liddie intently. Every so often the women would turn and look at them, then turn back to their animated conversation.

Beckley smiled in response to Henry's question. "It's all good, I hope!" He laughed.

"Yes, yes, indeed!" Henry laughed with him. "I think you've got Adelle sold on you, that's for sure!"

Reaching the campfire, they saw that most of the others were already there. Liddie was quickly surrounded by the women. Beckley stopped and stood quietly on the fringe, listening to the conversations.

"Another beautiful sunset — did you see it?

"Yes — weren't those the deepest purples and reddest reds you've ever seen?"

"Have you seen Liddie's friend?"

"I have — handsome, isn't he?"

"What? Chocolates! Are there any left?"
"Here, I brought the box with me. Anyone else want some?"

"Liddie, where is he?"
"I want to meet him, too! I hear he's the cat's meow!"

Beckley saw Liddie disentangle herself from the women and walk over to where he was standing on the edge. Just as she reached him, they both heard clearly from the group,

"Grass is growing!"

Liddie and Beckley burst out laughing and collapsed into each other's arms.
"See! See! What did I tell you?" she quietly exclaimed to him.
Beckley struggled to control his laughter as the two of them walked into the group around the campfire. Ten pairs of eyes focused on them. And all ten of the persons behind those eyes were especially intrigued, given that quick hug they had all witnessed.
"Everyone," Liddie began, "This is my friend Beckley. We met at an internship a few weeks ago, and he has come to visit."
"I'm so glad to be here," Beckley said to the group. "It's a lovely place. I've met a few of you already, and look forward to meeting everyone else!"
Mac was the first to step up and greet Beckley. He firmly shook his hand in welcome. Beckley remembered that he was deploying soon and thanked him for his service. Liddie told Mac about how Beckley also had that poem memorized. Mac nodded with obvious approval.
Stanley, aided by Anna, walked slowly up to Beckley and spoke only briefly before his cough took over. Beckley was able to ask Anna how the herbal treatment had worked, commenting that Liddie described finding the plant for her. Anna said that she had hopes for it, and thought perhaps Stanley slept better last night.

Mary and Sarah brought the box with its few remaining chocolates over and offered some to Beckley and Liddie.

"I know you've had some, but I thought you might like another before they disappear completely," said Sarah. "Thank you for bringing them!"

Liddie and Beckley each took a chocolate and savored the taste as they moved to sit together on a log.

Osmund and James looked over in Beckley's direction, but didn't move. When Beckley noticed them, they both nodded their heads in solemn greeting.

Mac and Bronia walked arm in arm up to the campfire. Mac set about laying the wood in a teepee shape and stuffing smaller tinder inside. He lit the fire, stepping back as crackling began and smoke swirled upwards. Then he sat down on a nearby stump and watched Bronia, who remained standing. The love in his eyes was obvious to all.

Bronia sighed deeply, locking her eyes on his. She began speaking slowly, still staring at Mac.

"Yesterday Mac touched briefly on how we met — how he memorized my phone number… about the circus, and dancing, and how it was a whirlwind. But he left out so much! You women know what I'm talking about!"

Here she turned to Liddie, Adelle, and the others. Liddie found herself nodding along with them — a bit too emphatically, she realized, when she became aware of Beckley's interested but slightly befuddled glance.

"So, given that Mac is scheduled to ship out in three days, I'm just going to enjoy talking about us. Perhaps it will ease the pain of our upcoming separation. There's nothing earth-shattering about my story. Just a simple, every day love affair!

"I was just nineteen years old. After graduation from high school, I worked various jobs — Hump Hair Pin Factory, Spearmint Gum, the Donnelly Company, where we created Life Magazine. I enjoyed trying out the different jobs. But my favorite was at International Harvester. They had changed most of their production to build equipment supporting the war effort. You all have seen that picture of Rosie the Riveter? Well, that was me! 'We Can Do

It!' That was basically the motto of all of us girls who worked there, taking up the slack of our men who'd gone to war. We all felt a lot of camaraderie, and honestly, we all needed each other's support.

"Anyway, the bosses must have thought I was good at the work, because they promoted me to section supervisor. That was a lot of fun, too, because I got to wander the floor and be a problem solver.

"I usually worked from eight in the morning through five o'clock. Most days, I would still have lots of energy and be ready to party after work. My girlfriends — let's see, there was Florence, Mary, usually my sister Celia — they were the main ones, but sometimes we would go out in big groups — we were always up for activities. Being young people in the big city of Chicago, there were lots of possibilities. But most of our interests lay in simple things — roller skating down the streets was a big one.

"Actually, sometimes we were a bit naughty. Some of us — I'm not saying which ones — would carry big safety pins with us. And as we walked through crowds on the streets, some of us would poke those pins at passersby!

"Ohhhhh, I can't believe I just said that!"

Bronia rushed over to Mac and buried her head in his shoulder, full of embarrassment. The initial universal gasp of the others quickly gave way to laughter and enjoyment and calls of "Hey, girl, haven't we all done things like that?"

Mac held Bronia tightly, then lifted her head and whispered, "I love you so much…"

Bronia smiled weakly and stood back up.

"So, I guess that's who I was when the circus came to town.

"My sister Celia worked in a newspaper office not far from International Harvester. They always had extra tickets for local events, and the workers got those free. That afternoon, she came home with a big fistful of circus tickets, so I rounded up Mary and Florence and several others. Celia couldn't go herself, but she was happy to give us the tickets.

"By the time we got everyone together and rode the streetcar downtown, the circus had already started, and the only empty seats were all the way at the top of the bleachers. Mary and I scooted in first, leaving Florence on the end.

"I'm not sure what act was going on — it seems to me there were some trick horses running around the ring. What I am sure of is hearing Mary shout, 'Oh, dear! Look!'

"She wasn't watching the horses. Her eyes were on a Navy ensign climbing the bleacher stairs. Immediately, all of our eyes were fixated on the tall, dark form, neatly clothed in his best Navy dress uniform. He held himself firmly erect, head high, hat in hands, just oozing confidence! But I think what awed all of us the most was his smile! At each row, when his eye caught the eye of someone sitting there, the most gorgeous smile appeared on his face. We were all completely transfixed. Our entire row of young women was held speechless, watching this hunk get closer and closer!"

Liddie was transfixed with Bronia's story. It was like watching a romance novel in living color! She peeked up at Beckley and could see his eyes as wide as hers. He was completely drawn into the scene.

Mac seemed to be thoroughly enjoying himself, listening to Bronia describe their meeting. He was one of those men confident enough to receive compliments, but aware enough not to give them too much weight. Liddie kept staring at him so she could get more glimpses of that smile. She was amply rewarded.

Bronia continued. "Florence could see that there weren't any empty seats below us. So she quickly pushed the rest of us further down the bleacher row, creating an opening on the aisle end. Being at the end near the wall, I was squished flat. Mary and I bent forwards, watching as the ensign came closer.

"Florence was ready. She had daintily crossed her legs, leaned back on the bleacher with one hand resting seductively at her side. She raised her chin, tilted her head, and turned slightly toward the aisle. Mac reached our level and studied her with a slightly bemused expression. But as she turned and feigned surprise, he flashed that grin, and she melted! Of course, we couldn't see her face, but her whole body seemed to slowly sink down into itself — melting…like putty.

"We could just barely hear above the circus loudspeaker. He was so polite —

'Hello there. Is this seat taken? I don't mean to inconvenience you.' Florence nervously laughed and scooted over some more, almost knocking Mary off the seat. Mac seated himself and seemed to become engrossed in the circus acts. Several times, he did turn to Florence and they discussed one or another of the activities. The rest of us moved on, back to watching the circus, assuming that he was now 'Florence's guy'.

"After the grand finale, including a big parade around the ring, we all stood up to go. Mary suggested we head to a new coffee shop for a bite to eat. While we girls were discussing it, Mac kind of hung around on the stairs, obviously listening to us. Once we had agreed on the place, he delighted Florence by asking if he could tag along!

"At dinner, he appeared even more to be 'Florence's guy' when he bought some flowers from a vendor and presented them to her.

"Afterwards, Mac walked us to the streetcar stop, still animatedly talking with Florence. I really had no conversation with him. A couple of other sailors happened by and engaged Mary and me, trying to pick us up, but we weren't interested.

"Just before the streetcar got there, Mac walked away from Florence, straight over to me, looked me in the eye, all the time smiling that incredible smile, and said, 'Would you want to go out with me?' I tell you, I was floored! I peered around him, trying to catch Florence's eye to see if it was okay with her. She shrugged her shoulders and nodded — maybe they hadn't really hit it off, after all.

"So that's when I said, 'Sure' and gave him my number. And no, he didn't write it down. So… I expected to never hear from him again."

Bronia paused and accepted a Mountain Dew from Mac. She took a sip before continuing.

"But he did call that week. He suggested we meet at the Palmer House on Saturday. Now, the Palmer House was about the fanciest place in all of Chicago! The building just dripped in ornate carvings, gildings, and all the fanciest people went there. They offered such exotic specialties in their Empire Dining Room! Gourmet dishes like frog legs, ox tails, salmon, and lamb. So, when he suggested the Palmer House, I thought, 'Whoa, he's the real deal!'

"Getting ready for our date on Saturday, I carefully arranged my hair in curls using those Hump hairpins. I wanted it to be extra wavy! But then, I started having second thoughts — I hadn't even really talked with this guy! Why had he picked me to invite out? What if this was a big, horrible mistake? So I grabbed Celia. 'Celia!' I said! 'You've got to come with me!' Oddly enough, she was willing to be the third wheel on our date. As we planned it out, we agreed on signals so if I wanted an out, she and I could head to a different party, but if I wanted her gone, she would know when to leave!

"We arrived at the Palmer House lobby. It was completely full of service men! Navy, Army, all kinds of ranks — I couldn't tell who was what! 'Celia,' I said, 'how am I going to find him? I can't even remember what he looks like — just his gorgeous smile...' We decided to have him paged so a bellhop could bring him to us.

"'Oh, my goodness!' Celia exclaimed when she saw him coming with the bellhop. 'You didn't tell me he was such a heartthrob!' That's when I gave Celia the signal for her to leave.

"And," Bronia ended, "that's how we met. It was a whirlwind as it became apparent to both of us very quickly that this was right. Somehow, we had been led together through chance encounters. But we both knew in our hearts that as unexpected and random a meeting as it had been, God had his hand on it. So we grabbed hold of the future and let him guide our steps together."

Mac jumped up. He swooped Bronia into his arms, the two of them lost in their embrace. Liddie's eyes widened as she watched them. Turning to look at Beckley, she realized how much she wanted his arms to swoop her up in that very same way.

She wondered why she had never noticed what a gorgeous smile he had.

Chapter 17: Osmund

Beckley turned and met Liddie's gaze. Rising from the log, he reached for her hand. She felt herself moving up to meet him. Each of them allowed their eyes to now express what they had only recently begun to acknowledge. Liddie's and Beckley's hearts were beginning to be entwined as one.

It was only a crashing sound from the fire that pulled their attention away. Henry rushed up to drag the fallen log back into the fire. James stomped out wayward embers. Liddie and Beckley quickly, self consciously averted their gaze from each other. They nonchalantly stretched their legs a bit and sat down again.

Osmund stood up and limped to the fire. He put a hand on Henry's shoulder, and Henry turned toward him with an inquisitive look. Osmund nodded solemnly, and Henry and James returned to their seats.

Liddie thought Osmund looked different, somehow. She thought back to the night before and how the mysterious figure had held him so tenderly. Previously, Osmund had given her the impression of being a withdrawn, restrained figure. And then, of course, there was the story Adelle told about the attack on Henry! Liddie was eager to hear what Osmund might say.

"The past couple of nights," Osmund began, "two different people said something that sounds, on the surface, like the same thing.

"Last night, Anna talked about getting through all of the struggles that she and Stanley encountered. She said, 'You do what you need to do. You just do what you need to do.' Hearing that last night, in the context of simply continuing to persevere, well, it hit me hard.

"Because, it was just the night before that Adelle, in telling a story, used a phrase very similar to that. She was quoting what her incredibly mean — I would even say 'evil' — father said after trying to murder her fiancé. He said, 'I did what I had to do. I did what I had to do.'

"I have to tell you all." And here, Osmund closed his eyes and hung his head. "I was that evil man. I tried to kill Henry."

There was no shock or outrage in the group. Perhaps they had all pieced the story together, much as Liddie had begun to piece it together. But also, as Liddie had noticed, there was a change in Osmund. Along with that change came an expectation, a knowledge that the evil which had happened could be turned to good. So it was with hopeful anticipation that the group waited.

Beckley was the only one who hadn't heard the full stories. But he was already feeling connected and almost a part of this strange assortment of people. He, too, waited eagerly to hear what Osmund would say.

"I'll come back to the two statements." Osmund began, "but first, let me give some background. My mother brought me — just the two of us — to America on a ship very much like the one James told us about. I was five years old. My grandfather lay dying in a Norwegian hospital for lepers. My father had disappeared. No one knew why. There was talk that he came to America separately and began a new life with someone else.

"My mother, like Anna, was a strong and courageous woman. She hoped that her brother, who had come to America the previous year, would help her get settled. That wasn't to be. Her brother, a leader in the church and community, shunned my mother. Again, no one knew why — or at least, I was too young to know.

"So we worked hard. I suppose we 'persevered.' My mother remarried, and two half-brothers came along. My mother made sure to take us boys to the local church, and we learned about God. I'll say that again. We learned 'about' God. We learned about all the rules we had to follow in order for him to accept us. We learned about laws, sin and the terrible consequences of what happens to those who do not follow the rules. We did not learn about love.

"When I turned twenty, I thought I had it all figured out. I knew the rules. I knew that if I just worked hard and kept the rules, all would be well. I said goodbye to my family and headed south from our little settlement in Illinois. I had a little money saved and planned to buy my own homestead. Along the way, I met Sarah, a young vision of loveliness. Without too much ado, we married and continued on, looking for land. Her parents journeyed with us.

"It was in the unworked frontier of Missouri that we settled. Sarah's parents found a place down the road. The early years were good, and we welcomed eight children. But something happened, somewhere along the way.

"I did my best, I tried hard, to do the works of a good man. But I could never really measure up. I just kept failing. And eventually, I realized that even when I did succeed at doing the right thing, it didn't make me good inside. It was almost like all my efforts to be good, to do the right thing — they were all imploding inside. And instead of good, I found this evilness growing in me.

"The children knew. They pulled away from me. One of them actually told a friend that she had been raised by a Norwegian devil.

"Sarah knew. I put her through such awful torment. After our ninth child was born... and died... due largely to my own failures... Sarah left us.

"The whole community knew. I was pretty much an outcast, known only for my total meanness. I was evil. I was the evil man who tried to kill Henry that dark night in the woods."

Osmund sank to the ground. He sat there, weeping.

Sarah was the first to move silently up to Osmund. She sat beside him, wrapping her arms around his shoulders. Henry followed, kneeling at his side. Adelle, then James and Mary, they all came and surrounded Osmund.

Liddie and Beckley moved up and stood on the edge of the circle.

The gentle presence of their love strengthened Osmund. He slowly stood. Turning to Henry, Osmund implored, "Please forgive me, Henry. I was so, so wrong."

Henry nodded, himself choked up, "All is well, Osmund. All is well."

Osmund then grasped Sarah's arms. Wrenching sobs filled their tormented bodies as they clung to each other. Again, Osmund pleaded for forgiveness. And again, it was offered, this time by Sarah.

Someone brought Osmund a Mountain Dew, and he gratefully drank it. Then, after everyone had found their seats, he continued.

"So, how I started, with those sentences — you can see how even though they sound the same, they were each motivated by different forces. Anna was motivated by good, by a reliance on God. She persevered by God's strength.

"I, well, I have to say that I was motivated by evil. I was a Norwegian devil, just like my daughter described. And when I said 'I did what I had to do' I was totally wrong, overcome by the evilness within myself.

"Two sentences so similar. But worlds apart. It wasn't until I actually met Jesus, the Jesus of the Bible, that I was able to see the difference. Before, all I knew were rules. And I was not good at keeping them.

"Now... now I know love."

Chapter 18: Who Are These People?

James began putting out the fire. Others moved quietly, gathering up their blankets and heading back. Liddie and Beckley each gave Osmund a hug before they started down the trail. Liddie pointed to the mysterious figure whom she spotted again, off to the side. Beckley gazed at him in the moonlight.

They walked in silence for a few moments, continuing to absorb the powerful scenes they had witnessed. Liddie hesitatingly began.

"Um… Beckley, um… I don't quite know what to say. Tonight was so heartrending. I am left with so many different emotions. I feel like my insides have been ripped out and tossed back in, not just once, but over and over again!"

Beckley stopped and looked at her. Despite all his courtroom training, he was at a loss for words. He had only been here the one day, and his emotions had been on a roller coaster the entire time. He had no idea who these people were, or which one of the scenarios Liddie had suggested might be real — were they all demented? Surely, they couldn't actually have lived their stories! What was going on? Yet, he also kept feeling that it was all good. That no harm would come from it.

"Liddie," he finally said, "that was one of the most emotionally draining experiences I've ever been through."

After a long pause, he continued. "Look, I've got to be honest. I don't know what in the world is going on here. I don't know who these people are. I don't know why your old family farm is populated by them. But, you know what? The really crazy thing is, part of me wants to stay here forever and live with them…"

"Really?" Liddie exclaimed. To the great surprise of both of them, Liddie jumped straight into Beckley's arms, and the two embraced in the moonlight.

The next morning, Beckley opened his eyes and stared up into the tree branches above his hammock. He smiled at the music of the spring peepers. Listening more carefully, he was able to pick out the additional calls of toads and grey tree frogs. Stretching his legs and pulling himself out of the hammock, he mused that the presence of all the frogs probably accounted for the delightful lack of mosquitoes.

He stood for a moment in the little grove of trees. The men had picked a beautiful spot for the hammock, close to the pond, but sheltered by oaks and hickories. Beckley watched a pair of wood ducks lazily swimming through the pond weeds. His thoughts returned to the previous night.

Certainly, he had never experienced anything remotely similar. He had lots of questions. He looked forward to discussing it again with Liddie.

Foremost in his mind, however, was the memory of their warm embrace on the trail as they walked home from the campfire. It was fortunate, or perhaps disappointing depending on your point of view, that Paula and David had happened along so soon after Liddie jumped into his arms. The momentary awkwardness of their meeting gave way to pleasantries about the stars and how nice it was that the full moon lit up the pathway. But Beckley did manage to reach out and grasp Liddie's hand. Every now and then, as they walked, he squeezed her hand ever so slightly. She would then turn to him, smiling, and squeeze his hand in return. A secret communication — would it lead to more, he wondered?

He glanced up as he heard a door open and close up at the house.

"Elizabeth! Wait! Don't wake up Beckley!"

Elizabeth ignored Liddie's call and barreled down the path. Beckley laughed and knelt down to greet the huge fur ball. When Liddie came around the bend, she found them rolling together on the ground, wrestling and having a wonderful time.

"Did she wake you up?" Liddie asked, concerned that it was still early.

"Actually, no. I've been up maybe half an hour. This is a beautiful spot. Did you know there are wood ducks here? They flew off once I started moving around."

"Why, no!" answered Liddie. "How about I run up and get us some coffee and we can sit on the dock watching for them? Perhaps they'll come back." She headed up the pathway.

Beckley set about shaking out his blankets. It would be nice having a coffee time with Liddie before he went up to shower and change in the house.

He sat down on one of the worn metal chairs on the dock. Elizabeth came and lay at his feet, presenting an appealing picture when Liddie returned. She carried a tray with two huge mugs of steaming coffee and a plate of pastries.

"Paula was just taking these scones from the oven!" Liddie exclaimed. "Don't they smell heavenly?"

Beckley quickly grabbed one and nodded as he took a bite. "And they taste heavenly!" He smiled in appreciation.

With full stomachs, Beckley and Liddie leaned back in the chairs. It was good to swallow the last of the coffee and sit in the peaceful surroundings.

Liddie was first to bring up the previous evening's campfire.

"Now that you've had some time to mull it over, Beckley, what are your thoughts about last night? Certainly, Osmund's story was much more intense than the others, and I'm still processing that one. But the whole experience, after meeting the people, do you have any idea what this is all about?"

Beckley reached down to get a burr out of Elizabeth's fur. He looked back at Liddie and shook his head, troubled that he still did not have any answers. So he began by laying out what he did know.

"I meant what I said last night, Liddie. There is a part of me that connects with these people. I don't know what it is — maybe their vulnerability, their total openness and acceptance, I don't know. But I would describe them as the most genuine, loving people I've ever met. It's disarming. And it makes me feel liked by them, welcomed into their community. That's why I said that part about me wanting to stay and live with them forever. It's kind of like an invitation to a blissful paradise.

"Now, having said all that, I do need to explore possibilities of what's going on, of who they are and why they are here."

Liddie found it interesting to watch how Beckley proceeded to describe the possibilities in a very lawyerly manner.

"First," he said, "my original fear was that they were squatters. That could be a dangerous thing. But I don't see any of that here. Didn't you say that David referred to having some kind of permission to be here?"

Liddie nodded. "Yes, that very first day. He said it in a strange way — something about having permission, but then he talked about how their time was almost done, and they would be gone before I needed them gone.

"I have no idea who gave them permission! When I suggested to Mom that they might be distant relatives, she didn't think that was the case. So it couldn't be Uncle Stan who gave them permission. The people at Frankie's didn't even seem to know that they were here, so anyone around here didn't give them permission. No one else would have the authority."

"So," Beckley continued. "They don't have permission from anyone we know who would be authorized to give it to them. Liddie, I hate to say it, but that sounds like a definition of squatters. When I researched Missouri law before I came out here, I found that squatters can lay claim to a plot of land after living there for ten years. It's called adverse possession. Do you know how long any of these people have been here?"

Liddie had not been aware of the possibility that her family could lose the land! This brought in an entirely new aspect of the situation. She struggled, trying to reconcile this possibility with what she knew and loved about the people.

"I have no idea, Beckley! Maybe we should check with that local farmer who clears the driveway. Maybe he can tell us how long they've been here?"

"All right, that's a good idea!" Beckley agreed. "But it's still early. Why don't you call your mom a little later and ask for his phone number?

"Now, let's try and figure out what this whole campfire thing is, and where these stories are coming from. I heard the two last night from Bronia and Osmund. You've told me brief descriptions of some of the other stories. Just based on the ones I heard, it certainly sounds like Osmund and Bronia believed they were talking about themselves. Would you agree that the others all thought they were relating personal stories about themselves?"

"Oh, definitely!" Liddie was sure about that. "I mean, even to the extent that they included each other in their stories. Like Adelle talking about Henry and Osmund, and even referring to Sarah leaving the family. Then, Osmund talked about the same things. And that was genuine remorse last night. Unless he is an extraordinarily good actor, he could not have pretended to feel and express those emotions.

"And, you know," Liddie continued, "when Sarah talked to me by ourselves that one day, she referred to things in her life that would have gone along with what Osmund said.

"So, are they all who they say they are in the stories? I don't know..."

Beckley frowned. "We could accept that they are talking about themselves, and that they might all be inter-related, as they seem to think, except for one thing, Liddie. Last night, Osmund talked about searching for a homestead in the unworked frontier of Missouri. Liddie, there is no 'unworked frontier.' There is no land that has not been owned by generations of people here. Assuming he might be in his seventies, he talked about leaving home at twenty, which would have been fifty years ago. But what he was talking about was not anything that could have happened in the past fifty years.

"And didn't the others all talk about different time periods? The potato famine, the Oklahoma land rush, Rosie the Riveter — none of that happened in the past fifty years. More like a hundred and fifty!"

Beckley stopped. He didn't want to face the possibility that they might all be unbalanced, albeit a very interesting situation of mass derangement. So instead, he brought up Liddie's original idea of a group practicing story telling.

"You had an interesting thought at the beginning, that maybe this is like a theater group — that maybe they are learning how to tell stories, or learning roles for some play. What do you think of that now, Liddie?" he asked.

"I suppose it's possible…" she began. "But I don't know. They would have to be totally immersing themselves in portraying these figures, and I think any good actor could do that. But, you would think that at some point, one of them would have slipped up and gotten out of character. Yet, I haven't seen anything to indicate that. I mean, even when they are totally enjoying themselves, like just before you got here, Beckley, and we were sitting in the living room discussing you, they were all so, so real! I just don't see it as an act they're putting on…"

Beckley turned with surprise. "Uh, discussing me?"

Liddie laughed. "They wanted to know why you were coming here. I think it was their way of trying to figure out our relationship!"

"Mmm-hmmm." Beckley answered. "And what did you say?"

"Why, the only thing I could say, Beckley! I said that you had rosy cheeks!"

Liddie looked up at Beckley and batted her eyes, totally aware of what she was doing. She was rewarded with a very rosy-cheeked flush as he was overcome with embarrassment.

"Oh, come on!" she pulled him up. "Let's walk the Pilgrim Path and head up to the Mountain Top."

Chapter 19: Phone Call With Mom

ate morning mist gave the Mountain Top an ethereal appearance. Liddie and Beckley disturbed several deer who had been lying down in the leaves. The deer jumped up and stood for a few moments, watching the two. One lowered its head and snorted.

Beckley motioned to the bench, and he and Liddie slowly sat down. Liddie began talking, reassuring the deer that they meant no harm, and after a bit, the deer disappeared down the other side of the Mountain Top into the Wetland.

Beckley brought them back to their discussion.

"Okay, then, I think we can discard the idea of it being a theater-type group studying different roles. That's too bad, because it would have been relatively harmless, I suppose.

"So, Liddie, I'm afraid we keep coming back to them being unbalanced in some way. But the really weird thing is for them all to be part of this one big paranoia. Because they all do seem to think they are related to each other. And even though some of them think they lived during one time period, like the potato famine, they don't seem to have any trouble thinking that they are existing with someone from another time, like World War II.

"I really don't have any background in psychology, but doesn't it sound like a mass hysteria?"

Liddie had not wanted to face this possibility, but she couldn't come up with any better explanation.

Nodding, she answered Beckley, "I'm afraid you're right... But I really, really don't think they are dangerous. I mean, no one has ever shown any threatening actions to me, or any of the others. As I've said before, there is just this atmosphere of love and acceptance over it all. And what about that mysterious figure?"

Beckley shook his head in bewilderment. "I just saw him from afar, so I don't know. But I do think you're right about there not being danger. At least not immediate danger. We don't know anything about the past. Like how they got here — I'm grasping at straws now — is there some treatment facility nearby that they might have escaped from? I could see, maybe, if they all got here at the same time, they might have developed alternative identities that seemed to fit, and they all kind of grew together."

"I'll need to ask Mom about any nearby facility," answered Liddie. "Although, it seemed pretty deserted for miles around when I drove here. Wasn't that your impression when you drove in? So I would think it unlikely. But I'll ask her when I get the caretaker's number."

Liddie shivered in the mist. Beckley removed his jacket and placed it around her shoulders, hesitating a moment as his arm encircled her.

"Let's get you back inside," he said. "These mornings can still have a touch of chill to them. Plus, I want to take my shower and change."

The two began walking down the pathway, hand in hand. Liddie felt very comfortable, warmed first by Beckley's jacket, and now by his hand.

"Oh, say!" she exclaimed with a sudden thought. "Let's look into the rest of those bins today. That's where I found the map with all the neat names. There may be other interesting documents. Certainly I should get them together to take home with me. I imagine Mom and Uncle Stan would want to see them."

Back at the house, they ate some more scones and enjoyed another cup of coffee. Beckley went off to take his shower while Liddie helped Paula clean up. Finished, Liddie stretched out on an antique wicker chaise lounge on the porch. Feeling very luxurious, she pulled up a fuzzy blanket, wiggled her toes under it, and dialed her mother's number.

"Liddie! How are you? I tried calling you yesterday, but my call wouldn't go through. Are you okay?"

"Yes, Mom. So much has happened since I talked to you! And sometimes the cell service seems to fade in and out. But, yes, I'm doing great!"

"And how are you and Dad?" Liddie added.

"Oh, we're fine. Your father had to fly out on another business trip, but he should be back next week. He made me promise to let him know as soon as I heard from you."

Liddie smiled. It felt good to be loved.

"So," Liddie's mom continued. "Tell me everything. Did Beckley get there? Any more campfires with stories?"

"Oh, Mom! I wish you could meet him!" Liddie exclaimed. "Beckley's the most gentlemanly guy I've ever known! And he is so good at helping me figure out what's going on here.

"And you should have seen him when he met the other women! He brought an enormous box of chocolates for them! Can you believe it? They all were so curious about him before he came — peppering me with questions. I had the best time with them — kind of like laughing with a bunch of girlfriends! They all absolutely love him!"

Liddie's mother leaned back in her chair, stared up at the ceiling and closed her eyes. But there was a big smile on her face when she opened her eyes again. No one could mistake what was going on with Liddie. Her mom remembered feeling the same giddiness when she fell in love with Liddie's father. She made a mental note to add this new development to her prayer list.

She responded carefully, trying not to pry. "Chocolates! Oh, Liddie, I'm sure everyone loved that!"

Liddie continued. "He's taking a shower right now. Apparently he slept well in the hammock last night — has he only been here the one day? I've walked him over most of the land and I've taken pictures along the way of different parts so you can use them in the listing. It really is a beautiful place. Very peaceful. Not like anywhere else I've ever been, even though geographically it's here in the Ozarks, so it should be just like where I was with the internship. But it feels different, somehow. Maybe the word I'm looking for is 'real?' I know that's a strange way to describe a place. But it does feel more real here."

Liddie frowned, trying to understand why that word came to mind. But then she moved on.

"Okay. The campfire. Yes. They've had one each night, and they seem perfectly happy to have me there. Well, more than happy — they encourage me to be there.

"So, two nights ago, one of the couples talked — a sweet old couple from Poland. He is really sick with a cough, but, Mom! I was able to find a specific herb growing on the land and show them how to use it. I think it might help him."

Liddie, pleased with the memory, continued. "Anyway, his wife, Anna did most of the talking for them. All about their struggles in life. Something I've begun to realize… most of these stories have some sort of helpful knowledge, something that maybe they've learned and want to pass on. I don't know, kind of like a 'Ten Best Lessons on Life,' maybe? Anna talked about how she learned that you just keep doing what you have to do. It sounds kind of simple, I guess. But also, given their struggles, it really got them through things.

"Oh, and Mom! Anna made the most incredibly delicious cookies! They were really flaky, with an apricot filling. I must have eaten eight of them all at once! I think she called them something like kolades? I need to get the recipe from her so we can bake them together!"

Liddie's Mom frowned. She interrupted Liddie. "Kolades… kolades… I'm trying to remember, Liddie. It seems my grandmother made something similar with apricot… Kolades… No! It was kolaches! That's what she made. Kolaches. I think the dough might have had cream cheese in it. Mmmm! I haven't had them in a long time. If it's the same thing, I can certainly see how you ate eight at one sitting. Yes, get the recipe! I'd love to make them with you."

"Yes, I think that was it." Liddie replied. "That's so neat that you've had them, too!"

Liddie thought a moment about which other stories to mention to her mom.

"Ah, yes!" she started. "Mom, one of the women here — Bronia — talked about meeting her husband. It was such a sweet love story. And this couple is gorgeous! You would like them, I think. Those old movies you like to watch — with the heart throbs? This couple looks like they walked right out of one. I'm afraid I stare at them a lot, just because they're so much in love and it's so beautiful."

Liddie heard voices from inside the house and realized that Beckley must be done with his shower.

"Mom, I almost forgot! Do you have the phone number of the caretaker — the local farmer who clears the driveway?"

"No, Liddie, your Uncle Stan takes care of that. But I can get it for you. Is there more work he needs to do?"

"Nothing more right now. I just wanted to check with him on how long he recalls these people living here — like did they just move in, or have they been here for years. Beckley did some research on squatters, and we want to check out any possible issues.

"Also, Mom, we still don't know who they are — these people. Beckley agrees with me that there is no danger. But our best guess, given the stories they tell, and their relationships with each other, is that they might be living in some kind of delusion. Like, they really believe they are who they think they are. So… we were wondering if you could also check with Uncle Stan to see if he might be aware of some kind of home or institution nearby for people like that. You know, like maybe they used to live there, and somehow ended up here."

Liddie tried not to alarm her mom by suggesting an escaped group of patients from a sanatorium. Her mother, however, understood exactly what she was saying. Liddie had heard her sudden fit of coughing which followed a very audible, sharp intake of breath.

After regaining control, her mom answered, "Liddie, of course I will check with your uncle. But I have to be honest, this idea concerns me — are you saying that they might not be totally grasping reality?"

"Well, Mom, I don't know. We couldn't come up with any other idea to explain what's going on. But Mom, like I just said, we are certain there is no danger."

Liddie paused, then continued. "It's interesting — what you just said. 'Grasping reality.' Just a few minutes ago, I described this place with the word 'real.' And now we're talking about reality. I don't know… it's just kind of weird, I guess."

Beckley stepped out onto the porch. Liddie looked up at him and smiled. Seeing that she was talking on the phone, he started to step back inside. Liddie motioned for him to wait and turned back to her conversation.

"Mom, um, Beckley just came out, so I should let you go. I love you, Mom."

Liddie's mother noted that Liddie's voice had changed from chatty to hurried. It certainly gave the impression that Liddie wanted to hang up and be with this young man. She answered with a quick, "I love you, too!" and put down the phone.

Liddie's mother reminded herself that from the time Liddie was a baby, they had been praying for her future husband, that God would guide him into being exactly who God wanted him to be, and that he would bring them together at the right time. Was this the time? She pulled out her journal and began writing intensely in her prayer list.

Chapter 20: Books and a Theory

"Liddie, you didn't need to get off the phone," Beckley said.

"I know," she answered, "but we really should get to those bins. Mom's going to ask Uncle Stan about the caretaker's number and about a sanatorium, so we'll just have to wait before following up on those."

Beckley moved over to sit next to Liddie. The two gazed at the pond a few moments, resting in the peacefulness. They were unaware of the two faces peering at them from behind the curtains. Paula and David stood there, hand in hand, observing the scene with great interest.

By the time Liddie and Beckley stood up, stretched, and came inside, Paula and David had disappeared. The house seemed empty. Liddie found the room where she had discovered the map and opened the door. Beckley glanced quickly around the room, noting the desk, bookcases, and finally stopping to stare more inquisitively at the stack of plastic bins.

"So, you said there are other papers and documents in those bins?" he asked.

"Yes," Liddie answered, but her attention was pulled away from the bins as she moved toward one of the bookcases.

"These books, they're covered in dust — be careful you don't breathe it in — but, Beckley, look at these titles!"

Liddie brushed the dust from a few books and read out loud, *"The History of a Norwegian Pioneer.* And here's another one — *History of the Norwegian People."*

She began leafing through the two books, noting that the *Norwegian Pioneer* included a long chapter on a voyage to America, as well as a chapter on the exploration of Missouri. Her mind racing with questions, Liddie reached for another book.

"History of Ireland," she softly read. "And here's another one, *The Polish Peasant in Europe and America."*

Liddie looked up at Beckley. Beckley's eyes held the same consternation that she felt in her heart. It was obvious that they were both thinking the same thing. These books, historical books of the very time periods and places where most of the campfire stories occurred — the coincidence was just too glaring.

Beckley picked up a book. He read, *"An 1888 History of Harrison and Mercer Counties, Missouri."*

"Beckley!" Liddie plaintively cried, "Henry referred to Harrison County when he told the story of the Oklahoma land rush! He said he lived there."

Liddie buried her head in her hands as she despondently sank down into the old leather chair. Beckley pulled over one of the plastic bins and sat on it beside her, his arm curling around her back. He didn't quite know why Liddie was reacting so strongly to the books. He thought the discovery nicely validated their thoughts of the people here.

"You know," Liddie finally began, "we had decided that the most likely explanation was some sort of mass delusion or psychosis. But we didn't really know. I mean, neither of us have studied any psychology, right? So it was okay to just kind of exist with that knowledge. I think I was fine with that...

"But, Beckley, these books — doesn't that kind of confirm that they must have all read this history, these books, and decided to be people from those times? This is just crazy! I think we've stumbled upon a whole group of people who have created their own world here, with new identities and relationships.

"And just who are they, actually? Are they listed on some kind of national missing persons database? Did they all really come from a sanatorium? Or did they just randomly meet up somewhere and decide they didn't like their previous lives, and this was a fun alternative?"

Liddie realized she was bouncing rapidly around from idea to idea. She stopped and was silent. Beckley, with lawyerly logic, explored the same options Liddie had just expressed.

"Liddie, I'm really at a loss. I agree, it seemed relatively harmless at first, when we came to the conclusion that they were all living in a delusion. Because we both agreed that there wasn't any danger here — remember?"

He didn't wait for a response. Liddie just stared at him in bewilderment, trying to comprehend everything.

"Okay, the books. Norway — that would be Osmund? He talked about coming to America with his mother. So he could have found all kinds of descriptions of life in Norway, the boat ride, and the American frontier. Then there is Ireland — you said that James and Mary told a story of immigrating from Ireland. Again, all of that historical narrative is in *The History of Ireland*.

"And this one — *The Polish Peasant* — doesn't that sound like Anna and Stanley? I mean, they certainly give that impression."

Liddie interjected, "Yes, and Anna referred to Stanley learning a shoe-maker's trade back in Poland! I suppose that would be a peasant's work."

"And, lastly, the Harrison County, Missouri history. That one seems most significant, I would think. These others — Norwegian, Irish, Polish — a lot of people might claim to come from those areas. But, Harrison County, Missouri? This entire book, why, look! It's over 750 pages long!"

Beckley thumbed through the pages, stirring up a cloud of dust which sent them both into sneezing fits. He placed the book back on the shelf.

"Harrison County," he repeated. "Why would Henry have said he lived in Harrison County? The only logical conclusion is that he read this book and chose to create his persona as someone who lived there."

Liddie was glad that no one else was in the house. She did not want to confront any of them, at least not yet. This evidence from the books would take some time to absorb. And she was sensing her own emotional reaction.

It was almost a feeling of betrayal — that the joy and camaraderie she felt with everyone here was somehow a big lie. The women with whom she had shared such fun and intimate details — was all that a lie? Bronia and Mac, who seemed so deeply in love — a big lie? Anna and Stanley — were they secretly laughing at Liddie's efforts to help his cough? And the cough itself — another big lie?

Concerned at Liddie's silence, Beckley retreated from his logical evaluation of the situation and tried to put himself in her place. Yes, he was feeling his own dismay about this book discovery. But how much more distressing must it be for Liddie? She had seemed so at peace in this place. And that seemed to have been largely due to her interactions with these people. They had been good for her. And now that appeared ripped apart.

Beckley reached for Liddie's hand and grasped it with both of his.

"Liddie," he said, "I am so sorry."

Beckley felt the warm splashes of her tears falling on his hands.

They sat in sadness. But for Beckley, the sadness was tinged, unexpectedly, with almost a sense of reverence.

"You know, Beckley," Liddie finally began, "I should have seen it when I found that map. It had all those names written on it. I should have put two and two together when I saw the name Lana na Null. The very first day, when Adelle and Anna took me on the walk, Adelle talked about how James and Mary were from the 'Old Country' and they called their living spot Lana na Null. They must have found that map. There's no other explanation for it…

"Okay, look!" Liddie squeezed Beckley's hand and stood up. "Enough of this! Let's finish checking out these bins, pack up and move on!"

Beckley was surprised by her sudden change of attitude. He assumed the emotional trauma was still there, but he was very impressed with her stoically choosing to press on. He took his cue from her and opened the bin where he had been sitting.

"I wonder what treasures we'll find here?" he said, reaching in and pulling out a manila file. Scanning the sheaf of papers within, he told Liddie they all looked like receipts for seeds and plants. "Nothing really important there."

Liddie pulled out a large spiral-bound book. It wasn't professionally printed, like the histories they had just examined. More of a private publication.

"*Barbro*," she read from the cover, "*A Redemptive Tale of Grace*. Why, look, Beckley! This must have been written by one of my ancestors! See — the last name is the same as my mom's maiden name!

"Huh!" she continued, a bit confused. "The author's first name is Paula. Interesting… That's not such a common name, is it? I wonder what kind of story this is — a novel maybe?"

She opened the book and began silently reading the first chapter. "Well, it appears to be about an old man, and he's having some kind of flashback, remembering stories about… maybe his parents, maybe his grandparents? It's a little unclear.

"Wait a minute! What? Beckley! Look at this! No, listen to this!"

Liddie began reading out loud.

James had married the lively Mary Halfpenny when they were both young and relatively carefree back in Portadown, Ireland. Together they worked hard and built a life for themselves, and later, their two sons. But it was without warning that the potato famine struck their native land. They, along with countless other tired and poor immigrants, sought refuge through that golden door to America.

"Beckley?" Liddie trailed off in confusion.

Beckley sat back down on another bin. He was just as confused as Liddie. They stared at each other, trying to make sense, once again, of the whole situation here.

"Um…" he began. "Um… may I see the book?"

Liddie handed it to him and leaned back in her chair with a deep sigh.

Beckley found the section Liddie had read. He continued scanning the pages.

"Here's more on Paula — I guess the author is writing about herself. Oh, no, Liddie! She starts talking about her husband — her husband is David! What is going on?"

He continued leafing through the book.

"And now here's a section where it mentions a Bronia, who is apparently married to that old man in the first part. Liddie," he said, putting the book down, "she calls him Mac."

"Okay," Liddie said, reassuring herself, "we can handle this."

She reconsidered their conversation when they discovered the history books. It made perfect sense that the people here had used those books to create a delusion. And now, this additional book was just another piece of the puzzle.

She bounced the idea off Beckley.

"So, this really supports what we were just saying, doesn't it, Beckley? I mean, we were thinking that it was some kind of mass delusion, right? And the history books kind of gave that a framework. Well, it makes sense that this book was used in the same way. They read it. They each found a character they liked. And they have, more or less, become that character in their minds.

"I would totally expect to find the rest of the characters — Osmund, Adelle — all of them, in the rest of the book."

She grabbed the book and began leafing through it again, stopping here and there as she recognized a name.

"Look — here's Osmund. And here — Anna and Stanley. Here's a section on Miss Holbrook. That was the teacher Mac mentioned! And here, why this is that poem he recited — the one you also knew!

"There are additional names that I don't recognize. For instance, Barbro — who was she? But the stories are here.

"So, I guess what I'm saying, they didn't just create their own delusions. They found this book — a book apparently written about my ancestry — and they took the personas of these real people.

"You know, I never knew anything about my ancestry. Mom and Dad just weren't into it, so it didn't seem important. But, all of a sudden, I find myself feeling protective over this book being used in such a way!"

Liddie thought about it some more. "I kind of feel, I don't know... kind of like something has been taken from me. Even though I didn't know anything about these ancestors, if indeed they are my ancestors, well, it just doesn't seem right to have other people use them."

Liddie got up and walked into the kitchen, telling Beckley that she needed a snack as it was already afternoon. They found some cheese in the refrigerator and shared the last of the scones, washing them down with some lemon water. Then they returned to the room with the books.

Beckley stood in the middle of the room, looking at the bins.

"Liddie," he began thoughtfully, "before we decided these people were all deluded, we talked about them possibly being a theater group. As I recall, the reason we discounted that idea was because they were so good at being their characters. It seemed unlikely that there would be a group of such really talented actors who never slipped up in their roles.

"I'm wondering, the idea of it being a mass delusion, where they all so perfectly play the different people, and fit together so perfectly, well, is that any more logical? I mean, doesn't a delusion imply some sort of lack of awareness of reality or not being able to function in reality? So how adept would someone like that be at acting out a role? I really don't know... but I want to revisit the idea of a theater group."

Liddie laughed, "I'm getting whiplash! But I like where you're headed with this."

Beckley continued, "It also occurred to me — I don't know why I didn't remember it before — they don't really have sanitoriums anymore. When we wondered if this group escaped from a facility, well, now I'm thinking it's just not possible. Years and years ago, maybe, but nowadays, you wouldn't find that kind of arrangement. I think people with needs are treated more individually now. This was covered in one of my classes — an early class, so maybe that's why I didn't remember at first.

"But let's look at this idea of a theater group. What if they really are great actors? They could seamlessly play out their roles. The question is why would they be doing this? Something you said this morning keeps coming back to me. You wondered if these people just didn't like their previous lives and saw this as a fun alternative — maybe a temporary escape."

"That's right," Liddie interjected. "Like one of those meetup groups where people get together with common interests. Maybe they were all looking for some sort of acting activity."

Beckley continued. "Let me tell you a story. I had a cousin — Fred. Fred was extremely creative and kept exploring new ideas where he could express that creativity. He got into some of the older games for a while — maybe you've heard of them — I think Dungeons and Dragons was a popular one that was played with dice. But then he wanted more and became part of the whole LARPing movement."

Liddie looked confused, so Beckley explained.

"Live Action Role Playing. Groups of unrelated people would create different personas. Then they would come together on weekends and act as though they really were those personas. I only know all this because Fred would sometimes take me along as an observer. The rest of the family kind of regarded him as some sort of super geek, but I rather enjoyed the experience. I never personally wanted to role play, but it was fascinating to watch.

"The interesting thing is that Fred went on to create an extremely popular derivation of this whole LARPing thing. He has an island off the coast totally devoted to the game, where people come for a week and live totally in character the whole time. He must be a multimillionaire by now!

"But, to get back to this group here. Liddie, given these books, especially this *Barbro* one, I could totally see a LARPing type group reading the book, choosing characters, and just taking a week's vacation to live it out. Is it possible this book was printed and copies given to other far distant relatives? Maybe that's how they found it."

"This could be it, Beckley," Liddie answered. "And it would tie together the strange things, like when I first came, and Paula expressed confusion — I think she said something about not recalling any mention of my presence. And maybe when I did show up, they were happy to adapt and welcome me to be an observer, kind of like you being an observer of your cousin. So I'm an audience?

"That would make me feel a lot better in terms of feeling like I was being lied to, or that there was some sort of betrayal. I might still be able to regard the closeness and connection as genuine. I like this idea, Beckley!"

Chapter 21: An Awkward Conversation

∾ ❧ ∿

Liddie and Beckley looked up, hearing voices in the house.

"It's up to you, Liddie, if you want to ask them about this. I'm not saying you should or shouldn't, but if you want to ask questions, I'll support you." Beckley was happy that Liddie seemed the more logical choice to start any conversation.

They went into the living room, where Bronia and Mac were already resting in chairs near Paula and David. Adelle busied herself, putting some cookies on a plate. They could see Henry out the window tossing a ball for Elizabeth.

"Oh, good!" Paula said when she saw Liddie. "I wanted to remind you of the service this evening in the orchard. Remember, I mentioned it the other day? Well, it's not really a service as such, like most people are used to. But it is Sunday, and it's a nice time to stop and focus. We'll have some turkey sandwiches there, kind of like a picnic beforehand."

"Yes, thank you for the reminder!" Liddie answered sincerely, because with the new discoveries, she had forgotten all about it.

"You know what?" she added. "You all have been so nice. How about if Beckley and I make the sandwiches and bring them up?"

"Oh, thank you!" said Paula. "What a nice offer."

She motioned to the scene outside. "I love seeing Elizabeth running

151

around."

They all turned to watch for a few minutes until Elizabeth plopped herself down to rest, totally worn out. Henry came inside and helped himself to some cookies.

Liddie commented on how good the cookies were, then turned to Paula.

"Um, Paula, remember when I first got here, and we found that map in the other room?

"Why, yes!" Paula answered. "Wasn't that exciting?"

"It was. It was." Liddie said quickly. "But… today… Beckley and I were checking through the other bins, thinking of getting things packed up to take to my mom. And we found a book…"

Liddie stopped and turned suddenly to Beckley, saying brightly, "Beckley! Would you get that book please? Maybe bring it out here? Maybe we can all look at it."

He jumped up, relieved to be given something to do. He was down the hall and back before Liddie lost her nerve. He handed her the *Barbro* book, and she held it in her lap.

"Yes, this book." Liddie held it up for the others to see. "We were confused when we found it, because, well, there's no easy way to say this… but we started looking in the book, and well, we found your names in it…" Liddie's voice trailed off.

"Imagine that!" exclaimed Henry. "What's the book about?"

Liddie was confused that there was not a strong response from any of the others. Nor was there any acknowledgement that they knew about the book. Not even feigned surprise that they had been found out.

"This is kind of weird," Liddie thought to herself.

She began again. "Well, Henry, it appears to be about you all. And it seemed really odd to us that your names were in the book. And not just that, but the stories you tell at the campfire — those stories are described in this book. Bronia — how you described meeting Mac. And Mac — your whole story about Mrs. Holbrook and your poem… Adelle, Henry — everything is in there, the Oklahoma land rush and the whole sordid story about Osmund…"

Liddie faced each one as she mentioned their names. She expected to see some sort of acknowledgement. Even a sheepish admission that the truth had been discovered. But there was nothing.

She felt helpless. Turning to Beckley, she whispered, "Beckley, this is bizarre. What do I do now?"

Beckley stood up. He always thought better, more efficiently, on his feet. He picked up the book and thumbed through it several times before handing it to Paula. Paula smiled faintly as she took it and fingered the book's covers, almost lovingly.

Beckley didn't see Paula's expression. He was busy formulating how to proceed.

"So," he started. "As Liddie said, we are both confused. We've grown very fond of you all. I know how much Liddie, especially, has developed an attachment here. And even being here just a day or two, I feel it also.

"But you have to admit that it's not realistic that you describe yourselves as living in completely different time periods, some over a hundred years ago. And, to find this book, with the exact same descriptions and names... Well, we're just hoping someone might help us understand."

Beckley looked around hopefully, but no one volunteered an explanation. Paula was still thoughtfully fingering the book. Beckley barreled ahead.

"Look, Liddie and I have gone back and forth, trying to figure out who you are and why you're here. I won't go into detail about our different ideas. I'll just say that after finding this book, we believe that you all must have found it, also, and are pretending to be those people — the ones described in that book.

"And really," he felt himself talking faster and faster, something he knew from experience he did when nervous. "Really, it's okay! I've had experience with role-playing game groups myself! Not acting, but watching my cousin and others. It's a lot of fun. And it takes an incredible amount of skill to carry it off as well as you all are doing.

"But, I guess... as I said, we — Liddie and I — we've begun to care about you all. And I guess we want to know the real you. Who you are outside of the roles you're playing."

Beckley sat down, somewhat unhappy about his efforts to explain. Liddie reached over and squeezed his hand. Then, before Beckley could continue, she jumped in.

"David," she said, "you and Paula were the first ones I met here. You welcomed me. You told me that you would be gone before I needed you gone. Can you tell me what it is you are doing here?"

David looked straight into her eyes.

"Liddie," he said gently, "you need to know that we all love you. We love Beckley. You have brought the brightest light to our time here. An unexpected light for most of us, to be sure, but one that has shone on us and has given us much joy."

Liddie was surprised to feel warm tears cascading down her cheeks. She didn't try to figure out why she responded so strongly. She simply basked in the love she felt pouring in from David's words.

"But more than that, Liddie, I can't tell you."

David stood and placed his hands on Liddie's shoulders. Paula softly lay the book on a chair and joined him. Adelle reached over and squeezed her hand.

Bronia kissed her lightly on the cheek and said, "See you later at the service…"

Then they were all gone, out the door, leaving Liddie and Beckley alone in the room.

Liddie sat, still holding Beckley's hand. He pulled out his handkerchief and wiped away her tears. They were no closer to understanding.

But, they each wondered, did it matter?

Chapter 22: Pictures of a Family

Rousing himself, Beckley looked out the window at the setting sun. He and Liddie stepped out on the porch to watch the changing colors. They sat in the comfortable wicker chairs, gazing across the pond. Elizabeth plopped herself at their feet.

Liddie suddenly jumped up, remembering the service they had been invited to.

"Oh, look at the time! We need to get started on those turkey sandwiches." She added, "I guess this service will replace any campfire tonight, wouldn't you think?"

They headed inside, rummaged in the refrigerator, found sandwich makings and got to work. Twenty sandwiches: bread, mayo, turkey, cheese, lettuce, tomato, bread, repeat. Liddie found it a gratifying experience, working side by side with Beckley. There was a warm bond which seemed stronger after their afternoon encounter with the group.

"Actually, I'm going to eat one of these sandwiches right now," Liddie said. "Aside from that snack earlier, we haven't eaten much at all today. And with all the emotional upheaval, I'm not sure how much longer I can last."

"Sounds good," answered Beckley. "We need to talk about timelines, anyway. I told the firm that I would be gone for a week. So that gives me three, maybe four more days here. I'd like to help you pack up everything so you can head home before I leave. Does that fit in with your plans?"

Liddie placed their plates on the table. She hadn't looked ahead enough to see that there would be an ending of their time together. The thought was not a happy one.

"I guess so…" she sighed. "I suppose I'll also need to start thinking of what kind of job I can get. At least Mom and Dad live near a big city. There should be something related to botany that I can do."

The two continued discussing her different job possibilities, until Liddie glanced out the window and noticed how dark it had become.

"Oh no!" she exclaimed. "We're late — I'm sure that service has started! And we missed getting the sandwiches out there! Well, let's pack up what's left and get going. Paula said it would be in the orchard behind the house."

Beckley and Liddie found the group sitting under the mature fruit trees. They quickly walked up. Seeing that people still seemed to be visiting with each other, Liddie went ahead and handed out the sandwiches. Beckley found a pile of blankets, picked out one with a Mexican design, and spread it at the back edge of the orchard. Liddie opted for a fluffy one and wrapped herself in it as she sat down next to Beckley.

A quiet settled on the gathering. It was a peaceful quietness, with an air of expectation.

"Oh, look, Beckley!" Liddie spoke very quietly so as not to disturb the silence. "Fireflies! Aren't they beautiful?"

Beckley put his arm around Liddie's shoulders and drew her close. They sat, entranced with the sight. The beauty of the night with its twinkling star lights and blinking fireflies combined with the peaceful calm. Liddie nestled herself down into the warmth of Beckley's arm. She wondered if anything could be so wonderful as this night. But her reverie was interrupted when she saw a figure approaching.

"Beckley!" Liddie whispered, "It's him! The mysterious figure!"

A strange glow accompanied the figure. Liddie and Beckley watched with interest as he moved slowly to the far edge of the orchard. The figure stopped and raised his arms.

"Oh, my goodness!" Liddie thought. "He looks exactly like that statue of

Jesus. The one on the Overlook Hill!"

She watched as those in the group at the front sat quietly. David and Paula raised their hands toward the figure. Osmund bowed his head. James and Mary bent down in reverence. Others knelt.

Liddie began to feel the light weight of a cloud coming down around her like a warm mist.

Time passed.

Liddie's eyelids slowly opened. She was lying on her face, still wrapped up in the blanket. Fireflies continued their twinkling light show around her. The quiet peacefulness was still there, enveloping her as she slowly sat up.

She looked around for the others. They were all gone, save for Beckley, who she saw on his back about five feet away. The mysterious figure was gone also.

Liddie slowly sat up. She had nothing in her experience to help her understand what just happened. She recalled seeing the figure, and then feeling the cloud descending upon her. But then, all she could remember was immense peace. She assumed that she must have drifted off to sleep.

She had no idea of how much time had passed. No idea of when the others left. Yet it didn't seem important. She wanted to stay within this lingering quietude as long as possible, savoring it.

Beckley began stretching. Liddie watched his unhurried movement silently, not wanting to disturb his experience.

He sat up and shook his head. Then he shook it again, as if to clear his mind. He looked over at Liddie. Beckley's wide smile said it all — that he also had just had a most wonderful, unexplainable encounter. Liddie nodded at him, but neither spoke.

The two silently gathered their blankets and walked back. A gentle wave of goodbye was all that was needed as Beckley headed down to his hammock and Liddie entered the house. Each was then carried off into the best sleep of their lives.

The next morning, Beckley woke up late and headed up to the house. He could see Osmund and Henry fishing on the pond, and he waved at them.

Opening the house door, he called out, "Hello? Anyone here?"

From down the hallway, he heard Liddie call back, "I'm here, Beckley!"

He stopped to fill a cup from the coffeemaker and proceeded down the hall to the room where they had found the books. There didn't appear to be anyone else around.

Liddie was leaning back in the big leather desk chair, looking at a worn photo album in her lap. She got up to greet him, and the two embraced.

"Wasn't that the most incredible experience last night?" Beckley asked. "I'm still trying to process just what happened."

Liddie agreed, "I've thought about it, but you know what, I'm content to just accept it — to know that whatever it was, it was good."

"I think so," Beckley replied with a grin. "But I'm going to hold onto that feeling as long as I can!"

Liddie sat down again. She reached for the photo album.

"Beckley, I need to show you something."

Beckley was intrigued by her slow, calm demeanor. There was an edge to her voice, but she seemed to have deliberately slowed down what she was saying. He pulled over another bin so he could sit by her chair.

"I woke up early and couldn't get back to sleep. So I came back to this room, looking for more information on what's going on."

She opened the photo album. It was quite old, with many of the pictures falling out. Most of them were faded black and white photos, many with ragged edges. Liddie turned a few pages, found the one she wanted, and handed the book to Beckley.

He stared at the page. He looked back at Liddie. She sat, expressionless, staring at the same photo. He turned back to the picture, focusing in on every detail. He carefully removed it from the album, turned it over, examined the back, and set it down.

He breathed deeply. He picked up the photo again and examined it once more.

"Liddie," he said, "this is Mac and Bronia…. No question about it. It's old

and poor quality, but there is no mistaking them. I mean, look at his smile —
that is him! And Bronia, why this picture could have been taken yesterday!
But it's obviously quite old — what would you say? At least a hundred years
old? I can't say for sure, but it's definitely not been taken in the past ten
years."

"Wow! Look at them!" he continued. "He's dressed in his uniform, just like
she described seeing him at the circus. And the way she's laughing, while
her arm is wrapped around his arm — what a picture. He looks so proud,
walking with her."

Liddie maintained her calm demeanor. Perhaps the unusual happenings
had taken their toll and nothing could faze her anymore. Perhaps it was the
simple realization that there was no way possible they could continue to
explain away what was going on here. And being unexplainable, was the
best course to simply accept? She was leaning toward that acceptance.

"Here, let me show you the other pictures," she said, taking the book back
from Beckley. She turned a few pages, stopping at one with a couple he
instantly recognized as Stanley and Anna. They were dressed in what looked
to be their Sunday best. Her hair was pinned up in circles. Stanley stood
tall and straight beside her. Written in the border of the photo was the
identification, "Stanley and Anna Jez, 1944."

"Why, it's almost like time traveling!" Beckley said. "How can this be?"

"That's not all, Beckley." Liddie turned another page and showed him a
young family. He again easily recognized Stanley with his tall pouf of hair.
And Anna sat beside him in the picture obviously taken by a professional
photographer. They were surrounded by four young children.

He read from the description, "Bernice, Adam, Anna, Cecilia, Stanley,
Walter Jez, 1932." Those must be their children."

"Look closely at the first girl," prodded Liddie. "The one labeled Bernice,
maybe twelve years old. Does she remind you of anyone?"

Beckley peered harder at the picture, holding it to the light. "Wait a minute,"
he said, quickly turning pages back to the photo of Mac and Bronia. He held
the two photos close together, and a smile touched his lips.

"Do you think that's Bronia?" he asked.

Liddie nodded. She motioned to the book they had found yesterday.

"Before I found the photo album, I went through some more of that *Barbro* book. Bronia was the girl's original name. It's short for Bronislawa. Her father, who I assume is Stanley, changed her name to Bernice to fit in better in America. But, the book implied that Mac always liked to call her Bronia."

Beckley sat back. He was at a loss for even a suggestion of explanation. He simply shook his head in wonderment.

"I want to show you two more photos," Liddie said. "Then we can try to figure all this out."

"This one, here," she said, flipping the pages again. "I absolutely love this picture. You see the writing on it? 'Patrick Henry McKay, 1918'. And the woman behind him? That's Adelle!"

"Patrick Henry?" Beckley questioned.

"According to that Barbro book, that was his name, but he went by Henry. Don't you just love the way Adelle is standing behind him, hands on her hips? I could just see her holding a rolling pin, ready to get after Henry for something or other. And he — he's just sitting there without a care in the world. I mean, from what we know of them — at least the 'them' that we've been relating to here — this totally captures their personalities!"

Liddie continued leafing through the photo album, stopping to admire some of the pictures. But then she found the last one to show Beckley. It was another family picture, much older than the one of Stanley and Anna.

"Here, look," Liddie said. "This one is from 1896. It's labeled on the back, but let me point out who's who. This old woman here — she's Barbro. Now Barbro was the mother that Osmund told about, bringing him to America on the ship when he was five years old. Here on the left — this bearded man — that's Osmund. He's younger here than how we see him at the campfires, but his features are unmistakable."

Beckley nodded in agreement.

"In the middle, surrounded by how many children — eight? — is Sarah… she was beautiful, wasn't she? And down here at the lower right, that's Adelle, maybe fourteen years old. But Beckley, on the back, the notation gives her full name. Liddie Adelle!'"

Liddie didn't know why that realization gave her such joy. She still wasn't totally sure that this book related her own ancestry. But she took great delight in seeing her name joined with Adelle's. Whatever the connection she might have to Adelle — the one in the book, or this person she'd come to know as Adelle — she was happy.

Beckley slowly ran his finger over the photo. Then he reached over and touched Liddie's face, very gently brushing back her hair. "You have her eyes, Liddie."

"Let's stop so I can figure out the relationships here," Beckley said. "I need a framework. This photo of Osmund and Sarah — that seems to be the oldest one? Their daughter was Liddie, who married Henry. Now who is Henry — where did he come from?"

"I remember that from the first day," said Liddie. "Adelle identified James and Mary as Henry's parents." She found a paper and pencil and started to draw out a rough chart.

"Okay, so who were Henry and Adelle's children?" Beckley continued.

"Let me look at some more of these pictures," said Liddie. "Maybe I can find one of them with kids.

"Oh, my goodness…. Look at this, Beckley! Here is Adelle, much older. It looks like she is peeling potatoes on a ramshackle old porch. This young child at her feet — someone has written in 'Mac'! What an adorable little boy, with all those blond curls. He talked about the poverty where he grew up. You can really see it in the worn down house and their clothes."

"So then, does that give us everybody?" David asked, beginning to count people on his fingers. "Mac married Bronia, and Bronia's parents were Stanley and Anna."

"But wait," Liddie interjected. "Who are Paula and David?"

"Didn't a Paula write the *Barbro* book?" Beckley asked.

Liddie mused, "Yesterday, when we were talking with them, Paula did seem quite moved when you handed the book to her. You didn't see her face, but it was much more reaction than I would have expected. I wonder if she's the author. Here, let me see…" She leafed through the front of the book, finally stopping at a preface. It had been stuck to the title page.

She read, "'I owe a great debt of gratitude to my father and mother, Emerald Raleigh McKay and Bernice Jez McKay. They inspired me by their lives and examples.'"

Chapter 23: If You Came This Way

"Well," said Beckley. "So I guess we have the relationships figured out. Paula's father is Emerald Raleigh. They must have called him 'Mac' because of his last name, McKay. And Paula married David.

"But," he continued, "it still doesn't explain this particular group of people living here."

Liddie began, "I've been thinking about that. Remember I said I was content to just accept all this, even though I couldn't understand it? Provided, of course, that it was good. I am convinced, especially after that experience last night, that it is good.

"So, I don't know. Maybe sometimes we don't need to understand fully. My Mom and Dad used to say that when I struggled — just do what you know is right, and let God take care of the rest. Like Jehoshaphat in the Valley of Blessing."

Beckley thought for a moment. "Could be you're right. Maybe we've been missing the whole point of what's going on here. I'm thinking back to our conversation on that Overlook Hill. We both noticed that the people here seem to talk a lot about God. And even you and I, who probably haven't even thought about God for years — we started talking about experiences we had where God was present."

He continued, "Taken all together, I think we have to ask, is there something supernatural going on here? And by supernatural, I mean basically something we can't explain. So, by that definition, I guess, yes — the answer is yes.

"But more than that: is it something supernatural about God? Is this a place, in time or space or both, where we need to pay special attention to what's going on, because maybe, just maybe, God is trying to reach us?"

Beckley surprised himself with his ease of talking about God and the supernatural. But he surprised himself even more when an old poem popped into his head. It was another one he had memorized because it sounded beautiful when he encountered it in his high school literature course. Now, though, there seemed to be more of a reality to it.

"Liddie," he said softly, "listen to this poem I'm remembering from long ago."

He began slowly, enunciating carefully, allowing the words to soak in, their meaning penetrating years of apathy toward God.

If you came this way,
   Taking any route, starting from anywhere,
   At any time or at any season,
   It would always be the same.

You would have to put off sense and notion.
   You are not here to verify,
   Instruct yourself, or inform curiosity or carry report.
   You are here to kneel where prayer has been valid.

And prayer is more than an order of words,
   The conscious occupation of the praying mind,
   Or the sound of the voice praying...

Beckley stopped. "It goes on," he said. "It talks about how we can learn lessons about God from stories of those long dead — those who have gone before us. It's quite a beautiful poem — a bit long. I believe it's labeled as mystical poetry because it carries really deep thoughts about God. T. S. Eliot was the poet."

But Liddie wasn't ready to talk about the author and what type of poem it was.

"Beckley, let me hear it again!" she pleaded.

He recited the poem again, this time even more slowly.

Liddie repeated one line.

You are here to kneel where prayer has been valid.

Again she repeated it. And once again.

"Beckley, this is so beautiful! It's like God is talking directly to us! Like the poem says, we don't need to verify — to explain any of this. What we need to do is receive, to recognize that God is here, for whatever reason he chose to be here at this point in time. And we need to embrace that presence now.

"Because I'm sure that's what it was last night, Beckley. That was God's presence! Beckley, that mysterious figure? It was Jesus…"

Beckley grabbed Liddie's hand, carried away in the excitement. Neither of them quite knew how to respond to this new revelation of God. Beckley lifted his eyes up and began talking, talking to God as if he was there with them. Which, of course, he was.

"I don't know how to begin, God. How do I pray? Here we've been so wrought up trying to figure out if these people were delusional, squatters, whatever. And you've had it all under control all this time. You must have orchestrated this whole experience.

"God, I feel such, such utter contentment. Like, how could I worry about anything? You are here. You are in control."

"Yes," Liddie added. "And you love us, God."

The two sat quietly — neither knowing how long it was. Neither caring about the time.

Later that afternoon, Beckley and Liddie started off on a hike to the old homesite. Liddie wanted to document more areas with photos.

Their path took them through the Wetland. A wild profusion of mosses covered the fallen logs and the open ground of the trail. Liddie had never seen so many shades of green. Beckley found the tiny plants fascinating and several times bent down to get a closer look at them. Liddie explained the difference between the mosses and the lichens that covered the live trees.

"The fact that we're seeing so much moss and so many different kinds of lichens means the ecosystem here is productive and beneficial to wildlife. See, every plant has value in the right place.

"Oh, look at this over here, Beckley!" Liddie bent down to pick up a rotting branch in their pathway. It had the pale green lichens, but also patches of a type of hairy green growth. Beckley touched it with interest.

"This is old man's beard!" Liddie exclaimed with great excitement. "It's hard to find because mainly it grows on limbs high in a tree. But you can see that this branch recently fell down, bringing the lichen with it. It's rare, being susceptible to air pollution. So, another indication of the healthy atmosphere here. I've read that the American Indians used it in a number of medicinal applications."

"Liddie," Beckley replied, "I love listening to you talk about plants. Your knowledge is so great, but what I really love the most is your passion. You start talking about these mosses and your whole face lights up."

"And Liddie," Beckley continued, "when your face lights up like that, why, you look just like a beautiful woodland nymph!"

Beckley intended the statement as a compliment, but he was suddenly struck by the realization that he didn't actually know the definition of a 'nymph.' He became quite concerned that it might mean something more than simply a beautiful woman, and feared that he might have inadvertently insulted Liddie. That was the last thing he wanted to do.

He began stammering, "I mean, uh, Liddie, I mean, I don't mean… I don't know…"

Liddie looked at him, confused. She hadn't even heard the "woodland nymph" part. She was fixated on "beautiful." But as she was still trying to understand what Beckley was talking about, she spied another log with a huge old man's beard on it. She bent down to pick it up.

"Liddie! FREEZE!" Beckley shouted.

Liddie stopped in mid reach, not even daring to turn her head.

"Liddie! There's a snake! Don't move! He's right down there — near that log. Don't move. I'll get it."

Beckley quickly found a long stick, and bringing it stealthily to the log, he prepared to thrash it on the ground, hoping to make the snake move away from Liddie. His eye was glued to the snake as he smacked the ground just behind the creature. Then again! Over and over again, thrash after thrash, Beckley pummeled that spot of ground.

Totally out of breath, he stopped for an inspection. It looked like the snake hadn't moved. "How could that be?" he thought. He gently poked the snake with the stick. Still no movement. Another poke. No movement.

A sinking feeling began to form in Beckley's stomach. He tried to look at Liddie out of the corner of his eyes, but couldn't quite see her face. Did she know that he had just made an embarrassing spectacle of himself? He hoped not. But there was no denying it now. The "snake" appeared to be nothing more than a tree root.

"Beckley," Liddie whispered. "What's going on? I can't see the snake. Is it gone?"

Beckley was momentarily tempted to simply answer, "Yes, it's gone!" but he fought off the temptation.

"Uh, Liddie," he said instead, "I may have been mistaken. You see… If you come over here and look…" Here Beckley noticed that Liddie was still frozen in her stance. He stopped immediately and reached for her hands.

"Oh, I am so sorry!" he said. "It was just a root. You must have been so frightened, with me making such a fuss yelling about a snake that wasn't even there, and you trying to stay so still. I am just so sorry. I don't know why I didn't recognize that it was just an old tree root!"

Beckley continued berating himself, stopping only when he felt a gentle pressure on his cheek. Liddie's hand was softly stroking his face. His eyes met hers. He found no condemnation of his actions.

"Beckley," Liddie whispered, "you have done nothing wrong. You, Beckley, were my hero. You thought I was in danger, and you rescued me. You protected me. Beckley, you were my knight in shining armor, swooping in to carry me away."

She gazed up at him in total adoration.

Now it was Beckley's turn to melt inside. Not exactly a swoon, but definitely a melting of what he thought were his strong male defenses. He felt himself becoming putty in this woman's hands.

Beckley wrapped his arms around Liddie, encircling her. She tossed her hair back and continued her gaze of total adoration. She closed her eyes, and there, surrounded by the lush green mosses and lichens, Beckley and Liddie kissed.

Time stood still as they were transported to an entirely new level of relationship. And when the kiss was done, Liddie's eyes fluttered open. She lovingly looked up at Beckley.

"Beckley," she said, "thank you for rescuing me."

Beckley returned her gaze, shook his head and replied, "Thank you, Liddie, for taking me to the moon."

Chapter 24: Henry Gets Out

With a sigh, Liddie and Beckley resumed their walk. Only now, their hands were firmly clasped, their fingers intertwined. Each one held the delicious anticipation of newness that this kiss brought to their relationship.

The path led out of the Wetland, through the Bottomland and up the hill to the Homesite. Liddie found it strange that they hadn't encountered any of the others on the walk. As they walked past a huge cedar log bench, she was glad to hear voices in the distance up ahead.

"Henry? Henry? What are you doing in there, Henry?" A man's voice was calling.

Beckley quickened his pace, concerned that Henry might be in trouble. Rounding the bend, they saw Osmund on his knees, peering into the ground. Before they could get close enough to see what was happening, a bellowed answer replied.

"I fell in! What do you mean, what am I doing in here? You think I got in this cistern on purpose?" It was, indeed, Henry calling up from the deep hollow of a partially filled cistern.

Osmund looked up as Liddie and Beckley approached.

"I was out looking for deer tracks," he said, "and I heard all this commotion — splashing, yelling — I couldn't tell what was going on!"

Henry called out, "Hey! What about me? Is anybody going to help me?"

Beckley and Liddie got on their hands and knees and crawled up to the edge of the cistern. It was about six feet wide and had a rough rim of stone around the edge, but they didn't want to stand too close for fear of ending up inside with Henry.

The cistern looked to be about twelve feet deep, with water covering the lower third. Henry did not appear to be in danger of drowning, although he certainly must be cold and he definitely seemed bothered.

Osmund called out, "Henry, I don't have a rope with me. But I'll tell you what. When I was building cisterns, I developed a special way of leaving toe holds in between the rocks. Others thought it was a good idea, so maybe this one was built that way. Run your hands along the rocks all around the sides. Feel any holes?"

There was a bit of silence, punctuated by "Yuk!" and "What was that?"

Finally, Henry yelled, "Hey, I found one!" And then, "Here's another one. Thanks, Osmund!"

More grunts and some splashing ensued until a few minutes later, Henry's wet and muddy head popped up out of the cistern. Osmund and Beckley grasped his arms and together they pulled him the rest of the way out.

Henry plopped down a safe distance from the opening.

"Someone ought to cover that, for sure!" he said. "I was just walking along, looking up at the birds, and 'whoops' there I was! Good thing I didn't break any bones!"

Liddie pulled some huge leaves from a nearby mulberry tree and tried to wipe some of the mud off Henry.

"We need to get you back to your house and into dry clothes," she said.

Seeing that Henry was beginning to shiver, they all agreed and quickly started off to Glen McKay, hoping Adelle would be home.

As soon as they got close enough, Beckley began calling, "Adelle! Adelle!" She came out from the garden area and started running toward them.

"Henry! What in the world happened to you? You were supposed to be delivering some bread to your parents!"

"I got out!" Henry shouted back. "Adelle, I got out! I nearly died, Adelle, but I got out!"

Henry was realizing that this would be a great story to retell. It would be interesting to see how much embellishment the story carried the next time Liddie and Beckley heard it.

Osmund stayed to help out, while Liddie and Beckley continued their walk. Turning onto the top of Carn Ingli, they saw the campfire area. It wasn't long until dusk, so they decided to stop and see if there would be another storytelling time. Liddie had again packed snack supplies in her backpack, and they sat down to a picnic on the hill.

A few minutes later, Beckley swallowed the last bite of his peanut butter cracker and sighed deeply. He watched as the first fireflies of the evening began their rhythmic blinkings.

"Liddie," he began. "I've been having such a wonderful time here with you. Despite all the weirdness and drama, it has been so much fun. And discovering that God is such a big part of what's going on — well, how amazing is that?"

She nodded contentedly, cleaning up the last signs of their picnic. "I know what you mean, Beckley. This time, just these past few days …well, I think I would call it transformative for me. What a word! I would never think to use that word for myself, except, now, it fits…"

Beckley felt a rush of love — was it really love? — as he looked at Liddie. It was certainly more than he felt when he jumped out to hug her at the gate. And that had been pretty intense, he thought to himself.

He leaned over and lightly kissed Liddie on her lips. Her eyes fluttered open and met his in a dreamy gaze.

"Oh, Liddie!" she thought. "You're swooning again!"

Paula and Bronia ambled up the pathway, closely followed by David and Mac, who quickly set to work laying a new campfire. Beckley jumped up to help them. Liddie was glad to see that no one indicated any uncomfortableness due to the previous day's conversation. Quite the contrary, Paula and Bronia entered into an animated discussion with her about the wetland area with its mosses and lichens.

As the talk of lichens slowed, Paula looked curiously at Liddie, who had been trying to hide her sidelong glances at Beckley.

Paula quietly ventured, "Liddie… you really like him, don't you?"

Liddie turned, looking a bit surprised. Blushing, she replied, "Does it show that much?"

Paula and Bronia smiled, first at each other, then at Liddie.

"Girl," Bronia said, "those are the same eyes I was making at my Mac when he took me to the Palmer House!"

Liddie nodded, then blurted out, "Can I tell you something?"

Without waiting for an answer she rushed right in.

"He kissed me!"

Her eyes glistened, full of stars, as she nodded emphatically in response to Bronia's and Paula's wide-eyed, grinning faces.

"Tell us more!" insisted Paula.

"Quick!" Bronia exclaimed.

"He kissed me — right there in the middle of all the lichens and mosses! We had been walking along that beautiful wetland path, and I bent down to pick up a branch with some old man's beard — that's a kind of lichen — and Beckley saved me from a snake. Well, he thought it was a snake. It was actually a tree root. But he thought I was in danger, and he rescued me! And then, well, you know how one thing leads to another… I ended up in his arms, and it… it… was just so, so, oh, just so amazing…"

Liddie trailed off, eyes closed, beginning to swoon right there in front of them!

"She's got it bad!" Paula whispered to Bronia.

The rest of the group straggled in. Beckley had finished helping with the fire and rejoined Liddie. They heard snippets of the good-natured conversations.

"Did you hear about Henry?"

"Yeah, I heard he went and got himself into trouble again!"

"Anna! When are you going to make more kolaches?"

"Well, now, when are you bringing me some apricots?"

"Everyone, did you hear how I almost DIED? And how I got out?"
   "Henry, why don't you tell us all about it. Again…"
   "What I heard was that Osmund rescued you!"

"Grass is growing."
   "And flowers, too! I love this time of year."

Liddie mentally counted down those members of the group who hadn't yet given stories at the campfires. She realized that Paula and David were the only two who hadn't spoken.

"What might they talk about?" she wondered.

There wasn't long to wait. Once the fire started burning and crackling in earnest, Paula and David stood up together and made their way forward. Their hands were clasped tightly together.

David began.

"We — Paula and I — want to talk about an extraordinary trip we took many, many years ago. Not so much a trip, as a pilgrimage. That's what we called it — The Pilgrimage.

"But first, we need to sing Happy Birthday to someone! I know it's not today, but, Liddie, don't you have a birthday coming up next week?"

Liddie was shocked. She couldn't remember saying anything about her birthday to anyone — even Beckley. But David was exactly right. Perplexed, she chose not to question, but instead gave in to the mystery of what was happening. So she laughed, waved her hand high in the air, and shouted, "Yes, that's me! Twenty-two!"

Shouts of "Happy Birthday!" came from all around, followed by a rousing chorus of the song. Liddie was secretly pleased, for even though she normally downplayed her birthday, it somehow seemed right to enjoy a celebration with this group.

When the singing was over, David began again.

"When our grandkids were young, I used to make jokes with them all the time. Perhaps too often; the younger ones learned early on to groan and confide in one another, 'Grandpa joke...'

"Especially when I would start talking about mustard. Do you know how many different ways mustard can be inserted into a conversation?"

Henry yelled out, "Mustard!" Adelle turned to shush him, but Mary had already taken care of it. Everyone else chuckled.

David went on. "I also wrote poems for the grandkids' birthdays. Silly poems. Lots of grandpa jokes. They seemed to enjoy them.

"Along with the jokes, I always included a reference to God's plans in their lives, and an encouragement to follow that plan.

"Liddie, you're not technically my granddaughter, but in honor of your upcoming birthday, I wrote a poem for you."

Liddie immediately sensed a change in the atmosphere. Surprised and touched, she sat up higher, listening more intently and watching David with expectation.

He smiled and continued. "I borrowed a couple of lines from a poem that I actually did write for one of the grandkids, but the rest are for you, Liddie."

He struck a pose and began reading from a paper in his hand.

Liddie is a botanist. A granny-woman, she.
  Look out for the lichens that are growing on that tree!
  God has plans for Liddie, plans so wonderful,
  To make her life amazing, to fill her heart so full.
  She's kindly and she's curious, she's pretty and she's smart.
  To think of what she can become just warms my dear old heart.
  We haven't known her very long, our newly precious Liddie,
  To think we'll keep on knowing her just makes me downright giddy!

Liddie and Beckley looked at each other with delight. She couldn't think of a better present for a birthday. Impulsively, she jumped up, ran to David and gave him a big hug.

Beckley filed this new information away in his memory — "Liddie's birthday, Liddie's birthday, Liddie's birthday. I need to get a present! Where can I get a present out here? Oh my, oh my! I'm not used to this!"

175

Chapter 25: The Pilgrimage

After Liddie was settled back in her seat beside Beckley, David started his story.

"I said we wanted to talk about the Pilgrimage. Paula and I — we were at a point in our lives where so much had happened, so many challenges, so much negative force coming against us, that we had to retreat completely from our regular lives.

"Some of you know that I'm a minister of the gospel. My entire life was dedicated to preaching and teaching about God. And it was the most rewarding life I could ever imagine. But at this particular time, following a particularly hard few years, we needed a break.

"We settled on the idea of a pilgrimage to find God. Not because he was lost, and not because we had lost contact with him. Indeed, God, and our reliance on him, was the only thing that saw us through those years. This pilgrimage was because we so strongly sensed our need for more of God — to know him on a deeper level."

David looked over at Paula, who picked up the story line.

"So we did lots of research, and finally settled on the idea of visiting 'thin places.' James and Mary, you might be familiar with the concept, because a lot of them are in Ireland. And Ireland was one of the places we planned to visit — along with Turkey, Wales, and Scotland."

James nodded his head and whispered something to Mary.

Paula continued, "A thin place is a place where there has been a special connection with God, where the ancient saints had felt his presence strongly. Sometimes they built chapels or even monasteries to mark them. The thin place is where the veil between heaven and earth seems thin and pulled back, and one can experience God easily. What we needed was that deep, healing experience of God.

"So we started off. First we visited one of our sons and his family in Turkey. Then it was on to Ireland. We were blessed to have another son with us on this part, and our daughter — she was a joy to have on the entire trip."

David picked up the story.

"We drove a small motorhome around Ireland, north and south for three weeks, focused mainly on visiting ancient Christian sites. At certain times we were very aware of the presence of spiritual entities, both godly and ungodly. We had experiences that neither one of us could explain. But, we came to realize that it was okay. The things of God can be mysterious.

"On Tara, there was such an overwhelming sense of God's love. The Hill of Slane also held God's presence, but in a different sense — it was holy, and powerful, but at rest, almost like a sleeping lion. And on a climb to St. Columba's Well in Glencolumcille, and again in Iona, our daughter had visions of angels.

"Paula, didn't you also see flames of fire on that Glencolumcille hike?"

Paula nodded and smiled as she remembered. "Yes. Some of those places were so intense, it was as if God himself had his arms around me — holding me and loving me.

"And remember the ancient turf labyrinth, David? We all walked it in silence. But the angels — they were there, surrounding us. And when we all reached the middle and the three of us hugged, there was such an exquisite sense of God's love and his arms enfolding us. It was like… I never wanted to leave that moment in time."

Paula's eyes glistened with tears as she gazed into the fire.

"So Ireland accomplished its purpose," David said. "Our eyes were widened to ancient paths and thin places, and it opened an appreciation for the history of the saints — those who had gone on before. It forced us to slow down, walking pathways with more awareness.

"But," he went on, "there were also other places that held a very strong sense of evil. We dealt with those situations through the name of Jesus. We learned to always be discerning as we sought God.

"The encounters with God are what stayed with us. Iona, a tiny island off the coast of Scotland, was a high point."

"Oh, yes!" exclaimed Paula. "I could feel God there without even trying. It was the most amazing experience."

David continued, "We were there over Easter weekend. What a glorious celebration. Hurts and frustrations put to death on Good Friday, then rising to a fresh new life of faith and possibility on Easter."

Paula interrupted. "That was the place where I heard a voice telling me I was healed from that stomach issue — remember, David? It was God."

"Yes, it was," David replied thoughtfully. "When you told us the story there on Iona, you were positively glowing!

"And I remember our walk to the Bay at the Back of the Ocean, and how it seemed like we wanted to spend eternity there."

Paula reached out to hold his hand. "And how you found that enormous piece of green Iona marble and carried it back for me as a remembrance! I can't believe how much you have loved me in so many little ways through our lives!

"Oh, and how could I leave out Wales — the hike up Carn Ingli — that's the namesake of this Carn Ingli hill. It's a mountain by the sea there in Wales. It was named for St. Brynach, who communed with angels on the top. Just a total feeling of timelessness, otherworldliness."

"Whoa," Liddie whispered to Beckley. "So that's what the name means. A place to commune with angels! Maybe we were right in thinking that God is doing something here..."

After a brief silence, Paula began again.

"David, you know, we've been talking about being with God, and that was the most important part of the Pilgrimage, but do you remember that castle? Oh, my goodness! What a night! I still think it was about the stupidest idea

I've ever had!"

Paula gestured toward the group with upraised hands. "Okay, let me set the stage. This was a genuine Scottish castle. Built in… was it the fifteenth century? I think so. This was our one big splurge on the trip — to spend the night in a real castle. It was so impressive as we toured the grounds, exploring the nooks and crannies and eating dinner in the gigantic hall. We wrapped up the evening with a chess game played with massive pieces in another great hall. I think we were the only people there, certainly the only ones on that floor.

"All that was great until… night fell. Our daughter had a bedroom at one end of the great hall. David and I were in another huge old bedroom up the spiral stone stairs at the other end. We made sure that our daughter could call us if she wanted to, and then we went to bed.

"Ten minutes passed. Fifteen minutes. The phone rang. Yes, she had decided that she wanted to come over to our bedroom. So David left to go find her and bring her back.

"I was left all alone, in this huge room, surrounded by all these medieval furnishings, at night, remembering all the history we had just learned about the place — you know, all that horrid stuff they used to do in the Middle Ages!

"I lasted one minute, maybe two, by myself. And then, honestly, I literally leaped across the bed, tore out of there and practically flew across the great hall to find David!"

Paula paused while the group laughed and exclaimed, imagining the scene. Then she continued.

"After we all got back to the one bedroom, maybe it was my imagination, but I tend to think it was an actual residual spiritual presence of so many who had suffered in that castle. I kept sensing weird things and presences until David finally told everything to stop and go away in the name of Jesus. And they did! The name of Jesus — that's all it took!"

David nodded at the memory. "Yes… the name of Jesus."

He continued. "You know, I've always seen this place — this Valley of Blessing — as a continuation of our pilgrimage. There we experienced thin places and retraced the steps of the saints who knew God so deeply. Here, we come closer to creating those thin places ourselves, by our own and each other's worship, community, and efforts at holiness. God is love. And by experiencing that love more fully, is it possible that a thin place develops within ourselves? Does the Valley of Blessing become a dwelling place for God's presence? Maybe a human attempt to recreate the Garden of Eden, as much as that is possible here on earth. A place where we walk with God in the cool of the evening…"

David's intensity and obvious yearning was palpable in the words he spoke. Liddie, as she watched him, could see out of the corner of her eye the outline of the mysterious figure beyond, on the edge of the clearing. It seemed to her that the figure and David moved in unison.

Paula responded to David. "I love you so much, David! Your heart is the closest to God of anyone I know. That's why I fell in love with you — your connection to God and your desire to find him in every way possible. Thank you for continuing to pursue God."

She turned back toward the group.

"There's something a little bit personal I want to share with you all. When David celebrated thirty years in ministry, our kids wrote a song for him. This is the chorus:

You held God's hand
  You sought his face
  You begged him, take me
  To your secret place.
  You asked God to tell you
  What to do.
  Now I ask God to let me be
  More like you.

"What could be a greater testimony," she continued, "than your children seeing the honesty, integrity, and passion for God in your life? And, in the seeing, want their lives to be like yours?"

Another silence enveloped the group, until broken by Paula again.

"I want to say something more about our time in Turkey. One of the amazing experiences was being able to have our daughter's high school graduation — she was homeschooled, as were all our kids — in the ruins of the ancient library in Ephesus. Of course, it was a moving ceremony in many ways. But part of what I said to her comes back to me. And I think it would be a nice way to end this evening.

"I gave her a brooch or pin depicting two horses running together. One is slightly ahead of the other one. And I told her that throughout most of her life, I was the lead horse, guiding her, nudging her on to find her pathways. But now, at her graduation, she had pulled ahead of me. She was running free, running the race. And you know, parts of a verse come to me, but I can't remember all of it. David, my Bible answer man, I know you can recite it — would you? The one on running the race?"

David nodded. "The one from Hebrews? Hebrews 12, I believe — a good one. And I think it applies to everything we've been saying."

Looking into the eyes of those gathered, he spoke the words.

"Therefore, since we are surrounded by so great a cloud of witnesses, let us also lay aside every weight and sin which clings so closely, and let us run with endurance the race that is set before us."

Chapter 26: Pursuers

Next morning, Liddie awoke to a strange sound. *Slap, slap, slap!* It was Elizabeth. The big St. Bernard stood by the bed, her jowls flapping back and forth as she shook her head. Liddie was amazed at how far out the jowls swung to each side. She even thought she saw a bit of drool fly onto the wall as Elizabeth continued to shake.

Tempted to simply pull the covers over her head, Liddie thought better of it and stretched in the warm blankets. Then she addressed Elizabeth.

"I guess I haven't been playing with you much, have I?"

Elizabeth stopped shaking and did her best imitation of perking her ears up. But her ears being so droopy, as well as her eyes and, basically, her entire face, they didn't move much. All Liddie saw was the same face she saw every time she looked at the big dog — a slightly sad, floppy mass of hairy brown and white wrinkles, highlighted by those huge eyes with their sagging lids. She rubbed Elizabeth's ears a bit absentmindedly.

Her thoughts went back to the night before. There was so much to think about. And now, looming over it all, was the knowledge that whatever this time had been, it was drawing to a close.

She remembered the conversation a few days before when she and Beckley talked about the timeline, and how he would need to head back to work.

"Would that be tomorrow?" she wondered. "Or the next day?"

Liddie grew pensive thinking about Beckley leaving. She had never imagined when she left the internship how this week would develop. It was supposed to be a simple stop for taking pictures. But here she was, thrust into a most unexplainable time, and surrounded by a new group of people who felt more like family than anyone except her mom and dad.

And Beckley! Well, who could have expected the intensity of that?

Liddie knew she liked Beckley back at the internship, and she knew how much she had grown to rely on him during these past few days, trying to decipher what was going on. But that kiss yesterday, in the wetland, surrounded by the vibrant new growth of spring, had taken her to a whole different level. She felt new stirrings in her soul, her mind, her body.

Liddie wondered, "What will happen when Beckley leaves? New York is so far away, and he'll be immersed in his new job. How can I leave this relationship, after discovering just how deeply I feel for him?"

She got up and opened the window blinds. Beckley was still asleep in his hammock by the pond. She gazed at him a moment through the window.

"Oh! I know," she suddenly cried out loud, knowing that no one was in the room except Elizabeth. "I'm going to make an omelete! Beckley probably doesn't even know if I can cook! Come to think of it, I'm really not sure if I can cook, myself, but how hard can it be? Maybe Paula is in the kitchen and can help."

Liddie dressed quickly and headed down to the other side of the house. Paula wasn't there. Nor was David. She peered into the other rooms, but there was no sign of them. She frowned slightly at not finding them, realizing a sudden fear as she remembered David's first words about how they would be gone before she needed them gone. She shook it off, not wanting to think about that possibility.

Instead, she busied herself making a pleasant clatter in the kitchen, opening and closing cabinets, finding bowls, searching the refrigerator for anything that might go into an omelete, and most importantly, looking for a cookbook. Hidden behind cans of beans in the pantry, she spied a tattered copy of *The Joy of Cooking*. Liddie recognized it as one like her mom had, grabbed it up, and quickly found a recipe for omelets. She sat down at the table to study it.

The door creaked and she looked up, expecting to see Paula.

"Why hello there, Miss Chef! What are you whipping up for breakfast?"

It was Beckley. Liddie's heart fluttered unexpectedly, but quite insistently. She jumped up and ran over to him. His arms opened wide as he laughingly embraced her. There was no question in either of their minds how they saw each other now.

"Oh Beckley, I wanted to surprise you with an incredible breakfast! But Beckley, I'm so sorry… I honestly don't know how to cook! I so wanted you to be impressed by my skills… You must be so disappointed in me. I mean, what girl doesn't know how to cook!"

"Liddie, Liddie, Liddie…" he murmured, caressing her face. "I don't care if you can't cook. The person I'm interested in is inside you — it's who you are. Cooking — that's a skill anybody can learn. And if you decide you want to learn, why, I am convinced that you will be the most incredible chef ever!"

Liddie felt her eyes close, mainly in reaction to the pure bliss of listening to Beckley's voice. She relaxed in his arms, simply absorbing his warmth and tenderness.

"So!" Beckley spoke again. "Suppose we make this omelet together."

"Yes! Look here, I've found a recipe." Liddie reached for the book.

"Well, actually," Beckley said, "let's just see what I can do from memory. I worked part-time in the college cafeteria and one of my specialties was the breakfast bar. Looks like you've gotten out the right utensils and ingredients."

"Is there anything this man can't do?" thought Liddie to herself, as she reached for a bowl.

The omelet was delicious, made even more so by their shared cooking adventure. Leaving the dishes soaking, Liddie and Beckley refilled their coffee cups and relaxed on the front porch. The pond sparkled in the morning sun. Every now and then a big bass jumped up, catching a dragonfly. Liddie watched the mini waves ripple from the jump outwards to the pond edges.

"I've been thinking, Beckley," she said. "Last night, do you remember how David talked about not needing to understand everything about what God was doing? Isn't that the same thing we were saying the day before? That it was okay not to know how to explain what was going on here?

"And David said he was a preacher — imagine that! I've never really known a preacher. He does... seem very nice, though... Anyway, he's a preacher. But he implied that he didn't know everything. Like, how can a preacher not know everything about God?"

Liddie shook her head in confusion, then continued, "But he talked about wanting 'more' of God. The funny thing is, I kind of know what he was talking about... in that service, the one in the orchard... it was such a surreal experience. The sense I felt there, of... of, I guess it was God's presence, of him being there, well... I think I would like to have more of that experience. Do you know what I'm saying?"

"I do, Liddie. I do." Beckley nodded. "I don't understand any of it. I can't explain it. But, you know, I believe we have been part of something remarkable here. What was it they called it last night? A thin place. Yes — a thin place. What I've been feeling here could be described that way. If all of this is about God, which I believe it is, then he is present here, just like in all of those places in Ireland.

"But why?" He trailed off into silence.

"Liddie," he began again. "Can I share something really personal?"

She looked over, a bit hesitant, not knowing exactly what to expect. Liddie liked where their relationship was going, but she wasn't quite sure she was ready for deep, dark secrets. However, she answered in the only way she could, in their blossoming intimacy.

"Of course, Beckley!"

"I listened to Paula talking about David last night," he started. "About how he pursued God. And their kids — Liddie, their kids wanted to be just like him. Do you know how unusual that is in today's world? I mean, I love my Dad, but he's got all kinds of faults! Why, there was one year he tried to get me to cheat on my taxes! I definitely do not want to be just like him. Certainly I admire him in some ways — he works hard, and that kind of stuff. And I'm grateful to him for raising me. But as for a moral compass? No...

"But that song! David's kids wrote a song about how he sought God. Just let that sink in. He must have actually lived out, every day, the things he taught — honesty, integrity, and the biggest one — pursuing God. And, he must have made the kids feel loved, by him and by God, through it all.

"I realized, Liddie, that I had planned my whole life out, and there was no place in it for God. My plans were all about me — law school, getting the right job, making me happy. So, Liddie, last night, as I lay in my hammock gazing at the stars, I asked God to take over my life. I asked him to make me more like David, and ultimately, more like Jesus. Liddie, I want to pursue God."

Liddie's hand reached for his. Their eyes met.

"Beckley," she softly answered, "last night, I did the same thing. I told God that I want to pursue him, too."

Beckley impulsively grabbed her up. This time in their embrace, they both felt the warm tears of joy tumbling down their cheeks.

Chapter 27: Floating on Love

"I feel, Beckley, like I've been transformed," Liddie said. "There's that word again — but it's like I'm not the same person I was when I left the internship. And I'm afraid, Beckley. Afraid that it's all going to end. I mean, I'll be leaving. You'll be leaving…"

Liddie looked up sideways at Beckley to see what reaction he might have to that statement, but he was gazing out at the pond. So she continued.

"And I'm worried. I haven't seen any of the others this morning. Normally, there is someone around. But this morning, the coffee wasn't even started! I'm worried that they may have all left — like David said they would leave — be gone before I needed them to be gone…"

She finished with a plaintive, "I want to be able to say goodbye…"

Beckley nodded, "I know what you mean," he said. "They're my friends, too. Close friends. I like them."

He got up slowly and gathered their coffee mugs.

"Here, I'll do the dishes, then maybe we can get those bins packed up and in your car." He continued, "I always find that if I do something active, it seems to let my emotions settle down some."

Liddie got up and the two of them washed the few dishes. She wandered over to the room with all the bins. Sitting down on the big executive's chair, she marveled at the soft leather and how it was still in such great shape. She read again the book titles on the shelf. Had it really only been two days since they discovered them? It seemed an eternity. Her eyes closed as she waited for Beckley.

He found her, almost asleep, and kissed her gently on the forehead. Beckley thought her smile was the most angelic thing he had ever seen. He stroked her arm as she continued to rest in the chair. Yes, she was swooning yet again!

Beckley noticed a thin old volume on the bookshelf and turned to reach for it. Liddie opened her eyes and shook her head, sending her hair swirling. She looked with interest at Beckley.

His face was full of wonder, joy, and excitement, as if he had just opened a long-awaited Christmas present.

"Look, Liddie," he said, handing her the small book. *"Dykcyonarz Polsko-Angielski."* He did his best with the language, stumbling somewhat, but there was no denying that it was a Polish-English dictionary.

Liddie opened it, turning to the publication page.

"Chicago." She read out loud. "1912."

Liddie smiled back at Beckley, reflecting his wonderment. Any confusion they may have felt two days ago was gone. Now, it was a simple acceptance, even an enjoyment at being part of an extraordinary story.

Liddie continued, as she carefully turned the crumbling pages, "This surely must be the dictionary Anna carried on the streetcar — the one she used when she knew no English.

"Oh, my goodness!" she exclaimed. "Beckley, look at this page. Down here — see this penciled-in check mark?"

Beckley came close to read the tiny print. Then they both laughed out loud with delight! For there it was — marked because of its great importance to Anna — the word 'apricot!'

"What a treasure!" Liddie murmured. "Here, let's put it and all the books in some boxes in my car. I know Mom will want to go through all this stuff."

Perhaps an hour passed as they worked hard gathering the books and papers. They were able to add some into partially filled bins. The rest they carefully boxed up.

Beckley shoved the last bin into Liddie's car. They congratulated each other on the packing job and went back for one last inspection of the room. Running her fingers over the empty shelves, Liddie felt herself growing pensive again. Beckley sensed the change in her.

"Liddie!" He spoke a bit too loudly, as Liddie jumped in response. "I'm sorry, I didn't mean to startle you. I've been thinking — tomorrow we will be leaving. And there's something I want to do before then."

Liddie looked over with interest, her pensiveness disappearing.

"I want to go out in the boat with you!" Beckley proclaimed.

Actually, Beckley had very little experience with rowboats or ponds. Boating was not on his list of favorite activities. But he was desperately trying to think of something to help Liddie distract herself, especially after she had described how worried and fearful she was about the future.

Liddie looked at him, tilting her head in a questioning manner. She, also, had never had a great desire to go boating. But, it did seem like a pleasant diversion.

"Why, yes!" she responded. "Beckley, that sounds like a perfectly wonderful idea."

The two raced each other down the pathway, laughing as their competitive spirits emerged, each trying to be first to the boat. Beckley briefly considered letting Liddie win, but at the last minute, he surged on ahead. It had been a long time since he felt the sheer joy of physical activity. At the dock, though, they both had to grab hold of tree branches to keep from falling headlong into the water.

Liddie bent over, catching her breath. "Next time!" she promised. "I'll beat you for sure!"

Beckley examined the small flat-bottomed boat tied to the dock. "How hard can this be?" he wondered. He started unwrapping lines, only to see the boat begin to drift away.

"Quick, Liddie!" he called. "Grab that rope — the one in the water! I think I untied them all too soon. Can you pull it back in?"

She found a long, dead tree branch and reached out into the pond, just catching the twigs on the floating rope. "Here we go, here we go… I think I've got it!" she exclaimed.

Beckley pulled the line from the end of her branch and drew the boat back in.

Liddie found two paddles leaning against a tree and tossed them into the boat. Beckley insisted that he should climb in first, because of the danger involved, and Liddie was happy to let him do so.

The boat rocked a bit more than Beckley expected. He carefully adjusted his body to the movement and scrambled in. Then he turned to help Liddie. She was already sitting on the dock's edge, legs dangling, ready to slide in behind him.

"Careful! Careful!" Beckley cautioned. "I don't want you falling in!"

Liddie laughed, recalling that first day when she did, indeed, fall into the pond.

Liddie sat down in the stern, adjusting the flotation cushion under her. Beckley carefully moved to the bow, picking up one of the paddles. Liddie reached for the other one and after a brief examination, decided to slide the big part into the water. She moved it back and forth, experimenting with the water flow it created.

Beckley, in the front, was also experimenting with his paddle. He quickly decided that he understood the physics of how the water responded. He called back to Liddie.

"Okay! Here we go!"

He launched into a flurry of strokes, all on the right side, because, after all, he was right-handed. Liddie watched with interest as the boat turned around, and around again, in a small circle.

"Wait! Wait!" Beckley called out. "I know! I need to paddle on the other side, too! Or maybe you need to paddle there?"

Liddie began paddling on the left, but Beckley had stopped his paddling and turned around to face her with a wry smile.

"Liddie, I have to tell you something… I really don't know anything about boats… um… what do you say we try and figure it out together?"

So the two of them pushed, pulled, and twisted their paddles, sharing their discoveries until each felt fairly confident of venturing out to the middle of the pond. They carefully switched seats, having determined that the boat responded better if the stronger person sat in the back.

Leaving the dock, they drifted along, discovering the peace of slow, aimless paddling. They crossed the middle of the pond and glided toward the far edge. Liddie pointed out cattails and explained to Beckley how important they are to red-winged blackbirds. Pulling up to a large buttonbush along one bank, they saw an enormous blue heron take flight.

Beyond the buttonbush, a fallen tree was partly hidden in the water. Beckley motioned to Liddie. She looked closely and spied three red-eared sliders sitting on the log. The sliders were one of Liddie's favorite turtles, and she set her paddle down to watch them.

Beckley stuck his paddle into the muddy pond bottom and pushed the boat slightly up on the bank. Liddie turned around in her seat, facing the pond and Beckley. They sat there in a comfortable silence.

Beckley reached out for Liddie's hand, caressing it gently.

"You have the most beautiful hands, Liddie," he began. He lifted his eyes to hers.

"But it doesn't stop there. Your hands are beautiful. Your eyes are beautiful. Your hair is beautiful. Your face is beautiful. Liddie, I think you are the most beautiful girl in the world..."

Beckley realized he was talking way too fast, but he couldn't help himself. His words just came tumbling out. He couldn't stop, for fear of not expressing what he was feeling.

"Liddie, even with all the mystery that we've been immersed in this past week, I find that when I go to sleep, you're the last thing I think about. When I wake up, you're the first thing I think about. I think about you constantly, Liddie — the way you toss your hair, the way you are so vulnerable in your feelings — how I can look in your eyes and see the depths of your soul, and know just how you feel.

"Liddie, do you remember when I told you the story of the constellation Perseus, and how he rescued Andromeda? Liddie, whenever I look at the stars now, I'm thinking of Perseus riding Pegasus, with Andromeda sitting behind him. Only it's you, Liddie, and me. You and me, riding our winged horse Pegasus — into eternity."

Beckley took a deep breath. He was leaning close, very close to Liddie, who waited, enraptured with his words.

"Liddie, what I'm trying to say is… Liddie, I've fallen in love with you."

Liddie, overwhelmed with her own emotions, tried to jump into Beckley's arms. They narrowly escaped capsizing, rocking the boat back and forth before settling into an embrace as they knelt in the bottom of the boat.

"Beckley," she whispered, "I love you, too. I never knew how beautiful life was until I met you. It's, it's as if you showed me all the magnificent colors of the world and made them all come to life for me. I love you so much…"

Hours passed. Beckley and Liddie drifted randomly around the pond, unaware of the time. Their newfound love blossomed, surrounded by the croaking frogs, singing birds, and gentle breezes rippling their hair.

Suddenly they both caught a faint whiff of… something… could it be? Quickly, they rowed back to shore, jumped out of the boat, and raced up to the house. Yes, it was stronger, and definitely the lovely, smoky scent of a campfire!

Chapter 28: The Last Campfire

Beckley and Liddie quickly grabbed jackets, blankets, and a few sandwiches, and started off toward Carn Ingli.

Brrring! Brrring! Liddie's phone sounded its classic ringtone just as they reached the Overlook Hill.

"Mom? Mom? How are you?" Liddie answered the call. She sat down on the Overlook bench.

"Liddie! I have the most exciting news!" her mom exclaimed.

"What, Mom?"

"Liddie, I'm coming out there to see you!"

"What? What? How?" Liddie's excitement spilled over as she whispered to Beckley, "Mom's coming out here!"

"I'm already on the way! I left yesterday and spent the night in a motel. You remember your Dad is on that business trip. And I decided it was just silly for me to stay there alone in that empty house while you were having all these adventures. So I just hopped in the car and took off! I wanted to see the land in person, and hear more about these campfires."

"Well, Mom, that's wonderful! You'll get to meet Beckley when you get here. Tomorrow?"

"Yes, honey. I've already stopped at a motel for tonight. But sometime late tomorrow morning, maybe early afternoon. I'll see how the driving goes.

Do you think I'll get to see one of the campfires?"

"I don't know, Mom. I hope so. I think the one tonight has just started, and Beckley and I were heading up there."

"Oh, then don't let me hold you," her mother said. "I love you and can't wait to see you!"

"I love you, too, Mom. This is the best news ever! Drive carefully!"

Liddie excitedly told Beckley that her mom expected to get there the next day, maybe early afternoon. Beckley shared the excitement, but he also felt a bit apprehensive. Would her mom approve of him? He had just told Liddie how much he loved her. What would this mean for their relationship?

The sunset's pink and purple stripes began to paint the sky above Overlook Hill. Liddie stopped to soak in the beauty. She wasn't sure how many more times she would see this hill — certainly none after the land was sold. But she could also see the distant flickering of the campfire flames. The knowledge that their time with the group was also coming to an end spurred her on.

"Let's hurry, Beckley," she said. "I don't want to miss anything tonight."

A little out of breath, they arrived at the campfire. Henry reached out, greeting them with a big hug. He looked directly at Liddie, his eyes twinkling mischievously.

"Grass is growing, Liddie!" he said cheekily.

She looked at him sharply. What did Henry mean, addressing her specifically with that trademark comment? Then it hit her. Yes, everything was as it should be. She smiled warmly in response.

"Thank you, Henry. I love that expression — it means that life is progressing just as God wants it to be. Right?"

"Exactly." He nodded, then continued, "Someone tells me that you two took a boat ride today. Have fun?"

Liddie looked demurely up at Beckley. He sensed lots of eyes peering at them. Indeed, a hush had fallen around the campfire. And it did appear that everyone else was watching them inquisitively.

"Um, yes..." Beckley began awkwardly. "It was a beautiful ride on a beautiful pond..."

Despite his inward discomfort at being the center of attention, Beckley reached out and wrapped his arm around Liddie's waist. He pulled her closer.

"But not just that!" he blurted out. "It was a beautiful ride with the most beautiful girl in the whole world, and... and I discovered that she is the woman of my dreams!"

Liddie burst into a laugh of absolute joy. Then she reached up and kissed Beckley — not a peck, not a brush on the cheek, but a full kiss that transported them both to a totally different plane, the two of them only aware of each other and their new love. Neither one heard the exclamations from their friends.

"My, oh my!"

"Wow!"

"Would you look at that!"

"Yeah, I'd say they had a good boat ride!"

An enchanting melody arose near the fire, mingling with the crackling of the burning wood. David stood there, eyes closed, playing soulfully on a tarnished silver flute. The melodious strains lifted and carried across Carn Ingli, bringing with them a presence, as if the Spirit of God was settling over them.

David continued playing, notes rising and falling more slowly until the music tapered out completely. Then he broke the silence, addressing Liddie.

"You know that our time here is almost done, Liddie. We will be leaving soon, as I promised you. A few days ago, I spoke of how you had brought the brightest light to all of us. Your presence was very unexpected, to be sure. But it was certainly intended by God. Just as, yes... the grass growing."

Murmurs of agreement moved through the group as David continued.

"We all love you so very deeply."

Liddie's tears flowed freely. She reached for Beckley's hand and held it tightly.

David turned toward Beckley, saying, "And now, Beckley — we have been given the immense privilege of loving you. Again, so unexpected, but so perfectly right."

Beckley nodded and squeezed Liddie's hand.

David thought for a moment, looking into the distance, his face brightening with a sudden idea.

"I want to sing something for you two. A blessing. Maybe more of a benediction, but the evening is just beginning, so we'll call it a blessing. This is the chorus of a song I wrote many, many years ago. It is for you… as we have been able to witness the beginning of your love."

May everyone that you love give you love in return.
   May strangers give you a welcome where'er you sojourn.
   May everyone you meet give you the hand of a friend.
   May wisdom guide your steps until your journey's end.
   And may love travel with you across the green sod,
   Until your time has come to gaze on the face of God.

Gentle silence followed the blessing. Liddie and Beckley sat quietly, absorbing its powerful impact. The silence was broken by James commenting to Mary.

"Mary, I know that tune — remember, I used to play it on the fiddle. It's called 'Lord Inchiquin'. But what lovely, lovely words he has put to it!"

Liddie gazed around the group, from one end to another. She thought there must be a mist in the air, for they all seemed a little blurry to her. Or, perhaps it was the tears still forming in her eyes. She spoke tentatively, not quite sure of what she wanted to say, but knowing she needed to give voice to her heart.

"When I came here, I was a young, confused girl. Now, I'm still young. But, even though this past week has been filled with so many mysteries, I see more clearly than I ever have in my life."

She again gazed around the group, lingering here and there to focus on them.

Mac, dressed in his Navy uniform, Bronia holding tightly to his arm.

Adelle — she was grinning back at Liddie, her face full of sisterly love.

Osmund with Sarah at his side, and all the others.

Liddie continued.

"You all… um… you don't really live here, do you?"

It was David who answered her. "Liddie, remember how Paula wanted me to quote a verse on running the race? The first part of that verse referred to a cloud of witnesses. Remember?"

Liddie nodded as he recited the entire verse.

"Therefore, since we are surrounded by so great a cloud of witnesses, let us also lay aside every weight, and sin which clings so closely, and let us run with endurance the race that is set before us."

He continued. "So, to answer your question — no, we don't live here now. Though we have, in the past. You and Beckley have read our stories, seen our pictures in those books and albums."

"That cloud of witnesses — we are a small part of that. And for whatever reason God has seen fit, he has given us this brief window in time to be here, for you… to show you that you're not alone.

"We have all lived our lives. Some of us sought God from the start. Others wandered, knowing the hunger for something more, only to find God at the end of a long painful search. But God was always there for each of us, calling us, wooing us.

"God wants you to know, Liddie, that he is here for you, too. And for you, Beckley. He has your times in his hands."

Liddie and Beckley sat, speechless. So it was true. All of their discussions, trying to figure out that which just did not make sense, had led them to the same basic conclusion. It could not be explained rationally. What was happening here was a step outside of time, outside normal reality. Yet it was the most real experience they would ever have. And, it was definitely of God.

Liddie pondered. Was there anything she could say? Anything worthy of following David's explanation? Her emotions made the decision for her.

"I don't want you to leave…" The cry of her heart burst forth. Again, "I don't want you to leave.

"I want life to go on and on and on just like we've known you this past week!

"You all have become so dear to me. You have taught me so much. Even when I did not know what I needed, you have given it to me.

"You see, my mom and dad — they're the greatest, and I love them so much. But I never felt like I measured up to what I should be. They are so accomplished, they can both do so much. And here I am, a jobless almost-twenty-two-year-old with a worthless degree! I guess I've always told myself how much I fall short.

"And then, at college — well, Mom and Dad, they taught me about God, all the stories of Jesus. But no one else in college believed it was true. I let the other students lead me astray. I guess I left God behind."

Liddie looked over at Beckley. His loving expression gave her comfort and encouragement.

"Beckley and I — we talked about this, how God didn't seem relevant to either of us anymore.

"All my life, I've loved plants, the woods, the fields, and how life all interacts and works together. That why I went into botany. To learn more about the world.

"But, could it be, that I found a substitute for God in my botany? That knowing about God, and still wanting him but not knowing it was him who I missed, and not having him in my life, I made nature become a god for me? I know that sounds kind of convoluted..."

"Yes! Yes, Liddie." Beckley jumped up, completely carried away with excitement. He began, almost shouting across the hillside.

Late have I loved you, O beauty ever old, ever ancient and ever new!

Beckley gestured expansively from the woods surrounding them up to the twinkling stars.

And behold, you were within, and I was without. And deformed, I ran after your world. These things held me back from you. Things whose only being was to be in you — ever ancient and ever new.

Liddie's eyes had popped wide open when Beckley began speaking so loudly. But then, the words began to make sense, and yes, it was exactly how she felt! Complete awe captivated her and all the others as Beckley continued, a bit more slowly and softly.

You became fragrant and I sought after you.

I inhaled and I sighed after you.

You touched me, and I burned for your embrace.

I inhaled and I sighed for you.

Beckley dropped back into his seat, totally exhausted from the pure emotion of connecting so deeply with God.

Liddie stroked his brow, making sure he was okay.

"Beckley," she said. "That was so profound! And exactly how I feel — that it's really God that I want! And I have found him here!

"What you said — was that something else you had in that heavy duty brain of yours? Something you memorized?"

Beckley smiled and, somewhat revived, answered, "Yes — it was from one of my last Sunday School classes. St. Augustine. Was it the 4th century? 5th century?"

Liddie turned back to David and the others.

"This is what you all have shown me. That there is more. And I want this more…

"It's like, when I started out on the Pilgrim Path near the house, I was confused by the curves, and why it wasn't cut straight. But now I see. The curves, they represent the exciting mystery of life, that we don't know what might be around the bend, but there is definitely more as we turn those corners. And what God shows us is that we can always find more of him. Like the first time I came around the curve at the Overlook Hill and first saw Carn Ingli in the distance, why, I knew something drew me there. It was God.

"And, and that smell on the pathway — from the sewage lagoon. Why, that just reminds us that there will always be something nasty that we need to face. But, if we keep our eyes on the pathway and follow it, God will lead us back out to the wildflower meadows!"

As Liddie completed her reflection, she noticed that the scene was looking blurry again. Through her tears she searched the faces around her intently, wanting always to remember.

Stanley strode up to her, with Anna on his arm. Liddie realized that she had heard no coughing during the evening. She asked him about it. He nodded and proclaimed, "I am completely healthy!"

Anna reached for Liddie's hand and gave her a small card. On top, she had written *Dla Liddiego*. Liddie could scarcely contain her excitement as she opened the card and saw the recipe for apricot kolaches!

"Thank you, Anna, thank you so much!"

Anna and Stanley hugged Liddie, repeating over and over, "*Cie Kocham!*"

James addressed Beckley, "You're a fine, strong young man, Beckley. Perhaps you will plant a garden one day."

Mary added, "You will have crabapple trees! Lots of crabapple trees!"

Liddie watched as they walked off after more hugs. She felt the tears flow again.

Adelle rushed up. "Now, child!" She said as she wiped away her own tears. "You just remember what that boy of yours said — you have my eyes. You keep those eyes looking at him.

"And what a hunk to look at!" She and Liddie laughed through their tears.

"And," Adelle continued, "don't you worry at all about measuring up to what anyone else thinks of you. Something I learned a long time ago — the only person to compare yourself to is the person God wants you to be."

Henry held his old hat and shuffled his feet. "Not saying anything here," he began hoarsely, "'cause I don't expect you to need this, but keep in mind — if I could forgive that old coot Osmund for trying to kill me, you two can forgive anyone anything! And remember that God used it all to bring good!"

Liddie nodded weakly and sank down in her chair after their embraces. Beckley was not feeling much stronger. He sat down beside her, just as Osmund and Sarah walked up.

"No, don't get up," Sarah insisted. "Here, we'll sit beside you."

"Sarah," Liddie said, "I need to thank you for sharing your story with me that day I came across you at the Pond Beyond. Your words started my journey of being open to God here."

"Yes," Sarah answered. "You know, it was only after I heard God tell me that I needed to forgive Osmund that things changed. I made myself forgive him. And God restored our relationship. It made all the difference…"

Osmund nodded. "I was the cause of so much pain," he said. "But in the end, when I finally came to God, it was like… like I was brand new." He shook his head in amazement. "The power of redemption…"

Liddie and Beckley jumped up for a group hug before watching Osmund walk off with Sarah.

From behind, Liddie felt something cold touch her arm. Whirling around, she saw the laughing, beautiful face of Bronia, who held two cold bottles of Mountain Dew. She was pressing them up against Liddie and Beckley just like she must have stuck those pins in the crowd as a schoolgirl!

"Oh, Bronia!" Liddie cried as she fell into her arms. The two stood motionless for several moments.

"Liddie, I want you to remember something I learned all those years with Mac away in the Navy," Bronia said. "I always tried to see Jesus beside me in every situation. And whatever I did, I did it for Jesus."

Liddie nodded, biting her lip to keep from crying more.

Mac stepped up, stopping in front of Beckley. Beckley stood at attention. The two men looked intently at each other. No words needed to be exchanged.

Mac continued to stand, then smartly saluted, turned on his heel and strode off into the night.

Beckley stood silently, slowly raised his arm and saluted the retreating form.

Liddie, however, could not keep herself from running after Mac and giving him a hug full of the love she felt.

Looking around, Liddie could see that she and Beckley were now alone with Paula and David, who were working on the campfire.

"Will you be walking back with us?" Liddie asked.

"No," answered David. "We need to finish putting out the campfire. Don't want any loose embers, do we?"

The four of them moved the logs back and forth in the fire. It was not an intense effort to quench the fire, but more of an attempt to gain a few more moments together.

"I've got a question." Liddie suddenly broke the silence. "So much has happened here. And we are so grateful to you both for welcoming us and teaching us about God.

"You probably think this is weird, but I'm still confused about something my mom referred to — something about a funeral. Something strange that happened some fifty years ago, maybe? I haven't been able to ask her for more details yet, but maybe you can tell me. What happened?"

David grinned. "Oh, child," he said. "That's another story. Another story for another time. You'll find it taking you on yet another journey in another place. But, that one is not for here…"

He paused, then continued. "Ask your mother about the old journal she was given."

Liddie hugged Paula. Then she hugged her again, not wanting to let go. "Paula," she said, "thank you for writing that *Barbro* book. And the other one — for putting all of those stories together… and thank you, thank you for the story of Jehoshaphat!"

To David, she simply said, through their hug, "Thank you, David, for letting me see Jesus through you."

Liddie and Beckley tore themselves away, forcing their legs to start the quiet, moonlit walk back to the house. Behind them, back at the campfire, they heard the strong clear voice of David, singing.

Lord, help me enter in, that I may worship you.
  Lord, help me come into your holy place.

Help me forget myself, conscious of only you,
That I may lose myself seeking your face.
Help me to think, help me to feel,
Help me to act, help me to speak,
Help me to live all of my life so as to honor you.
Lord, make me clean, fill me with light,
Fill me with love, fill me with life,
Let people see, looking at me, nothing but you.

Chapter 29: The Cloud of Witnesses

Liddie woke before dawn. She sat on her bed, watching the day break. Not wanting to go down to what was most certainly an empty kitchen, she continued to sit, counting the different shades of pinks and reds in the sunrise. Her final tally was three pinks and two dark reds, with a deep yellow mixed in. The morning blue peeking out from behind the wispy clouds was the deepest turquoise she had ever seen.

Elizabeth flopped down onto Liddie's feet. She wiggled her toes against the soft fur.

In a way, Liddie welcomed the coming return to her parents' house. So much had happened, so quickly, that she felt the need for a quiet retreat to process everything. Certainly the drive back would provide some processing time.

"But for now," she told herself out loud, "I need to finish packing and get things ready for when Mom gets here."

She put her bed sheets and towels in the washer, leaving it to run while she wandered down to the kitchen. She started a pot of coffee. Then she checked through the refrigerator, taking stock of what foods should be removed before they left. There wasn't much — no eggs, milk, or other perishables. Just a jar of flour and a box of oatmeal.

Out the window, Liddie could see Beckley still asleep in his hammock.

She thought back to the image of him saluting Mac last night. An almost irresistible urge came over her to race up to Carn Ingli. Maybe, just maybe, all of this would not have ended, and she would find the others still there.

Liddie knew it was a hopeless idea. Last night had been final. But, still, she had to go back one more time.

"Let's go, Elizabeth!" she called. "Come on girl!"

Grabbing a thermos of coffee, she headed quietly out the door, so as not to wake up Beckley. She picked up the twisted walking stick on her way.

Crossing Coneflower Field, Liddie and Elizabeth turned off toward the Pond Beyond. Liddie watched the mist rising off the water. She felt the quiet solitude of the woods. But as she neared Sarah's garden, where they had that first chat, there was nothing. No garden, no lean-to house, no sign of any human habitation. Liddie kicked around where the garden had been. No sign of Sarah's pea plants.

Liddie ran on, finding the path to Carn Ingli and racing up it. Again, nothing to indicate any activity other than quail fluttering up from their coveys. Liddie paused briefly to gaze out over the green valley. She then called Elizabeth and continued on to the old homestead where Adelle and Henry had lived.

The house was still there, but the walls had crumbled. Only an old chimney was standing. Liddie sighed, shook her head, and walked on toward Lana na Null. Even before she reached it, the scent of the remaining crabapple flowers wafted toward her. There weren't many left, but they still held their sweet perfume. Liddie couldn't help smiling, remembering Mary's insistence that they should have lots of crabapple trees. Yet, even here, there was no sign of human habitation.

"Well, Elizabeth," Liddie said, "I guess that's it. As wonderful as this week has been, I guess it's over..."

She hugged Elizabeth, burying her face in the dog's fluffy fur.

"But, wait a minute!" she cried out. "You're still here! You were there. Paula and David knew you, but you didn't disappear with everyone! I am so, so happy you didn't leave me, too!"

The realization brought back all the raw emotion from the night before, and Liddie found herself sobbing as Elizabeth did her best to lick her face and comfort her.

Beckley had already awakened and showered when Liddie returned to the house.

"Oh, I am so glad to see you, Liddie!" he said, greeting her with a lingering kiss. "For a minute there, I thought maybe you had disappeared, too!"

Liddie chuckled. "It's not that easy to get rid of me!" she joked.

Beckley and Liddie cooked up the last of the oatmeal for breakfast.

"It's looking pretty empty here, Beckley. Nothing in the refrigerator. I guess it's just another indication that it's time to leave…"

"At least there was still enough coffee!" Beckley answered as he refilled his cup.

"Liddie," he continued after a sip, "I don't want us to be separated for too long — I mean, I'll be heading back to New York. You're going south to find a job. Is there any way you might look in New York for a job? I mean, we could see each other more often then."

"I know, Beckley…" Liddie answered. "I've been dreading being away from you, too. But what kind of job could I get in New York? And isn't it terribly expensive to live there? I suppose, maybe in a National Park. I haven't looked into being a Park Ranger, but that might be a possibility. Then I would have lodging as part of the job."

"Liddie," Beckley asked, "What would your dream job look like? I mean, if you could do anything in the world?"

Liddie pondered thoughtfully. She had never considered it that way. Always before, the question had been, what job could she find that was already out there?

"Well," she started, "I think it would definitely have an outdoors component — one where I could walk in the woods a lot. And discovering new uses for plants — like in my medicinal teas. I really love doing that. And teaching, yes — the internship showed me how much I enjoy connecting with young kids."

"Then let's start there," Beckley began.

Just then they were interrupted by the crunch of gravel on the driveway. Liddie jumped up.

"Mom!" she shouted. "Come on, Beckley!"

The two ran around the house just in time to see the car door open. Joyful shouts filled the air.

"Mom!"

"Liddie!"

"Mom!"

"Liddie!"

Beckley stood back a bit and watched the reunion with pleasure. It was heartwarming to witness their love. Liddie pulled her mom over to Beckley.

"Mom," she proudly stated, "this is Beckley!"

Beckley, feeling a bit like a specimen in a science project, stood up as straight as he could and reached out his hand.

"I am so pleased to meet you, Ma'am. Liddie has told me much about you. I look forward to knowing you in person now." He motioned toward the car. "May I carry anything for you?"

Liddie's mother couldn't help herself. She tilted her head, eyes slightly narrowed, lips pursed, evaluating the young man. But it only took an instant before she nodded emphatically. Beckley had passed muster.

"Why yes, Beckley, thank you!" she answered. "I seem to have gotten here earlier than I thought — my motel was only a couple of hours away."

She handed Beckley a grocery bag. "Look here, I brought a rotisserie chicken. Perhaps we can have it for lunch."

"What a great idea, Mom!" Liddie said, leading her mother into the house. "We're totally out of food. Here, I'll put it in the refrigerator. There's so much I want to show you! And tell you! This has been the most amazing adventure!"

Liddie opened the refrigerator to place the chicken in it, but she stopped, staring inside.

"Beckley," she asked, "did you put anything in here this morning?"

"What?" he asked. "No, there wasn't anything when we looked for breakfast. Is something wrong?"

Liddie shook her head 'no' and motioned to the refrigerator, smiling wistfully. Beckley came over, peered inside, and silently shook his head.

"Amazing adventure? Yes, Liddie, and it doesn't seem to be ending, does it?" he answered.

Liddie's mom eyed them curiously. She came up, looked inside, and said, "Why, that's wonderful! You do have something left. Three bottles of Mountain Dew! And the old glass bottles, too. I haven't seen these in such a long time!"

"This house is lovely!" said Liddie's mom. "Why, look at the huge windows, and the pond, and all the flowers beginning to bloom. What a gorgeous place! Can we take a walk around and you show me everything? You did get pictures, right?"

"Sure, great idea, Mom! Yes, I got plenty of pictures for Uncle Stan."

Liddie and her mother started down the Pilgrim Path. Beckley hung back a few steps, giving them time to visit without him. And, sure enough, as soon as they were out of earshot, Liddie's mom turned to her.

"I think he's a wonderful young man, Liddie! So polite, so handsome, and he seems to really like you."

Liddie blushed slightly. "Mom, I do really, really like him… Mom, we're in love!"

"Oh, Liddie!" her mother gave her a huge hug. "I couldn't be happier for you! Watching the two of you interact, it just seems like a match made in heaven. Tell me more — this is so exciting!"

Liddie proceeded to tell her mom all about Beckley, starting with his rosy cheeks. The two women turned and squinted at him, confirming that, yes, his cheeks were a robust shade of red!

Liddie continued, detailing all the things about Beckley she loved — how he knew almost everything, how they were interested in all the same things, and most importantly, how he made her feel so special and loved.

By the time they got to Overlook Hill, Liddie's mom was certain that her first impression of Beckley was correct — he was a good match for her daughter. They sat down on the bench and waited for Beckley to catch up.

Liddie pointed out the statues of Jesus and Jehoshaphat and asked her mom if she knew the story. Before waiting for an answer, Liddie plunged right into telling her all about it.

Beckley walked up just as Liddie was finishing.

"Isn't that a great account of God's provision?" he asked. "The whole idea of letting God fight your battles is one that I will continue to keep in my life."

"Um," he continued, "how would you like me to address you, as Mrs. —"

Liddie's mother interrupted him. "Call me Mom," she said. "Mom is perfect!"

The three continued their walk, pointing out the different parts of the land and how it might be shown in a real estate ad. It wasn't until they reached the top of Carn Ingli that Liddie brought up their friends and the campfire. Beckley pulled over some fallen logs, and they sat, looking out over the Valley of Blessing.

"I was waiting to ask about them," Liddie's mom said. "What with seeing you again and meeting Beckley and seeing the house and all, I didn't want to rush into it. But please, I want to know what has happened. It sounded so mysterious on the phone."

So Liddie and Beckley did their best to chronicle the week for her. They told her all about meeting everyone, finding the books, coming up with different theories, and finally having their conclusions confirmed at the last campfire.

"It all sounds incredible," Liddie finished. "It's hard for me to believe, and I lived through it. But Mom, it wasn't a dream. We didn't imagine it. It was real. And I'm convinced it was God — that he was calling me back to him, showing me how much I need him in my life."

Liddie's mom put her arm around her daughter. "Liddie, I know beyond a shadow of a doubt that it was indeed God. I can feel his presence here — with you, with Beckley, in this place. So, yes, embrace this time. Hold onto it. What you have experienced and learned here will guide your life into the future."

She continued, "I'm sad that I didn't get to be at any of the campfires. What an incredible experience it must have been! And I'm sad that I never really learned anything about our ancestors — for I'm sure that is who they were. You said you have the books to bring home?"

"That's right," Liddie answered. "Oh, and Mom! Somehow, David knew, a couple of nights ago, at the last campfire, that my birthday was coming up! I don't know how. But he made up a birthday poem for me.

"How did it go? Beckley?"

Beckley scrunched up his forehead. "There was something about you being a botanist... then, wait! I've got it...

God has plans for Liddie, plans so wonderful,
 To make her life amazing, to fill her heart so full.
 She's kindly and she's curious, she's pretty and she's smart.
 To think of what she can become just warms my dear old heart.

Liddie smiled with the memory. It was a simple poem, but carried such love.

Liddie's eyes were on Beckley, so she didn't notice the shocked expression on her mother's face. But the cry and deep weeping drew her attention.

"Liddie!" her mom sobbed. "Liddie... that... that was my grandpa... Liddie, those last two lines... He wrote them for me when I turned ten years old..."

Liddie's mom continued sobbing, her heart wracked with the pain of long lost memories. Liddie and Beckley hugged her, knowing the same pain in their hearts.

Their walk around the land continued to the homesite, with its sad derelict house, on past Lana na Null and through the Wetland. At each place, Liddie and Beckley laughed as they recalled stories of the characters they met.

"Oh, Mom!" Liddie said as they headed back to the house. "You said on a phone call something about a funeral, like it was a very strange occasion. I asked David about it, and he said I should ask you about a journal. Do you have a journal? What exactly happened at the funeral?"

Liddie's mom looked thoughtful. "Well, I'll tell you... No, no I won't. Not here. Not now. But I will look for that journal and show it to you when we get home.

"There — now let's go eat that chicken!"

Before sitting down to lunch, Beckley checked his phone. He sighed.

"I had hoped we might be able to change our plans and stay another day," he said. "But there's a message from my new boss, wanting me to get started on the job. So I guess I do need to leave today."

Liddie and her mom agreed. It made sense to get on the road after lunch.

After the long walk, they all appreciated the ready meal and devoured the chicken and Mountain Dews. Beckley cleaned up in the kitchen while Liddie and her mom checked through the rest of the house. Elizabeth was sleeping soundly on Liddie's bed, but she jumped up and greeted them, especially Liddie's mom, whom Elizabeth recognized instantly as a dog person.

Beckley made sure all electrical and water connections were set right. Liddie's mother found keys in a kitchen drawer and locked the house.

"Mom," Liddie said as they reached her car. "See all these boxes of books? These are the ones we were telling you about. Look, here's that *Barbro* book — the one with stories of the ancestors.

"Oh!" The book slipped out of Liddie's hands and landed on the gravel. Beckley quickly bent down, picked it up, and began brushing it off. Before closing it, he stopped to skim the page where it had fallen open.

"Mom, Liddie, look at this!" he started. "It seems to be a chapter on Mac and Bronia's 50th anniversary… one of Mac's grandchildren wrote a poem about them. It's long, but seems to be about visiting Mac and Bronia on the farm — here — the Valley of Blessing. Let's see… Mac is getting them to help with clearing brush, promising them a trip to Frankie's store! The writer describes riding in the pickup together. Can I read some out loud? It might be a fitting end for our time here."

"Why yes, Beckley, I would love that," Liddie's mom answered quickly.

Liddie, of course, welcomed anything that would delay their departure.

Beckley began.

Grandpa would sit in the front seat,
　　With his brown hat on his head,
　　And a toothpick in his teeth.
　　And he would sing "The Blue Tail Fly."

Liddie smiled. "What a great memory for a grandchild!"
　"But, wait," said Beckley. "There's more."
　He continued.

And when we were all done,
　　We would go and get our drinks from the store.
　　And we would take them out in the yard
　　And open them up, out by the back door.
　　And as we lifted the ice-drenched bottles to our dried lips,
　　Grandpa would look back as he turned to go in.
　　And you know,
　　You could just see his reflection
　　In that bottle of Mountain Dew.

Liddie's mom stood up. She walked over to her car, silently opened the back door, and rummaged around in a trash bag. Coming back to Liddie and Beckley, she held within her hands a precious treasure.

"Here," she said, giving them each an empty green bottle. "Let's hold on to these."

She returned to her car. Sitting down inside gave her time to absorb what she had just experienced. It also gave Liddie and Beckley time to say their own goodbyes.

Beckley hugged Liddie tightly. His love for her had grown leaps and bounds even in this last day. Their lives, so intertwined, so guided by God's hands — how could they leave each other now? He shook his head, at a loss for any solution, torn between the demands of his new job and his love for this beautiful woman.

He gazed over at the Coneflower Field. "It really does seem like the Garden of Eden, doesn't it, Liddie?"

He sighed deeply.

"I'm going to miss you so much. And I'm going to miss being here."

Liddie answered, "It's funny. I can almost feel the cloud of witnesses. It's like they are still all around us. Do you feel it, Beckley?"

His answer was a prayer.

"Lord God, thank you so much for this time. Thank you so much for my love, Liddie. Help us to be more of what you want us to be."

Beckley was first in line to head up the driveway. Liddie followed with both Elizabeths, stuffed and real, in her car. Last came Liddie's mom, looking wistfully out the side window at the field of tall grasses blowing in the breeze.

Rounding the bend, they saw seven deer standing in the driveway, five does and a pair of twin fawns. One of the does turned and fixed Beckley with an unwavering gaze.

Beckley, in the lead car, stopped, then moved slowly toward the deer. No indication that they would budge. He got out of the car and began to walk toward them, but something stopped him. Turning, he looked back at the house, nestled down below the driveway. His gaze then turned toward the top of Carn Ingli, visible just behind the Pond Beyond. His eyes closed, his head tilted up toward heaven. Tears streamed down his face.

Liddie saw the deer and watched Beckley get out. She wondered why he didn't just shoo them away. She opened her door and stepped out to see if he needed help.

Beckley's eyes flew open. He ran the few steps back to Liddie's car. He grabbed her up in his arms and kissed her. Passionately, he kissed her. Again, and again, they kissed.

And then, Beckley dropped to his knee. He tenderly reached for Liddie's hand. His pleading eyes looking up into hers, he began.

"Liddie, I cannot live without you. My life would not be complete. Without you, I would leave here an empty shell of a man. Liddie, please, will you marry me? Will you be my wife?"

Liddie's mom, head poking out her window, watched Beckley delightedly.

She climbed out just in time to hear Liddie's soft and breathless answer.

"Yes, my love!"

Liddie melted into Beckley's strong arms. She was swooning yet again.

A hawk's persistent shriek called to them from the south. They turned to watch it swoop down toward the house. Above the roof, nestled in the drifting clouds, another unfolding scene drew their attention.

The heavens had opened up. Waves of light cascaded down. The River of Life flowed over the edges of the clouds onto the Valley of Blessing below. All was brilliantly illuminated by the glory of God. Standing in the opening was the cloud of witnesses, singing and praising God. All of them, covered in glory, waved at Liddie, Beckley, and Liddie's mom.

Beckley waved at them, joined by Liddie and her mother.

"We'll be back!" he called out. "We'll be coming back!"

Epilogue: Ten Years Later

Liddie wandered down the Pilgrim Path, reveling in the warm sunshine of another gorgeous June day. She bent down and clipped some yarrow, placing it carefully in her basket.

"Davy!" she called, "Can you find the echinacea? Remember, it has the long lance-like leaves? You might find an early purple flower on it."

A small boy raced ahead to a small green patch next to the pathway.

"Here it is, Mommy! And look, some coreopsis right beside it! You want me to pick some?"

"Good job, Davy! You went right to it. Yes, but only pick five or six. We want to save some for later."

Liddie glanced over at a young girl sitting in a large patch of clover. She was diligently picking the fluffy white flowers and tying them into a long chain. Liddie smiled, enjoying the peace and simplicity of life that surrounded her.

"Adelle," she said, "when you're done with your pretty necklace, can you get some of those plantain leaves, please? We need some for the class tomorrow. What do you think we'll be making with them?"

"Oh, Mommy! That's easy!" Adelle answered. "A healing salve! Will we be using some wax from my bees?"

"Of course! And thank you for letting us use it!"

Liddie's thoughts went back to Beckley's question of ten years ago, asking her what she thought her perfect job would be. She still found it hard to believe that she was now living out that perfect job.

What was it she had said? Walking the land, learning more about plants, and teaching others about them. And not only was she teaching others in weekly classes, but she had her own two little apprentices! Life was so good.

Liddie proudly called herself a granny woman, the Ozarks term for someone who used wild plants for healing. It may have been more accurate to say she aspired to be a granny woman, being only thirty-two years old. However, Liddie had been immersing herself totally in learning the folk wisdom and ways of country people. And she was already teaching others, so she felt good about the name.

Liddie heard the house door slam and, looking up, saw Beckley striding down toward them. He always took her breath away, even now, after these ten years of marriage.

"Liddie," he called, "how about catfish for dinner? The kids and I can go fishing when it gets a little later."

"Oh," she answered. "That sounds lovely! But don't you have any more appointments?"

"Nope! Last one just left, so I'm free for the day."

Beckley ran his tiny practice out of the house. In this small community there were enough simple wills and trusts, occasional real estate sales, and minor disputes to keep him occupied, even as he developed a growing reputation in environmental law. It certainly didn't bring in the financial rewards the New York job would have, but Beckley never looked back on his decision to settle here. He embraced, instead, the rewards of spending his time with Liddie, being able to fully partake in the joys of fatherhood, and the freedom he had in wandering the Valley of Blessing, living in the presence of God.

Liddie ambled over to where Beckley stood near the pond.

"I saw them again today," she said. "Every now and then, I'll be looking at the clouds, and one of them appears. It's very faint, but very clear. Do you know what I mean?"

Beckley nodded. "Yes, I know. Once you become aware of the cloud of witnesses, it seems they are always there. I saw your mom this morning.

Very faintly, but she was up there…"

Beckley reached out and held Liddie's hand. The two of them walked to the patch of clover where Adelle was still making her flower chain. Davy had joined her, industriously creating his own string.

"Mmmmm. If you get really close and take a deep breath," Liddie said, "what a heavenly fragrance you find."

The children held their flowers up to their faces, inhaling the lovely scent.

Beckley smiled and leaned back, eyes closed, sinking into the soft green clover. Slowly, ever so slowly, he recalled and spoke out the words of long ago.

We may shut our eyes,
But we cannot help knowing
That skies are clear,
And grass is growing.

Appendix: The People Behind the Stories

Therefore, since we are surrounded by so great a cloud of witnesses, let us also lay aside every weight and sin which clings so closely, and let us run with endurance the race that is set before us. — Hebrews 12:1-2

The characters described as being in the cloud of witnesses are based upon real-life people. They were my ancestors. In 2022 I privately published a family history in which their lives were chronicled. In 2012 I privately published *Barbro: A Redemptive Tale of Grace,* which followed my own journey of discovery as I researched and learned about my ancestors. The books mentioned in Chapter 20 are all real books I used as resource material in my genealogical work. The songs and poems quoted were all written by the people I attribute them to in the story.

For all the family stories, I am deeply grateful to my mother and father, Bronia and Mac McKay, and to my aunt Jewell McKay Johnson, who recorded a great deal of research and personal interviews for the McKay and Weltha history.

I have tried to make the characters' personalities consistent with family historical anecdotes. But, while based upon real people and stories, *Witnesses To Love* is a work of fiction. I have taken liberties with my development of the characters. Liddie represents one of my future great-grandchildren, not yet born.

The underlying theme of the cloud of witnesses, as well as references to the Bible and Christian faith, are based upon my understanding and beliefs as a Christian.

You, the reader, may find it interesting to know more about the characters in my book. To that end, I have written a short biography of each one, including representative photographs.

James McKay (1822-1875) and

Mary (Halfpenny) McKay (1820-1907)

Mary McKay around 1905. No photos of James exist.

James and Mary lived in Crabtree Lane, Armagh County, Ireland. They immigrated to America in 1850, after the potato famine hit their homeland. The journey took six weeks in an open boat. One child died at sea. Another died as they made the trek west in a covered wagon to Eagleville, Missouri, where they homesteaded a plot of land.

Osmund Weltha (1853-1927) and

Sarah (Belmore) Weltha (1858-1909)

Osmund and Sarah with their children and Osmund's mother Barbro, 1896. Liddie Adelle is at bottom right.

Osmund was five years old when he and his mother, Barbro, left Norway and immigrated to America, settling in the Fox River Norwegian settlement in Illinois. He met and married Sarah in Indiana as he traveled to Eagleville, Missouri, looking for land. Their lives were hard, even by the standards of the day. He was a Lutheran when young, and there are some reports that at the end of his life he gave his land to the church. But in between, indications are that he hardened and lived an angry, wicked life. One of his daughters did refer to being "raised by a Norwegian devil."

Osmund and his daughters must have achieved some kind of peace once they were grown, because he ended up spending his time visiting each of them in their homes. It was during one of those visits to Adelle and Henry that he made a child's rocking chair out of spare wood for baby Emerald (Mac). That little rocking chair now sits in our living room.

Sarah's father was a farmer and part-time preacher. He and his wife Jane traveled with Sarah and Osmund from Indiana to Eagleville. Family research and interviews with neighbors portray an extremely difficult life for Sarah in the marriage, and for her nine children. There were allegations of abuse. Osmund's actions led to Sarah leaving him. She did maintain a connection with the children, visiting them when Osmund was traveling. I like to believe that the apparent reconciliation with his children and the story that he left his land to the church indicate that he came to faith in his later years.

Henry Patrick McKay (1863-1935) and

Liddie Adelle (Weltha) McKay (1883-1944)

Henry and Liddie McKay on their farm in Eagleville, Missouri, 1918

Henry McKay was born the youngest of eleven children on the Eagleville farm his parents, James and Mary, homesteaded. By all accounts he was a happy-go-lucky person. He was part of a local group that made a run for the Oklahoma Strip. I found a local newspaper article from the time detailing such a trip, although Henry is not mentioned by name.

Adelle's full name was Liddie Adelle Weltha. She was fourteen when her mother left home, and she did take over most of the household chores. The story about her father, Osmund, hitting Henry on the head with a log is based on family lore. Osmund did not want them to marry. Henry was twenty years older than Adelle and they did elope in order to escape Osmund.

Stanislaus Jez (1881-1945) and

Anna (Wojnarowski) Jez (1894-1983)

Stanley and Anna Jez outside their home in Chicago, 1944.

Stanley immigrated from Poland in 1905. His father was a shoemaker, and Stanley as the oldest son would have taken over his father's business. But he left for America and gave the store to his brother. He settled in Chicago and worked at the Calumet shops upholstering train chairs. It was there he inhaled asbestos and developed the chronic emphysema that led to his death.

Anna was the only grandparent I knew. She immigrated, alone, from Krakow, Poland, in 1911 at the age of sixteen, and found work as a domestic servant. She was introduced to Stanley by her employer. After Stanley got sick, she did work as a cleaning woman at the Field Building on State Street. I treasure the Polish-English dictionary she used, which I recently received from my mother. It really does have the word for apricot checked! She was an excellent cook and sent us boxes of Polish treats on Easter — eggs dyed with onion skins, homemade Polish sausage, and kolaches. The story of her chasing down the purse snatcher was true, as told by my mother.

Emerald "Mac" McKay (1919-1995) and

Bernice (Jez) McKay (b. 1922)

Emerald "Mac" McKay and Bernice "Bronia" Jez in Chicago, 1941.

Mac served in the Navy until 1950. He transferred to the Naval Reserves as a Lieutenant Commander and worked in the federal government. In 1975 he and Bronia retired to a farm in the Missouri Ozarks. Part of their farm is the setting for this book.

The story of Mac and Bronia meeting at the circus and their subsequent dinner at the Palmer House is accurate. They married about a month later, in late 1941, shortly before Mac was deployed to the Pacific Theater in World War II. Mac's stories about his teachers are taken almost verbatim from a recording of his own words.

Bronia, when she met Mac, was a real-life "Rosie the Riveter." She had begun working as a drill press operator in the International Harvester Company, and was promoted to a supervisor at age 20. Her father, Stanley, changed her name from Bronislawa to the more American 'Bernice,' but Mac always called her Bronia.

David Wentz, Paula (McKay) Wentz, and The Valley of Blessing

Paula and David Wentz, 2023

David served as a Methodist pastor for thirty-four years before retiring to the Valley of Blessing. There he has written and published eight books as of this writing, some for pastors and others on Christian growth and maturity. He founded and leads a small nonprofit providing free books to pastors in developing and minority-Christian countries, mainly in Africa. He wrote the Blessing/Benediction song and "Lord Help Me Enter In," cited in the story, as well as numerous other Christian worship songs. Our children did write a song for David featuring a chorus in which they asked God to let them be more like him.

The account of The Pilgrimage is accurate. It was a wonderful time of finding God at a deeper level.

I (Paula) homeschooled our five children. When David retired from serving churches, we moved to the Valley of Blessing, the back eighty acres of the farm in the Missouri Ozarks where my parents, Mac and Bronia, had raised horses and cows. We have restored the pastures to native grasses and wildflowers. Our goal is to recreate, as much as possible, a type of "Garden of Eden" where we can walk with God. All the places named in the book are actual paths, fields, hills, or ponds on the property. The statues of Jesus and Jehoshaphat are also real, as well as the "Thus Far" rock (1 Samuel 7:12), which reminds us that God has guided our paths thus far and continues to walk with us into the future. The photo on the book cover was taken by me in the Valley of Blessing.

About the Author

Paula Wentz lives in the Missouri Ozarks with David, her husband of over fifty years. After a busy career homeschooling four sons and a daughter while actively serving as a pastor's wife, she is making the most of retired life. Paula loves planning new projects in the Valley of Blessing and gazing at God's beauty around her.

1998 winner of the national adult beginner Celtic harp championship and graduate of the Music for Healing and Transition program, Paula created *A Celtic Journey With the Saints: From Desolation to Consolation*, a Christian musical worship service combining traditional Celtic tunes with lyrics by her husband. She has privately released two CDs of her harp music and three books based on her genealogical research.

Witnesses to Love is Paula's first publicly released book. If you liked it, please tell friends. If you can post a review, that would mean a lot. And follow Paula's Facebook page for photos of the Valley of Blessing and new book updates!